A Numina Parable

A DAUGHTER of the TROLLS

McKENZIE CATRON

Whimsical Publishing

A Daughter of the Trolls

Address Whimsical Publishing, whimsical publishing.ca

ISBN: 978-0-9869373-7-8

Edited by: Micheline Ryckman, Dylan Garity & Jenny DePierre

Cover art by Micheline Ryckman
Interior Illustration of the elder chair by
Paulina Tloczek - @tloczuss (IG)

To Mom and Dad,
Thank you for loving me and being proud of every accomplishment of mine, big or small.

THE GLADE

My days usually begin with thwarting an attempt at kidnapping. And today is going to be no different, because the minute I reach the center of the glade, I find the trolls plotting.

They sit on the ground in a cluster, moss-covered backs hunched over, heads bent together, bulbous noses practically touching the heart clutched between the eldest troll's palms.

"That's not what I think it is, is it?" I push my wheelchair closer to their gathering spot.

They glance up in alarm, scrambling to help hide their newest creation within his large, knuckled hands. "Ah, Sparrow! My dear!" they crow in unison.

I park my chair in front of them, careful not to edge my front wheels over the smooth stone path and into the grass. "Come on now, let's see it." I cock an eyebrow and hold out a pale hand.

The trolls all share a look, their bodies tense, hesitant. They know they're caught; all they have to do is admit defeat. With a huff, the eldest troll, Bramwell, thrusts his thick arm toward me, sending a shower of dirt onto my lap. With care, I take the heart from his green, weathered fingers. It's crafted from the sturdy gray twigs of an elder tree, woven to resemble the fragile heart nestled within my human chest. I turn it over, studying every angle, searching for the telltale glow of a golden troll charm.

Luckily, it hasn't yet been imbued with magic. Had they succeeded in fabricating a body for the twig heart before I happened upon them, we'd have a little changeling babe, ready to be swapped with its identical human counterpart. I can't have them adding another creature to the list of ones I already have to keep out of trouble.

The trolls tend to devote every waking hour to crafting their sons and daughters. Yet, they barely spare a minute for the completed ones that don't get exchanged for a mortal child. My mother and I have kept a vigilant eye throughout the years, making sure we don't end up with parentless changelings or human babes in the glade. Not only would the babies add a heap of work for us, but the folk who live in the villages, hours away from our secluded home, don't take too kindly to having their babies kidnapped or swapped for hand-cobbled faeries.

That's not to say the changeling babies aren't sweet wee things, they are, but they have the same temperament as any baby, which means one second they're nuzzled in your arms napping and the next they're kicking you in the ribs and screaming bloody murder. Unfortunately, this doesn't bode well for the patience of timeworn trolls, and they're quick to give up caring for them. Thankfully, the rascals do grow up, and you can never tell the difference between them and humans. All of the changelings the trolls had made in the past, before my mother and I put an end to it, have moved on and created lives for themselves outside of the glade. Not a single one is left.

I turn the newest creation over in my hands. "You know, this heart could be the best child you've made yet." I grin. "Too bad you won't be able to use it."

I brush off the dusting of dirt still on my trousers and twist in my wheelchair to put the changeling heart in the bag strung along the handles. "This is going with the rest of them, just for safekeeping. We can't have any disgruntled folk come searching for their stolen child. Nor can we care for a changeling—they drove the gnomes crazy the way they used to tromp through the garden."

The trolls let out a collective groan. I know they spent days molding the heart into the perfect shape to sit inside a host. It's a weekly job deterring them from whisking away distressed human babies and leaving indistinguishable changelings to live in their place. I don't blame them, though. It's just the nature of trolls.

It's almost like breathing—they cannot stop themselves from creating.

As I finish squirreling away the heart and turn back to face the trolls, I hear the soft pad of slippered feet approach. My mother comes up behind me, smooths the short, dark waves of my hair, and stoops down to kiss the crown of my head. She smells like freshly baked bread and honey, and she gives me a warm smile. "Hello, my little bird." Then her dimpled chin turns toward the trolls. "Are they causing trouble?"

"No more than usual." I return her smile.

She steps into the grass in front of the circle of trolls, supporting a fruit-laden basket on her hip, tucking a stray lock of ochre-brown hair into her bun as she gives Bramwell a knowing, though loving, look. The grizzled troll smiles. Then, in a synchronized motion, all the trolls reach toward her while emitting a humming noise similar to the buzzing of bees. The creatures move and speak with a hive-mind drone. My mother bends down, and Bramwell cups the side of her face while the other trolls still reach out toward her. "Ah, Daughter," the trolls all sigh in unison.

My mother turns her head into his palm and pats his rough hand with her perpetually berry-stained fingers. After my eighteen years of coexisting with all sorts of faeries, I know my mother holds a special place in her heart for the trolls. Even though she's human, they raised her, and as a result, she became a dutiful daughter, a caretaker and protector of the faeries. And my mother's hard work and devotion never ceases to amaze me. She tucks any creature looking for safety beneath her wing and offers them a home. There are *things* out in the world wreaking havoc, searching for blood, and sticking together offers us all a layer of protection. The glade is a haven for all who wander here.

My head tilts up as I watch my mother straighten back to her willowy height and reach into her basket. She retrieves a plump sack of gooseberries and presents it to the trolls, plopping the bag in the middle of the group. "Why don't you all take these and enjoy the last couple hours of sun. Sparrow and I have a few more things to do before the Moon shows her face."

Then, my mother turns on her heel, her homespun dress twisting around her knees as she pulls my chair away with her one free hand. I feel a small surge of frustration at being moved without permission and grasp my rickety chair wheels.

"It's okay, I can push myself." I straighten my shoulders.

My mother lets go and presses her hand to the floral-printed apron around her narrow waist. "Oh, Sparrow, I'm sorry. I just don't want you to wear yourself out. You need to be wary of your heart, honey—you've been working too hard."

I shake my head and start pushing myself along the paved path, heading toward the old timber barn. Even a decade after my heart weakened and put me in this wheelchair, she still frets. "Mother, my heart feels fine. I'm not tired yet. I even helped some of the goblins fix the water mill earlier. I feel just dandy." I chuckle, and it earns me a disapproving stare, so I temper my next words. "I only have a couple chores left, then I promise I'll rest."

She stops me with a hand on my atrophied legs. "Are you sure, sweet girl? You could always go back to the house, do some baking and turn in early."

I let go of one wooden wheel to put my hand on top of her wrist. The difference between her sun-kissed, freckled skin and my ghostly, blue-veined complexion is stark. I squeeze her arm. "I'm okay. Really. I'm just going to go leave a treat for the brownies to find and make sure the imps leave them alone. I'm sure the critters are feeling attention-starved by now."

The edges of my mother's hazel eyes crinkle as she laughs. "I think so too. Here, take these." She hands me the palm-sized elderberry cakes I baked yesterday. "I wrapped them up in cheesecloth to keep them fresh."

I take them from her, setting the goodies onto my lap so they won't get smooshed in my bag. Then, just as I grasp the creaky rims of my wheels, my mother stops me once more. "Oh, I almost forgot—if you are feeling as strong as you say, can you check the perimeter and reinforce the salt barrier for me before it gets dark? I need to finish picking the spring garden and take the preserves down to the cellar in case it gets too hot. Summer will be here in the blink of an eye." She gives me a weary smile.

I know she has a lot of responsibility around the glade, things I don't have the endurance for, and it's rare for her to ask me to do more, so I know she needs the help. "Of course. I have my salt pouch in my bag. I'll start as soon as I'm done in the barn."

I watch the weight leave her shoulders as her body loosens. With a parting kiss to my forehead, she strides down the snaking pathway toward our rugged house. I can just make out its honey-colored wood and the slowly rotating water mill pressed against its side. It took a lot of goblin patience and persuasion to get the giant wheel moving again, but now it's good as new, ready to grind all our wheat for us.

I peer up at the sky, past the canopy of trees, to see I have just over an hour before the blue of day starts fading into a balmy evening pink. I lost time earlier today, reading while I ate lunch. It's always so easy for me to get sucked into a book; today it was Arabian princes and murderous kings, and I nearly forgot to eat the food in my hand. It was worth it though, even if the time loss left me hurried. I only had just enough daylight now to visit the barn and take a lap around the property to check the salt barrier before keeping my promise to return home and rest.

The ring of salt trailing around the entire glade is the only thing keeping Black Annis out. And my mother dedicates every evening to making sure we're shielded from the poisonous witch. There were nights though, as a child, when I gazed out my window to watch for her. I used to turn my nose to the air to see if I could smell belladonna berries on the wind. I'd heard stories from the gnomes around the glade that the witch ingested the poison as if it were candy. They said it made Black Annis's lips lethal, a true kiss of death.

Sometimes, I swear I've seen a flash of her blue skin, or the flying banner of her long hair streaking past, just outside the ring, stalking us like prey. Other times I think I can feel her just watching us, anticipating the night we slip up and forget to reinforce the salt. I imagine her waiting to sink her iron claws into our flesh and strip us of our skin, so she can add it to her macabre leather collection.

From where I sit now, I can see her far-away home, the tips of the bare white banshee trees encompassing her cave. The dead forest is notorious for housing Black Annis; the witch is territorial and only seeks out victims from surrounding villages. Our glade just happens to be her favorite place to haunt, with the way all the faeries group together here.

Humans and creatures alike, far and wide, know to stay out

of the vicinity of the witch's home. Banshee branches reach high into the sky like a giant's finger bones, a constant reminder to me, and all the faeries, that death and danger are never far.

I shiver, tearing my eyes away from the dark scene, propelling myself toward the barn, where we keep our harvested wheat stalks and house the brownies. My ramshackle chair bumps its way over the paths my mother and the trolls cobbled together. They created them for me when I first became wheelchair-bound, so I could get around easier and do my chores. But even with the paths, I feel the soreness in my hips and legs from sitting in my wheelchair all day. I can't wait to take my boots off and stretch out my lanky frame before bed.

But first, I must make the rest of the trek to the barn and prepare the brownies for their nightly duties. Only then do these nocturnal fairies help by threshing wheat for the mill. One of my chores is to leave them treats to wake up to, like hunks of hard cheese and slices of their favorite yeast-risen bread. We learned fast that if we wanted to keep the brownies content in the glade, they had to be rewarded for their handiwork. And they had to be kept away from the imps and their bothersome pranks. Brownies not only have the appearance of tiny old men, but the crotchety attitudes to match, and pranks never sit well with them.

Just as I reach the wide double doors to the barn and prepare to slide their heavy weight aside, the panels wrench open. Startled, I sit back into my chair as three emerald-green goblin girls tumble into the waning sunlight. I recognize them as the mischievous sisters who steal all the flowers from the planters on my bedroom windowsill. They're tugging mercilessly on each other's pointed ears and black corkscrew curls while winking in and out of sight, and they giggle as they run from whatever trouble they've left inside.

Said trouble strolls out of the barn with his hands stuffed in his pockets and a fond smile on his handsome face—Rush, the goblin girls' half-human brother. His eyes widen when he spots me. The white shirt he wears underneath his tan vest is rolled to his forearms. and his tan vest is thrown open wide, showing off his skin. As he twists to face me more, his skin shifts from a cool, deep umber to an iridescent green. He appears tired, most likely from chasing his sisters all day.

"Rush! I didn't know you were visiting," I say, trying to rein in my surprise.

"I'm just passing through." He rubs at the back of his neck. "I'll admit I got a little turned around this last month. I'd planned on going up to the mountain settlements for the next year or so but somehow just wound up walking back to the glade. I don't know why, but something always pulls me back here."

"Is the nomadic wayfaring life not as thrilling as you thought?" I give him a wry smile.

"Oh, it's great! I just rely too heavily on my goblin ancestry and sense of smell to take me where I think I need to go." He gestures to his mildly pointed nose.

"I'm sure Posy, Primrose, and Poppy are happy to have you back."

"Speaking of—" He turns to see how far his sisters have gotten. "I better go, before they get into more trouble." Rush saunters backward in the direction they raced off in while he points toward the barn. "You might want to get in there quick, I think they gave the imps the idea to wake the brownies up with a toasty fire." He laughs at the shock on my face before winking a silver eye. "Bye, Sparrow." The ghost of his cinnamon scent trails behind as I watch him turn to jog after his sisters.

It's been a couple of years since I last saw Rush around the glade. During that time, he's changed—his once-lean body is now corded with muscle, and his jaw is more defined. I notice he's finally grown into the long-rippled goblin ears he inherited from his father.

When we were younger, Rush and I were best friends. He'd follow me everywhere while I did my chores, and we usually ended up playing games instead of working. Somehow, we always found a way to get into trouble together, and we always had fun doing it. However, as we got older, and Rush was gone longer and longer, we simply grew apart. Now, I miss those days.

A small jolt lights through my frame as I remember the half-goblin's warning. I tear my eyes away from his retreating form to push my way into the barn, using the tips of my aching toes to quicken the process. I roll into the middle of the open structure and look up to the lofted ceiling. Hanging from their tufted tails in the rafters, already anticipating my arrival, are the imps. And once they see me staring back at them, the flock begins scaling the wooden beams along the walls, making their way to the ground at my feet. Some of the imps release small chittering sounds, pushing one another, trying to be the first to reach me. Many of them already cling to my legs and chair, ascending into my lap.

"Hey, be careful," I yelp as I scramble to rescue the covered cakes from beneath their furry rumps. A few of them are wrestling for a spot on my bony knees when the first lick of fire is let loose. Chaos ensues as they attempt to knock each other off their perches on my legs by spitting volleys of tiny flames from their fanged mouths.

I swat at the imps. "Behave! If I see so much as another spark, none of you will get to eat these cakes."

The imps sit as rigid as statues. I glance at each of their bat-like faces and give them the most matriarchal stare I can muster. Then I shoo them off my lap until they all stand before me in an orderly line.

"That's more like it." I nod. "Now, if I give you these cakes, you must promise to leave the brownies alone tonight. No mischief, and absolutely no fire."

From the gurgling noises escaping their round bellies, I know I've gotten their attention. I unwrap the cheesecloth surrounding the cakes. Strings of sticky honey come away with the material. Each cake is fluffy and golden, the outsides brushed with shining honey and the insides dotted with dark purple elderberries. The sugary smell wafting from them is enough to make my own mouth water, and I handle my creations with reverence before surrendering them to the grimy paws of the imps. After snatching for the cakes, they scatter to the darkest corners of the barn to feast. I hope their favored treat will once again be enough to pacify them for the night.

I glimpse the darkening sky outside as I turn in my chair to reach inside my bag. The bones of the bodice I wear over my tunic dig into my sides as I feel around for fabric-wrapped parcels. Then, with a grunt of triumph, I pull out the food I brought for the brownies, along with my full pouch of salt. I unwrap the cheese and bread and lay out the linen handkerchief they were swaddled in. Arranging the provisions on top of the cloth, I make sure the brownies can't miss them when they wake. Then I see the darkening sky again—I don't have a second left to waste. The sun is almost set, and I need to check that barrier.

Dropping the salt in my lap, I hustle into the twilight. I steer my wheelchair toward the paths lining the outermost edge of the glade, using my feet to pedal as much as possible, to help launch me forward and lessen the burning in my biceps. As I glide around the border, I search for breaks in the salt ring. Here and there, I use my brimming pouch to reinforce the salt in the areas where it seems to be spreading a little too thin.

Mother always tells me, if the sun goes down and there's a line through the salt, it's a welcome sign for a bogeyman like Black Annis. We call all the things that go bump in the night bogeymen, but witches are the most dangerous of all—there's nothing they won't do for a scrap of power. And Black Annis is known to murder humans and faeries around the surrounding villages just for sport, adding their skin to her belt like trophies. This thought alone sends shivers down my spine, but I push on.

It's nearing dusk now, and I've almost made it around the barrier when I come upon the garden. My mother has picked it completely bare of its spring fruit and vegetables, and as I get closer, I can just see the top of a gnome's red mushroom-capped head. He's bustling along the empty trellises where the snap peas grew, hunting for stragglers.

Then he disappears from view.

When I reach where he was, I see a foot-wide hole in the ground. When I was younger, a gnome named Fern told me how, deep below the earth, they built themselves a series of gnome-sized tunnels to help them travel fast and deliver messages throughout the forests. As a result, gnomes became the couriers of the faeries. They deliver letters to anyone and anything, as long as they have tunnels connecting to the area.

I'm approaching the last portion I need to check when my chair jolts. My teeth click together as my body is thrown sideways. I have to grab onto my wheels to keep myself from tumbling to the ground. When I gaze down, I see that one of my wheels has gone off the path and into the grass, and it's less than an inch away from the salt barrier. Annoyed at my carelessness, I grumble, trying to pull my wheelchair back onto the stone. But no matter how hard I tug, I can't get it out of the deep grass. The only thing I can do is try to gather enough momentum to bring my wheels over the lip of the pathway.

I hear my mother call down the trail. "Little bird. It's time to come home."

Night is almost upon me now, and I don't want to be left alone in the shadows, especially so close to the barrier. My lifelong fear of coming face-to-face with Black Annis is enough to make my fatigued heart race as my hands grip the rims again, tight. I edge both back wheels into the grass, so I'm no longer lopsided, then pull them back a few inches more before thrusting all four wheels forward, pitching my chair back onto the path.

Without a backward glance, afraid I might see the witch lurking behind me in the dark, I push my way to the safety of my home.

UNDER ATTACK

I wake up to a roaring in my ears. My heart is racing as I lie on my wool-filled mattress. The pounding against my ribcage is enough to make me cringe in pain. I take deep breaths, trying to get my heart to slow down as I glance around, but it's pitch black except for the small sliver of firelight coming from the other side of my bedroom door. I can barely make out the furniture sprinkled around my room. I know there's the worn trunk at the end of my bed, an oak desk a few goblins made, and a cabinet filled to the brim with my books. Each of them bears scratches from me pushing my wheelchair too close. Everything seems normal—

A shrill scream makes me snap up straight in bed, my quilted blanket pooling around my waist. I strain my ears, trying to listen for more, but I can't hear anything over my building anxiety. I pinch my arm just to ensure I'm awake, but the sting I feel does little to soothe me.

Again, a scream comes from somewhere outside in the dark.

I drag myself across my bed to the square window, searching for the source of the shrieking. Squinting, I try to see past my sleepy reflection. I can't help but notice the harrowed look in my jade eyes and the lack of blood in my lips. This spark of nervous energy is making me nauseous now.

Without warning, a shadowy shape darts across my line of sight. It's close enough to make the flowers on the windowsill sway in its wake. I fall to my side, hiding underneath the window, my breath coming in ragged puffs as fear courses through my sore body. What is going on?

I don't know if it's curiosity or insanity that makes me rise onto my knees to look out the window again, but there's nothing outside this time. I scurry to the edge of my narrow bed and swing my legs over the side, onto the bare wood floor, leaning forward to grab the seat of my wheelchair. I pull it closer until it hits my knees. With a swift movement, I turn from my mattress and sit in my chair. I have never been more thankful for my mother taking out the rug in my room. It was impossible to roll over, just like the grass; my wheels would sink right into it.

I try to be quiet as I wheel myself to my door. It creaks on its iron hinges as I guide it open and poke my head out to look for Mother. There's a fire blazing in the stone hearth of our living area, but she's nowhere to be seen. Usually, this time of night, she works on a sewing project while she warms herself by the flames.

I push myself farther into the room and call out for her. "Mother? Are you okay? I heard yelling."

The only answer I receive is another scream from outside. I freeze in my spot by the kitchen table, too afraid of making the floorboards creak. Then the front door flies open, bouncing off the wall from the force of the entry. My mother bolts through the doorway, her long hair out of her usual bun, tangling around her face as she scrambles to latch the heavy lock.

"What's happening?" Fearful tears start to pool in my lashes. I've never seen my mother in such a state.

She runs to me, throwing her arms around my thin frame.

The strength she puts into her hug is enough to send my heart thumping faster yet. Then, she releases me from the embrace and crouches in front of me like she used to when I was a child. "Sparrow, I need you to listen very closely. We're under attack."

"Attack! What do you mean?" The glade has always been secure—we've never once been attacked. Bogeymen always creep along outside the ring, but nothing has ever been bold enough to get past the barrier and come inside.

She hushes me. "I don't know how, but Black Annis is here. She got in by the garden."

My back goes rigid, all the air leaving my lungs. Black Annis. Our living nightmare is in the glade. How could she have gotten in? I checked and reinforced the barrier. It had been solid, intact —or I thought it was. "I don't understand." I shake my head. "How did she get in?"

My mother grips my upper arms and squeezes until the tips of her fingers turn white. "There were two lines through the salt by some of the gnome holes. I don't think they would've purposely let her in, but we can't afford to waste time thinking about blame right now."

My breath catches—I had been out by the gnome holes in the garden when my chair went off the path. Did I put the lines through the salt while trying to get back on it? I'd been too afraid to look behind me before I left, imagining Black Annis standing at my back.

The truth hits me like a blow to the chest. This attack is all my fault. My fear is going to be the glade's undoing. Anxiety starts to burrow itself under my skin, settling in for the night.

My mother stands from her crouch and goes to the window next to the front door. And as she moves the gauzy curtain to see outside, I notice her nightgown. The white cotton is covered in blood. I let out a cry, which sends her stumbling over to me again.

"Sparrow? What is it?" Her eyes frantically search my face.

I reach out toward her dress. Guilt and fear send tremors throughout my body.

"Are—are you hurt?" I pat at her blood-splattered sides, looking for any signs of an injury, but she doesn't even flinch.

Her lower lip wobbles before she clamps down on it with her teeth. Sorrow glazes her words. "No, no, it's not mine. Black Annis is slaughtering the faeries as we speak. I tried to help some of them, to stop the bleeding, but it was too late." Her eyes look wild now. "I need you to listen to me. I need you to—" She's cut off by a sharp knock at the door.

I jump in my seat and clutch onto her nightgown.

My mother pries the soaked material from my fingers. "It's okay, it's just one of the trolls coming to help."

She runs to the door and unlocks it, pulling a thickset troll into the house. Once he crosses the threshold, my mother locks the door again. She presses her body against the wood and takes a deep breath before walking back to me. Then she cups my face between her clammy hands and presses her thin lips into a line. "My little bird, I'm going to need you to be brave for me, okay? I must go outside and search for survivors. I need you to stay here, to stay safe."

"What? No! I'm going with you," I argue.

"No, my love, it's too dangerous. I couldn't live with myself if you get hurt. I don't even want to risk the chance of Black Annis seeing you."

"Mother—" I start to protest. I want to help. I don't want to sit idly by while the faeries I care about get murdered by a witch, especially when it's my fault.

"Hush now. I need you to promise me you'll stay put. Okay?"

I say nothing. My mother jostles my face, which is still held in her hands. "Okay?" she asks again.

"Fine."

She inclines her chin. "There's my girl." Then her lips crush against my forehead, and I can't tell if the tears dripping into my lap are hers or mine. Her voice is almost inaudible. "I love you with my whole heart. I'll be back as soon as I can." Letting go, she steps back toward the door and turns to the troll waiting behind her.

"Copsewood, I need you to stand outside and guard the door. No matter what, I need you to protect Sparrow. Can you do that?"

"Of course, Daughter." His voice rumbles through my taut body as Mother lays her hand against his craggy chest and gives him a firm nod. A moment of understanding and gratitude passes between them, and by the expressions on their faces, I fear they're saying goodbye.

With one last glance toward me, my mother gives me a grim smile and unlocks the door. She cracks it open, peering outside, checking to ensure it's safe before she steals away into the night. I see her shoulders heave as she steps outside, and then she's gone. Copsewood lumbers out after her, sending a pointed look between me and the latch as he yanks the front door closed behind him.

It takes a moment for my brain to catch up. Black Annis is in the glade, and my mother is outside with her. Tears race down my face as I push away from the kitchen table and scamper back into my bedroom. I vault from my chair onto my bed, letting the wheels slam against the wooden sideboard.

Clambering to my knees, I smoosh my face against the window, cupping my hands around the sides of my eyes so I can see through the glass clearly. I spot my mother's stained nightgown glowing in the moonlight, making her look like a wraith as she runs across the grass, herding frightened faeries. She gives the creatures reassuring touches on their shoulders and backs while trying to push them in the direction of the barn. I also spot a few goblins running toward her, and I recognize them as the ones who helped repair the mill earlier today. One of them is hobbling on an injured leg, straggling behind the others. I can see a curling ribbon of skin and muscle peeled from his calf, flapping with each step. The sight makes my heart lurch, but then it flies all the way up into my throat when Black Annis materializes behind him.

Like lightning, her hand punches through his back and out his chest, her iron claws cleaving through him like fresh butter. His blood soaks her blue flesh, making it appear as if she's wearing an elbow-length satin glove. I throw my hands over my mouth to keep my scream from spilling out.

For a moment the witch blinks out of sight before emerging behind another goblin. With little effort, Black Annis disembowels the female using just the flick of her wrist. Again, she disappears and reappears, picking off her victims one by one. The remaining faeries wail at the sight, sprinting away from the ghastly scene in search of safety.

"Go! Run!" I hear my mother yell, waving the faeries forward before following at their heels. She's going to get herself killed—the barn is too far away to seek cover. I start to bang on the window. "Mother! Mother, come back inside!"

She doesn't hear me; she keeps running after the faeries until I can't see her from the window anymore. But someone does hear me, and my body vibrates when I meet Black Annis's gaze through the glass. She's too far away to make out all her features, but close enough for me to see her growing grin. The witch wipes her hands over her open mouth, smearing blood across her face. She looks toward my mother, then back at me. Her body turns in the direction of the barn, and then she vanishes.

"No!" I almost fall headfirst off my bed, barely catching myself as I hurry back into my wheelchair. The hag is going after my mother. I don't think I can stop her, but I must do something. I can't let my mother face her alone.

I slide my way out of my room, hitting the table and chipping a corner off one of its legs as I barrel toward the front door. I open the latch and pull it open only to be met by a very large, very green back.

"Copsewood, we need to go help my mother!" I try to squeeze my chair between his leg and the door jamb, but the troll isn't budging. I kick at the weak point at the back of his knee, but even that doesn't make him move.

"Please," I cry.

Finally, the troll turns around and looks down at me. "Daughter said to protect you. Go back inside, Small One."

I push against the burly creature again. "Please. Please! Black Annis is going after her." Tears of frustration and terror mix as they sluice down my cheeks. The trolls love my mother as much as I do. I can't believe they'd sit back and let her get hurt . . . or worse.

With a sad, stony look, Copsewood leans down, placing his large hands on the arms of my chair, pushing me back into the house. "Safe," he says as he steps outside again and shuts the door behind him.

I wheel forward and tug on the door, but it doesn't open. The troll must be holding it shut from the other side. I want to cry and scream and throw myself against it, but what good would it do? Even if I got outside, how could I truly help? I imagine I'd only succeed in getting both my and my mother's skin stripped from our bodies. I'm a liability in my chair—I always am.

All I can do is make the house safe. I glide into the kitchen and grab a hefty bag of salt from the cupboards. Little grains litter the floor as I drag it through the house, salting every window and crevice I can find. When I'm done, the house will be as impenetrable as the glade should've been.

A fine layer of sweat coats my back and forehead by the time I make it to the front door. I spill the last quarter of the bag in a neat line across the wood and toss the empty bag on the table behind me. There's no way the witch can get in now, and hopefully the others have found some kind of safety too.

I look up at the door and see it's still unlocked. I stare at the latch for a while, hoping Copsewood will open the door and my mother will walk in behind him. But I know the door won't open until the hag is gone and all the faeries are safe, so I raise a trembling hand, letting it hover over the latch. I don't want to leave my mother outside to wade through the butchered faeries and hide from Black Annis, but I have no choice.

Sobbing, I shove the latch down, shutting out everyone and everything I've ever loved, leaving them all to the mercy of the witch.

DEATH ON THE DOORSTEP

It's been hours. Dawn is just around the corner, and I'm still sitting in my wheelchair by the front door. Throughout the night, I heard more screams in the glade and couldn't help wondering which of the faeries, the ones I spent years living side by side with, had died.

I think of the trolls, the brownies, the gnomes and imps and goblins. I think of Rush, the boy I've always been drawn to. I think of my mother and refuse to believe that one of the cries was hers. I convince myself she's found a safe place to hide out, that she'll be back any minute.

I curl up in my chair, knees tucked up under my chin, palms pressed against my ears. After a minute, I hear a loud thud and groan at the front door. Slowly, I set my bare feet onto the floor and creep, leaning forward to press my ear against the wood.

Nothing but silence.

"Copsewood?" I whisper, tapping my finger on the door.

No answer.

I listen for anything: a pained breath, a sigh, or even another scream.

Nothing.

Then the door shudders underneath my head. Someone—or

something—is trying to get inside. I pull back fast, staring at the wood with wide eyes as the scent of sickly-sweet berries seeps through.

"Mother?" I whisper. At this point, I'm pleading for it to be her.

The only answer is an aggravated hiss before the jostling of the door stops. Quiet as possible, I spin my chair around so I can look out the window. But as I peel back the curtain, I'm blinded by blue light. I shade my eyes in response, squinting through the glass, and the image that meets my gaze is nothing short of my worst nightmare.

Black Annis stands in front of my home, surrounded by a host of statues. But these statues aren't made of stone—they're made of fear and witchcraft. It's unlike anything I've seen before. Faeries of all kinds stand completely frozen, cocooned in a bitter blue light. They float behind Black Annis like will-o'-the-wisps as she walks away from my salted door.

The witch sees me watching her and pulls one of the statues closer. Panic roils through my veins as I recognize my mother. Black Annis holds her against her gaunt body with a wicked grin and takes a deep whiff of my mother's hair.

The sun is rising behind the hag. It's just on the cusp, and Black Annis follows my line of sight to see her impending doom. For a moment, I'm filled with hope—maybe we can all survive this. But before I can blink, the witch turns back, waves her glinting talons, and disappears with her collection of prisoners.

No. This can't be happening. I let go of the curtain, and with numb, bloodless fingers, I reach up to unlock the front door. Drawing in a lungful of air, I swing it open, expecting an empty glade, but with a keening sound, the breath rushes out of me. The glade is not empty, not fully. On the doorstep, lying in a lake of blood, is Copsewood.

Tears fill my eyes, blurring the gruesome image of the troll and his entrails on the ground. I press my hands to my mouth as my stomach rolls. His stout belly has been cleaved open from his hip to his chest in four ragged lines. I was too low where I was sitting at the window to see his body on the ground when I looked out.

Poor Copsewood.

I try not to glance at the troll's corpse as I roll closer to him. I bend forward as much as my chair allows me and plant my hands on his blood-drenched side. I shove as hard as I can to try and clear a path, but his body won't budge. My mouth waters with nausea—I'm going to be sick. I need to get out of here, but there's no way I can move the troll, and no way to get around him. I peer past the doorway and out into the glade. "Hello?" I call, my voice barely louder than a whisper. "Hello?" I try again. "Is anyone still here?"

I hear muffled footsteps approaching from the side of the house. My eyes dart around, but I don't see anyone. My hands start to sweat.

"Hello? Who's there?"

"Sparrow?" a bodiless voice says.

I flinch and roll backward into the house.

"Sparrow, it's okay. It's me."

"Rush?" I move forward to peek around the corner.

"Yeah, I'm here."

I can't see him anywhere. "Where are you?"

He materializes right in front of me.

My heart lurches, but only for a moment until I remember that, like all goblins, Rush can conceal himself.

"I'm sorry, I didn't mean to scare you," he says.

I look up at his face, but his eyes are trained on Copsewood, sprawled in his cooling blood.

"I can't move him," I murmur.

Rush meets my eyes before letting his gaze rove over my body, checking for injuries. "Are you okay?"

I nod. "Just stuck."

Taking another glance at the troll, Rush walks over to his feet and bends to grab his ankles. With a grunt, he digs his heels into the ground and pulls. As Rush drags Copsewood off the doorstep, I stare at the blood trail smearing the dirt in his wake. The next thing I know, Rush is before me, putting his hand on my shoulder. "Are you sure you're okay?" His thick brows are furrowed.

"I will be. I just have to go find my mother." I shake my head, brush off his hand, and begin to push myself across the threshold, straight through the salt and sticky blood. All I can think about is how the blood will stain the light wood of my wheels, especially if I don't clean it soon.

"Sparrow, wait, about your mom—"

"I saw what happened to her," I interrupt him. "I have to go find her." I continue to push myself, heading farther out into the glade, onto the path I hope will lead me straight into my mother's warm arms.

"Sparrow!" Rush chases after me.

"I need to get her back, Rush."

"Sparrow, wait!" The half-goblin grabs onto the handles of my wheelchair and yanks me to a stop, making my body pitch forward.

I turn in my chair to give him an incredulous glare. Nothing irks me more than people touching my chair like that, especially without permission.

He throws his hands up in apology. "Look, I'm sorry, but you aren't listening to me. You can't just leave the glade. You're in no way, shape, or form prepared." Rush scrapes his hands over his mouth and across his jaw. I notice then how haunted and tired he looks.

"Did you see her? Black Annis?" I ask.

He answers me with a nod.

"Where were you?" I can't keep the tremors from my voice.

"I was on a walk on the other side of the glade when I heard screaming coming from the garden. By the time I got there, bodies were everywhere. Black Annis tore apart most of the gnomes before they could run to their tunnels." Rush shudders. "It was awful, Sparrow . . ."

"Did you see what happened to my mother? How she got caught?"

Rush shakes his head. "I left the garden to go find my pop and sisters." He deflates. "But I didn't find them at home, so, I concealed myself and snuck up to your house to make sure you and your mom were okay. When I got there, Black Annis already had her, and then I saw the witch kill Copsewood. It happened so fast. He didn't even see her until it was too late." He turns to glance at the corpse we left behind. "Then Black Annis started pulling on the door. I thought for sure she was going to get inside. I've heard a lot of tales in my travels, but nothing would've prepared me for seeing her in person . . ." His eyes glaze over before he continues. "She looked like a queen of Purgatory the way she was drenched to her elbows in gore. Her smile was so wicked . . . and her eyes. They were solid black."

The description sends my skin crawling. I knew I'd smelled something cloying through the door, and to know my head was pressed against the wood while the belladonna-soaked hag was on the other side is terrifying. The worst part is, my mother was with her, watching her try to reach me. She must have been terrified. "Rush, you know what this means, right?"

The half-goblin gazes into the far distance, searching out the banshee trees surrounding Black Annis's home like he knows what I'm going to say.

"I have to go get my mother and all the surviving creatures back. If Black Annis didn't kill them all while she was here, she'll save them as playthings for later. I might still have time to save some of them if I leave now." I heard rumors around the glade while growing up that the witch worships the hunt. She'll pick creatures outside the barrier off one after another, and only when she grows bored of her mass destruction does she save victims for later. These stories always resulted from missing loved one. Their bodies had to be going somewhere, and Black Annis was sure to be that answer.

"I thought you might say that." Rush puts his hands into the pockets of his olive-green trousers. "Come on then." He jerks his head back toward my house. "Go pack a bag."

I give him a skeptical look. "You say it like you're coming with me."

"Of course I'm coming with you." He sighs.

I cross my arms. "Do you think I'm not capable of going alone because I'm in a wheelchair?" I know it's an illogical time to argue something like this, but for some reason I can't help myself.

Rush gapes at me. "Of course that's not why . . . I don't know, it might be part of it, but it's not—"

"Hey! I'll have you know—"

"That's not what I meant."

"Just because I can't walk—"

"No, Sparrow!" Rush groans and throws his hands up into the air. "Black Annis took my family." He pauses. "I'm going with you because she has my family."

All the fight leaves my body. "Oh." I was too caught up in my worry about my mother; I hadn't even seen his father and sisters in the blue-glazed crowd.

Rush rubs his hands over his short, tight-curled hair. I wheel closer to him and put a hand on one of his elbows. "I'm sorry," I breathe.

He lowers his arms and grabs my hand, then peers down to study my fingers curled within his own. His casual show of affection reminds me of when we were kids. He was always tactile, pulling me into sticky hugs and playing with my hair. I follow his gaze. My hand is practically dwarfed by his broad palms, and the difference between our skin is sharp but beautiful. The way our fingers are laced together reminds me of piano keys.

He lets out a long exhale. "Thank you." His silver eyes glow in the rising sun as he meets my stare. The way the light catches on the highest points of his face shows the glimmer of green sitting under his skin. It shimmers so soft in comparison to the vivid green of his full-goblin sisters. Then he releases my hand and puts his own back into his pockets. I fold mine into my lap, praying they didn't feel clammy in his, before I flick my head toward my house. "I'll go pack that bag now. Do you want to come inside and wait? Or do you need to grab your things?"

"I only have the clothes on my back. It makes my—what did you say—*nomadic wayfaring lifestyle* easier." Despite everything we just faced, and will face ahead, a corner of his mouth tilts up, and I notice the deep dimples this creates in his cheeks.

I nod with a small smile in return. "Of course. I'll lead the way."

Turning my chair, I roll back toward my home, trying not to blanch at the sight of Copsewood lying along the side of the house, collecting flies. As my wheels bounce over the doorway, I can't help but wince over the tracks of dirt and blood I'm leaving on the floor. I can only hope that, in a week, I'll return to the glade with my mother and help her scrub them from the floorboards.

When I reach the open door to my bedroom, I turn in my wheelchair toward Rush. There's an almost-wistful quality about him as he stands in the front room and takes it all in—the worn areas on the floor, the empty hearth spilling ashes, the closed door to my mother's bedroom, and the vase of peonies sitting on the kitchen table. I feel like he's trying to imagine our daily lives inside this house. There seems to be a hint of longing in his silver eyes.

"You can help yourself to any food in the cupboards if you're hungry. Or you could help me by packing enough for us to eat along the way." I point toward the tall wooden doors lining the far walls of the room.

"Sure, I can do that."

After giving Rush a nod, I guide my chair into my bedroom and close the door behind me. I sit for a moment, staring at the morning light now streaming across the floors from the window.

Everything looks so normal.

Meanwhile, outside these four walls, a massacre has taken place. It feels wrong for this home to appear so ordinary when life is in ruins around it. Before I can think about it more or risk crying again, I roll over to my trunk. The warped wood lets out a squeal as I hoist the lid. Inside, folded in neat piles, are my clothes. The familiar black and earth-toned fabrics greet me with open arms, giving me a false sense of security.

I peel off my nightclothes before slipping on a black tunic, lacing up a bottle-green bodice over it. I wriggle into a pair of charcoal-colored trousers and flex my feet before lifting my weakened legs into a pair of tall black boots. I close the trunk with a snap and grab the bag sitting on the desk by the door. Flipping open the top flap, I take inventory of what I already have packed inside. I only find half of a salt pouch left, along with an empty waterskin. The troll's changeling heart has been removed, though. Before going to bed, I sealed it away in the short trunk my mother keeps under her bed. It nestled perfectly alongside the other sibling hearts we confiscated over the years.

I close my bag and swing it onto the handles of my chair, making a mental note to refill my salt pouch. After giving my room a once-over, my eyes snag on my cabinet of books. Lines of colored leather spines stand up straight in neat rows like soldiers. Their embossed titles glitter in the morning light. After a short internal debate, I pluck one off the shelf and slip it into my bag. I'm not sure I can do without at least one book. I need it

—I often find myself delving into fantastical worlds full of make-believe pirates and princesses when my anxiety is at its worst. It's calming to slip away from my worries, even if it's just for a little while.

I hear Rush rustling around the cupboards in the other room. Closing my eyes, I can almost imagine the noise is my mother making breakfast before a long day of chores around the glade. I can picture myself sweeping in and baking her favorite sticky buns, the ones I usually save for Christmastide mornings, just because I know they'll make her eyes gleam. My pulse races. Maybe if I reach her in time, maybe if I get us all back home safely, I'll have the chance to do just that.

I open my bedroom door and push into the living room just as Rush pokes his head out of the cupboard with his arms full of food and an empty waterskin. A stack of cheesecloth hangs from his teeth.

"Think you found enough?" I shake my head with a small smile.

"You tell me." His reply is muffled by the cloth.

After closing the cupboard doors with a foot, he walks to the kitchen table and sets out the food. Before me lies cheese, hard-tack, nuts, dried fruits, meat, and leftover sweet pastries. We rarely have milk at the glade, since my mother's trips to the village are so few and far between, so I've been trying out recipes without dairy and eggs. I've made the pillowy, pocket-sized, blackberry-jam-filled treats many times, and I think I finally perfected them. Lucky for us, they keep for quite a while.

Taking the cloth Rush grabbed, I wrap up the various foods in their own little sacks. Without being prompted, Rush takes the wrapped food from my hands and stands behind me to put them away in my bag. Then his hand, the one holding my waterskin, materializes next to my head. I take the skin from him and roll back over to the cupboard to find salt to refill my pouch. Pushing jars to the side, looking high and low, I find none. I must have used the last of it to cover the windows and doors. Passing back and forth through the front door scattered the thick line I'd poured there, and all that's left is the little drifts along the windows, hardly enough to fill the pouch.

"Can you hand me the salt in my bag?"

Rush roots around for a while before setting it in my hand. I thank him and make my way to the window by the front door. Opening the pouch, I run the side of my hand along the sill, scooping the grains into the bag. It doesn't even make a dent.

"What are you doing?" Rush asks.

I raise a brow at him. "Didn't your father teach you to bring salt with you everywhere? Especially on your travels?"

His eyes dart off to the side. "He might have mentioned it once or twice."

"I have a creeping suspicion you don't often listen to him."

"Ah, not particularly, no." He gives me a sheepish smile.

I tisk. Having spent his time out in the world, away from the specific dangers that haunt our home, has made Rush lax. He probably hasn't had to salt a house in quite a while.

The amount of salt I end up collecting is pitiful. My mother was meant to go to the village tomorrow, and I know purchasing more to stock the larder was on her list. If I'd only thought about it, I'd have conserved some. Salt is purifying, lethal to anything rotting on the inside, like witches. I don't know how just yet, but I'll probably need to use this pouch against Black Annis. Heaving a sigh, I take one last glimpse around my empty home and hope this will be a temporary absence, that my mother will have another chance to go into the village again. Then, I turn over my shoulder. "Ready?" I ask as I hand Rush back the secured salt pouch.

"Good to go."

We leave my house and Copsewood's body without a backward glance. Thinking of leaving him to the elements makes my throat feel thick, but we don't have the luxury of burying him right now. Rush and I couldn't move him to better cover under the barn alone, and we are truly on borrowed time.

According to the gnomes and their tunneling system, it takes eight days to get to Black Annis's home and back. This means Rush and I have four days of travel ahead, and we can only hope nothing happens to our families before we get there.

We stop at the mill to dip our waterskins into the stream before making the trek to the edge of the glade. I'm already feeling a slight strain in my arms from the fast pace, but thankfully the smooth, paved paths make it easier to glide along. Then, like a stone sinking into the pit of my stomach, I start to dread reaching the edge of the glade, where the pathways end. I hardly remember a time I've gone past the barrier since I could still walk. I've never had to try to push myself through a forest. I learned as a child how hard it was just to roll over soft grass. I got my wheels stuck multiple times, having to wait until my mother or one of the trolls could come to my rescue. I can only imagine how much harder pushing myself through a forest will be—not to mention the dangers lurking out there. The glade has always kept me safe from bogeymen. I imagine Black Annis will be preoccupied with her recent captives, but that doesn't mean something else won't stalk us. Rush and I will have to be careful. We'll need to find shelter to protect us every night, and use the salt in my bag sparingly.

Before I know it, we reach the end of the path and the barrier sits at my feet, blinding white, mocking me.

It's now or never.

With a deep breath, I steel myself for the journey, for the monsters I might face. I'm about to traverse into a world that isn't built for me.

WHEELCHAIRS DO NOT LIKE THE FOREST

I knew I was in trouble the moment my wheelchair left the path.

It took barely ten minutes before I broke out into a sweat. Now my arms are on fire as I try to push over the spongy forest floor. My wheels sink into the loose dirt, and every rock and branch littering the ground catches my chair and wrenches me to a stop. I try to use the tips of my toes to help me along, but it does nothing to lessen the battle. And I feel my feeble heart palpitating with all the effort.

During these ten minutes of agony, Rush walks alongside my chair, keeping with my slow pace. He doesn't say a word, just saunters with his hands inside his pockets, as usual. For some reason, his placid posture is infuriating, and I can carry on no longer. I'm fatigued, anxious, and frankly still a little nauseous from seeing my first dead body.

I stop pushing myself to rub at my aching arms and catch my breath. Rush stops, waiting next to me. From the look on his face, I know he wants to help, but the way I reacted when he touched my chair earlier must have been enough to make him hold back.

More than anything, I loathe feeling incapable. When I first became wheelchair-bound, I refused all help. I'd stubbornly push myself across the glade no matter how sick or exhausted it made me feel. I even tried to return to my childhood antics, but it wasn't long before I realized I would never again run through the grass over hills with the changeling children, dance in the summer storms with the goblins, or climb trees with the imps. I fell into a long depression and developed intense bouts of anxiety. Over time, I pulled through the worst of it, coming to terms with my new limits, but I'll admit, even now, my anxiety still lingers. Especially when I'm stressed or afraid—which, in the last twelve hours, has been inescapable. Tucking my pride away, I twist toward Rush, resigning myself to ask for help. "Well, it's beginning to seem like I require your assistance."

"Finally!" Rush howls. "You have no idea how painful that was to watch."

"Oh come on, it wasn't that bad."

Rush pins me with a pointed, joking stare. "It was downright tragic."

"Yeah, yeah, get back there and push me before I change my mind."

Needing no further encouragement, Rush practically skips behind, grabbing the handles of my chair with a smile. They creak and groan under his grip.

"Wow. How old is this thing?" Rush blurts as he starts to push. The going isn't smooth, but with his natural goblin strength, he isn't having as much trouble getting me over the constant obstacles on the footpath.

"You know, I'm not sure. I've had it for ten years, but I'm pretty sure the trolls went out and stole it from some elderly folk. I can only hope they had no use for it anymore."

"I do too. Those trolls have thieving issues." Rush sniggers.

We carry on in silence for a time until I feel a cloud of tension at my back. From the way Rush's body stiffens as he pushes me, I can sense hesitation, and I have a feeling there's something more he wants to say. I cross my arms and relax into my chair, resting my sore arms as I leave Rush to say what's on his mind when he's ready. I never like to push people—I just want them comfortable and cared for. It's probably why I bake so much, because feeding people puts them at ease.

The thought prompts me to remind Rush of the pastries in my bag, just in case, and then I ask him to pass me my book. Reading is the best thing I can do to take my mind off what we left behind, and what we're heading toward--off of the suffering I imagine my mother might be enduring. I tuck my near-shoulder-length hair behind my ears as I read. It's long enough now that it's tickling the sides of my neck. I like to keep it cropped to my chin, but my mother hasn't trimmed it for me in months. I fight the itch to scratch at my prickling skin along with my spiraling thoughts. I'm worried about her.

A few minutes later, I hear Rush swallow the last of the pastry he pilfered from the bag before he takes a breath. "Sparrow? Can I ask you something?"

"Of course." I close my book.

"I don't want this to sound insensitive . . . but what happened to you?"

I almost feel him wince at the way he asks his question. Rush and his father didn't live at the glade when my heart gave out. They showed up just before spring, months after I first started using a wheelchair. Rush, being only two years older than me, had a childlike curiosity about my chair, wanting rides especially, but he never asked about my health. I imagine the worms we dug up and mud cakes we made were far more important to him at the time. After Rush's father remarried, and his half-sisters came along, Rush began setting out on adventures. Alone. Sometimes he'd be gone for weeks, then it became months—the last stint was two years. As a result, we never had the chance to get to know each other as teenagers. Best friends turned to friends, and then friends turned to acquaintances . . . I take a deep breath. "Well, I'd always been a sick child, and my mother found out early on I had a weak heart."

The handles of my chair creak as Rush readjusts his hands. "Oh, so you weren't always in a wheelchair?"

I sigh. "No. The autumn I turned eight, I was out in the garden with Fern, one of the messenger gnomes, and felt my heart begin to pound. It was so painful it took my breath away." I pause as my memories resurface. "I remember thinking for a fleeting second I was dying."

"You must've been so scared," Rush murmurs.

I huff out a laugh. "Utterly terrified. I ended up collapsing among the vegetables that day. I got a huge mouthful of soil."

Rush lets out a half-awkward chuckle.

"Afterwards, in slow increments, I lost the ability to stand on my own. If I tried, my heart would explode with pain and I'd lose consciousness." I swallow. Sometimes I forget how traumatic those times were.

"The day I lay in the dirt with the pumpkins, that was one of the last times I remember walking. I spent the next month lying on my bed in oblivion. When I finally came around, my mother and the trolls had started creating the paths, and they had this chair ready for me to use."

"I can't even imagine just accepting a new version of life like that. You're very brave." I can't see Rush's face, but I can hear the sorrow in his voice.

"I wouldn't say I'm brave. Bravery doesn't have anything to do with being suddenly disabled. I'm not any braver than you." I laugh and put as much kindness into my tone as I can. I don't want Rush to think this is an upsetting topic. "I just wake up in the morning and get into a wheelchair instead of walking out the door. It also doesn't make me any less capable. I have a fully functioning life, and I don't think being forced to live it requires bravery."

Rush sucks in a breath. "You're right, I'm sorry. You just handle it so well. I think I'd be mad at the world."

I turn in my chair to give him a polite smile. "No harm done. I have days where I mourn my old self, but in the end, I just have to carry on, and live."

There's a moment of silence as we continue through the forest. I get through another few pages in my hefty book, trying hard not to think about the danger my mother is in before Rush speaks again. "I always thought people used wheelchairs because their legs didn't work. All the villages I visited had people with injured spines and legs, or they just happened to be born that way."

I mull over my thoughts before I speak. "Not always. Some of us just need our chairs to help us get around a little safer and easier." I raise my feet from their rest on my wheelchair and wiggle them in the air. "See? Everything's in working order."

"Except for your heart?"

"Except for my heart." I agree.

"I'm sorry it took me so long to ask. I've always been curious, but I didn't know how to bring it up. I figured now would be a good time as any, given we'll be stuck together for the next four days."

"You say it like it's a bad thing." I laugh for the first time since the attack.

"It was easy to get along as kids when we had everything in the world in common. We don't exactly have dug-up worms and games of Fire Ball with the imps to bond over anymore." I hear the smile in Rush's voice.

I sit up straighter in my chair. "I've been told I'm great company nowadays."

"Oh yeah? By whom?" Rush prods at my back.

I wave a hand. "Lots of people. Especially the brownies."

"The brownies, huh?" His voice is full of mirth now. "Those

grouchy creatures don't like anyone, and no one particularly likes them either."

I turn my head to the side so he can see my smirk. "Well, maybe cranky personalities agree with me."

Rush lets out a bellowing laugh this time, and I like the sound; it eases my stress and anxiety more than even my book. His voice lowers as he replies, "I'm sure they do, Sparrow. You're a special one."

I turn my head forward and flit through book pages, glad he can't see the blush spreading across my pasty skin.

It's so easy to fall back into laughs and good memories, but my happy-go-lucky attitude is quick to dissolve again. I know for a fact my mother isn't laughing right now, neither are the faeries.

Rush readjusts his grip on my chair, sensing the change in mood as we bump over another patch of moss and stones. "Care to read out loud? A story might help to—pass the time."

I can hear some of last night's horrors still haunting Rush's tone, and I'm happy to share my book with him—maybe it'll work to ease both our souls. His request also makes me hope for a new level of connection and friendship with him, one that doesn't include mud pies. My mother has always encouraged my passion for reading, but she's never really been interested in sharing the experience with me. Having someone around who's also passionate about stories could be refreshing. "Once upon a time . . ."

-

WE SPEND the next couple hours trading stories, me from my brown leather book about a beautiful woman under a sleeping enchantment and Rush from his own memory. He's seen many lands, traveled by river, and explored the mountains. He's lived in an ancient fishing village where people's homes were built on stilts in the water. He's stayed in smoky cities where people sell their wares from brightly colored tents on the streets. He even once stopped in a place where vineyards full of grapes stretched as far as the eye could see. The number of people and creatures he's talked to is dizzying, and he's heard so many intriguing fables, stories passed down from generation to generation.

I've only left the glade a couple of times, and I was young enough that I hardly remember those trips now. All I can remember is strange people and even stranger smells. There wasn't rolling grass like in the glade, but dirt-packed streets and not even a hint of the fresh ground spices from the tented city Rush told me about. Just hay-thatched roofs, horse droppings, and the memory of clutching onto my mother's skirts for dear life.

Rush has experienced a whole world I will probably never see, but it seems he's never stayed in one place too long. It makes me wonder if he'll ever settle down, if he'll ever enjoy having a home like my mother and I. Still, I soak up each new tale, wishing I could write them down and keep them in a book on my shelf. Maybe one day.

The rumble of his voice behind my back as he tells of his experiences, along with the gentle bumping through the forest, is almost enough to lull me to sleep. I haven't slept a wink since I heard the faeries screaming outside my window last night. At some point, we'll have to settle down for the night. Neither of us wants to stop, though, I can tell—we're afraid of what hides in the shadows and dreading that every moment wasted sleeping is time Black Annis has to hurt our loved ones. I can't even bear to think of the possibility of my mother already being gone, and I'm sure Rush feels the same about his family.

We take short breaks, allowing us to rest and eat for only a few minutes at a time. And despite the effort, I transfer from my chair to sit on the mossy ground with Rush, so I can stretch out my sore legs. Hours of sitting in my wooden chair are making my lax muscles throb, and I already feel a bruise forming on my tailbone. Rush and I split the hardtack and cheese into small portions to conserve food for the days ahead, and we try to take sparing sips of water now, hoping we'll soon come across a spring to refill our skins.

When we resume, I also try to conserve my patience. It's hard having someone else pushing me; the lack of control and constant jostling is starting to knock the kindness out of me. Over the decade of being in a wheelchair, I've developed a keen awareness of my surroundings. I know when my chair will fit through a particular space, and I know what surfaces to avoid rolling over. Rush, on the other hand, does not have this honed understanding, and he keeps running me into logs or failing to maneuver me around larger rocks. I don't want it to bother me, but it grates on my nerves. I know he's doing this out of decency, and I know I shouldn't complain, but there's still a couple hours of sunlight left and I think I might burst.

I try to focus on reading again, but the next bump pushes me to my limits, and right as I'm about to suggest we stop to find shelter, I hear a metallic rattling. It's a very out-of-place sound in this forest. I look up from the book in my lap, scanning our surroundings. I don't see the source of the noise, but then I hear it again.

This time it's closer.

I look ahead of us, then turn to the left and the right, but there's nothing. Just obstacles made of towering trees with roots weaving in and out of the ground, sticking up like a looping labyrinth.

"Hey Rush," I pipe up, "you should steer clear of those exposed roots." They're a clear danger to a rickety chair like mine.

"Yeah, I see them," Rush mumbles, but I can tell he's distracted by something. Maybe he heard the sound too?

We get closer to the trees, and my palms start sweating. There's a dense cloud of foreboding in the air, and as Rush continues to push me a little too close for comfort toward the twisting roots, the hair on the back of my neck pricks. Twisting in my seat, I lean to my right to see past Rush's body.

A pair of sulfurous, yellow eyes peer back at me from the shadows.

I keep my voice low, whispering to the half-goblin, "I believe we're being followed."

As Rush turns around to see what I'm talking about, a giant wolflike dog emerges from the trees. It's the height of a garden shed, with sooty black fur that seems to move in a nonexistent wind. A collar of chain hangs from its thick neck, and the links clink against the massive shoulders with every step it takes.

I hear a curse slip from under Rush's breath as he begins to push me faster. He steers me erratically as he keeps looking back over his shoulder at the dog. We're heading straight for the trees I've been worried about, and I know Rush isn't sparing the roots a single thought. Not that I blame him—the creature behind us is more than enough to take up my panicked thoughts as well.

Still, I look ahead for both of us. "I'm not going to fit through there," I warn.

"We'll make it," Rush assures me with a glance forward. He continues to push me straight for the trees, and I hear the dog's steps pick up.

"Rush, watch out!" I yell.

It's too late.

The grinding of my wheels as they barrel between two thick roots is deafening. I come to a jarring stop. Rush keeps trying to push me farther, but my wheelchair doesn't budge.

I twist in my chair, fast. "I'm stuck." Despite its impossible size and the amount of ground it could cover, the dog is a few paces away, approaching us menacingly slow. I swear I can hear a growl coming from its chest. A dark green flush spreads over Rush's cheeks, all the way up to his pointy ears as he shoves at my chair again. I think I hear him begging the trees and Fate to release my wheel.

His prayers are answered with a loud crunch.

The great dog behind us snarls.

My wheel does pop up and over the roots, but as soon as Rush pushes me forward again, I know the spokes haven't come away unscathed. A violent shudder goes through my chair and the wheel wobbles beneath me. I clasp a clammy hand down on my book as Rush breaks into a run. My wheelchair's sputtering noises, paired with the thunderous bark sounding behind us, are the worst symphony I've ever heard. That is, until I hear the crack of splitting wood, and see the slope we're heading straight for. "Rush?"

"I know, I know!"

Dread bubbles from my stomach, lodging itself in my throat. "What are we going to do?" There's nowhere to go, and the huge monster of a dog is getting too close to turn around now.

"I'm going to lower you down, okay?"

If only Rush could see the dubious look on my face as I yell at him. "Lower me down?"

Without warning, he tilts me backward, so my feet are lifted off the ground and my face is parallel with the sky. I try to protest, but my lips are clamped tight with fear. His steps are stilted as he lowers me down and tries to keep his footing behind me.

The dog howls.

Surprised, Rush slips, causing my chair to skid forward and clip a large rock jutting out of the grass. My wobbly wheel gives out. Rush loses his grip on the handles and they slam into the ground, making my head snap backward. As my chair rolls down the slope, I'm tossed to the ground to tumble head over heels. I try to catch myself on my hands, but I'm only rewarded with rocks jabbing into my palms and knees. When I hit the forest floor, I land on my back, hard. Pieces of my chair settle around me as I suck in a pained breath. Turning my head to the side, I see my book and Rush sliding after me.

The book comes to a gentle stop in the grass while the half-goblin skitters toward me with his arms pinwheeling. "Sparrow! Are you alright?" He helps me sit up, leaving a protective hand on my shoulder.

The dog bays from the top of the slope before it prowls downward. The bogey-like creature has its head low between its shoulders, its eyes smoldering, and each time a colossal paw strikes the earth my heart gives a paltry thump. I sit frozen, my muscles turned to solid ice.

Ever so slowly, Rush reaches forward until he gets hold of my book. He weighs it in his hands as he stares down the dog. I see a flash of teeth as Rush cranks his arm back and heaves the book at the creature. But before the weighty tome can make contact, the dog dissipates in a cloud of howling mist.

Rush is breathing hard. "What in Fate's name was that?"

A manic laugh bursts from my chest. The absurdity of what I just saw and the pure unadulterated fear coursing through my body makes me tremble. I can't even begin to comprehend what the creature that chased us was. But when I shift my thoughts from the ghostly dog to the broken mess around me, my laugher dissolves. The tiny, fractured pieces of blond, bloodstained wood that used to be my wheelchair lie scattered over the ground. Frustrated tears well in my eyes, and I press my knuckles against my face, trying not to cry. My anxiety grows. I'm stressed, I'm afraid—I have no idea how I'll ever save my mother, or Rush's family, or the rest of the faeries. And now I don't even have a chair to take me there. I rub at my temples.

Turning back and leaving everyone to die at the hands of Black Annis isn't an option either.

Rush puts his hand back on my shoulder. "Are you okay?"

I peer at him through watery eyes. I don't have an answer for him. He plops down in front of me and hooks his arms around his knees.

Somehow, I find my voice. "What are we going to do, Rush? It's not like I can walk the rest of the way."

He takes a deep breath through his nose, his pointed ears twitching as his brows knit. Then, with a sudden head jerk, he sniffs at the air like he's caught a scent. A small smile replaces his furrow. "Have you ever heard of the Elder Mother?" he asks.

"I can't say that I have." My voice is only a croak as I'm still trying to weave my frayed nerves into place.

Rush pokes his finger into a hole in the knee of my trousers. They must've ripped while I flailed my way down the slope. "Lucky for you, I have." His straight, pearly teeth are in full view now.

Despite everything, I give in to the joy on his face. It makes me think of all the times his grin got me into trouble as a kid. "Who is she?" I know he's dying for me to ask.

"The Elder Mother is said to be the guardian of all elder trees. Legend has it, elder trees can ward off evil. They grow full of purity, life, and magic. That's why the trolls use twigs from elder trees to make changeling hearts. The magic living inside the branches helps to power the troll charms."

"Bramwell never told me that." I've always wondered why they only used pieces of elder trees to craft their children's hearts, but I never thought to ask.

"It's true. Folk I've talked to say the Elder Mother lives in a cottage somewhere in a forest. Her home is surrounded by a grove full of elder trees. Since they ward off evil, nothing like Black Annis can get inside. We'd be safe for a time, and maybe she could even help us with . . ." His voice trails off as he looks around at the wreckage.

I exhale a heavy breath. "This is fascinating, Rush, but what does it have to do with anything right now? It's only a story."

His answering smirk is borderline mischievous, once again reminding me of our childhood. "Thanks to my pop, I have a wonderful sense of smell, and I just picked up on something."

Now my interest is piqued. "What would that be?"

"Hundreds of blooming elder trees. I can smell the flowers a mile away."

What he's implying dawns on me. Could one of the tales Rush has collected be true? "Are you telling me you think the Elder Mother is real and lives in this forest? A mile from where we're at right now?"

"Why yes, yes I am." His dimples are on full display, and he seems to almost buzz with excitement. "It's worth a look, Sparrow." His expression sobers. "Night is almost here."

I nod, teeth gritting at his last statement. "How are we going to get there?"

"Well, milady, I can carry you there. With your permission, of course." Rush presses a hand against his chest, trying to imitate the perfect gentleman.

I feel delirious. I've gone through a whole range of emotions in such a short time, and I don't quite know what to do with myself, nor my lack of wheelchair, but that's a thought for after we find cover. I give my head a small shake before shrugging my tired shoulders. I suppose all I can do is hope the Elder Mother is real, and that she's friendly enough to offer us shelter for a night. I shove at his legs. "Why are you still sitting there? Let's go."

With a cheer, Rush rises to his feet. He recovers my book, places it inside my bag, and straps it to his back. Then, he stoops down to thread an arm under my knees and around my back. After a decade of my body atrophying, I've lost a considerable amount of weight, but I still marvel at the ease with which Rush holds me.

I feel the muscles of his chest and arms against my side as he starts to follow his nose, and I can't remember a time I've ever been carried this way. It's odd, but also intimate, and I will myself not to fawn over this young man I grew up with but hardly know.

-

THE SUN IS SETTING when we arrive at a clearing. Rush's nose led him true. Before us are hundreds of elder trees, ranging in size from twenty-foot pillars to small shrubs. Each of them teems with clusters of white flowers that fill the space with the creamy smell of impending summer. Some of the more mature trees have even begun to grow small, dark purple elderberries. I know from experience how wonderful they are in honey cakes, and my mouth waters involuntarily.

Rush weaves us through the trees, pausing here and there, letting his nose lead us to shelter. Each tree stands like a guard, tall and proud, but they all appear so alike, it's hard to judge our progress. The waning light lets me know we've been in the maze of elder trees for a while. But over time, Rush's steps become more confident and quicker, like he's caught a new scent now. And just as the sky darkens, we're spit out into the middle of a clearing surrounded by tall grass. Squinting and looking straight ahead, I can see a quaint forest cottage a few hundred yards away.

It takes Rush awhile to cover the distance, but once we're close enough, I can see the house is made of large gray stones, with ivy climbing up the walls like lace. The roof is engulfed in moss and other small bits of foliage, and I can tell, from the smoke drifting out of the chimney, that we caught someone at home.

I glance up at Rush to share my thoughts but stop when I see the wonder on his face. It's the same look I noticed when I invited him into my house, and I can't help thinking, despite his constant wanderings, that this boy *is* yearning for a place to settle down and call home.

Rush gazes down at me, his silver eyes reflective in the waning light. They look the same way a wild animal's eyes do at night. The jagged edges of his ears and cheekbones glitter green. He looks like a faerie prince. I clear my throat, hoping the fading sunshine masks the color rising to my cheeks. Then I swallow before I whisper, "I think we made it."

He dips his chin like we're sharing a secret. "I think so too."

We wade through the grass toward the cottage, and it sways around Rush's knees, brushing against the toes of my boots as he cradles me to his chest. Moths of all sizes flee the safety of the grass, rising up into the warm twilight sky. The air feels charged with magic.

"Can you feel it, Rush?"

He gives me an amused look. "What?"

"The magic." I wave my free arm through the air as if the magic were tangible. I imagine my fingers passing through enchantments made of silk. "It's extraordinary." A moth flutters its way past my hand, landing on the tip of Rush's long ear. He shivers as I brush it away, and I let my fingertips linger for just a moment longer than necessary. I remember how captivated I was by his ears when I was child. I'd never met a half-faerie before, and I knew the first time I saw him, I wanted him with me. There was a pull I just couldn't escape, and I demanded right then and there that we be best friends. We even sealed the deal with a spit-slick handshake.

As we draw nearer to the house, I can smell herbs and

boiling berries wafting from the smoking chimney. The scent reminds me of the days I've spent making preserves with my mother, and my near-empty stomach pines for scones smothered with clotted cream and homemade jam.

Rush jostles me. "What are you thinking about?"

My face burns. "Scones," I mumble.

I turn my head away from his amused look to see how close we are to the cottage. He walks forward until I'm within arm's reach of the arched doorway, and I raise my fist to knock on the intricately carved wood.

Without warning, the front door swings open, and a voice greets us from the shadows. "What do we have here?"

THE ELDER MOTHER

An elderly woman steps into the moonlit night. She's silhouetted by the blaze pouring from her doorway, and it creates a glowing halo of messy, braided hair around her head. Her thin olive skin wrinkles heavily around her eyes and mouth as she gives us a gap-toothed grin. "I haven't had visitors in years. It's been awfully dull." She beckons us with a wave of her hands. "Come in, come in."

The stranger herds us into her cottage, and a wall of heat hits us as we cross the threshold. A fire is roaring in the hearth, which sits in the middle of the single-roomed house. I can see and smell a small cauldron of elderberries boiling over the flames. Scones cross my mind again, and my stomach renews its rumbling.

Rush moves to set me in a plush chair seated in front of the fire.

"Are you injured, dear?" the old woman asks me.

"No, ma'am. I haven't been able to walk in almost a decade."

"Ah. I see."

There's a small lapse of silence as the woman studies me, then takes the mismatched chair across from where I sit. She sinks into the floral-printed seat with a wiggle, making herself comfortable.

Sitting this close to her, I realize her eyes are different colors. One is a warm amber-brown, and the other a blue so cold it reminds me of a winter sky. They're stunning. Each has a depth I can only imagine holds much wisdom.

"Do you not have a wheelchair to aid with your mobility?" she inquires.

"I do—or I did. It got damaged during our journey. We left it about a mile back." I tuck my hair behind my ear out of nervous habit. "I'm sure it's been scavenged by animals and creatures by now."

Rush shuffles forward. "Excuse me, but are you the Elder Mother?"

"Is that what they're calling me now?" The woman titters. "Yes, I suppose it's me. The keeper of these trees."

Rush smiles. "I've heard many tales about you and your home of elder trees. That's how we ended up here."

The Elder Mother stands up on creaky knees, the hem of her black dress brushing against the ground. She crosses the floor to where Rush stands and peers up at him. Then she grabs his chin and yanks his face down to her level. I let out a surprised laugh as she tugs on one of his extended ears and turns his disgruntled face from side to side. The green shimmer under his dark skin shifts in the firelight.

"You're a goblin boy, eh? But only half of one." With a nod, she turns on her heel and lowers herself back into her seat, elbows braced on the arms of her chair. I watch with amusement as she shimmies, trying to find a comfortable position again.

Once she's situated, the Elder Mother looks me up and down. "And you, dear, are—"

"Human," I answer.

She hums and props her soft chin upon her hands. "How did you wind up with that one?" She glances at Rush.

Rush's eyebrows scrunch together. He sits on the edge of her kitchen table, legs crossed at the ankles and arms against his chest. I don't think the Elder Mother is living up to his grand expectations. Especially after groping him like that.

"My mother and I live with all types of faeries in our glade. Rush and his family are just some of the goblins living with us."

"Your mother, is she human?"

Her odd question confuses me. "Yes, ma'am. She was raised by trolls."

The Elder Mother's eyes flicker. "A daughter of the trolls . . . I see. The troll folk often use branches from the likes of my trees for their charms. But I'm sure you know all about that, don't you, dear?"

"I've seen them craft changeling hearts. Though we try to curb their kidnapping habits and keep the babies to a minimum. There hasn't been one in the glade in years now."

The older woman fiddles with the end of her braid, deep in thought.

"Sparrow and I were hoping you could provide us with shelter for the night?" Rush mumbles from the table. "We still need to figure out how we'll make the remainder of our journey without her wheelchair. A good night's rest would sure help."

"Where is it you're traveling to?" The Elder Mother raises a thin gray brow.

"Up north, to the cave surrounded by banshee trees," Rush answers.

The Elder Mother sniffs. "Are you daft? A witch lives there!"

I swallow. "Unfortunately, we know. Black Annis took our families and most of the faeries from the glade. The rest were all slaughtered."

She shakes her head. "Don't you know to protect your homes with salt?"

Visions of my chair going off the path flash before my eyes. "Yes, ma'am." It's my fault there was a break in the barrier, and while I've tried hard not to think about it—there are more important things to dwell on besides blame right now—the guilt is still eating at me. I haven't even told Rush yet.

"Sparrow's mother found lines through the salt barrier. Black Annis waited until it was completely dark before she attacked."

The Elder Mother pinches the bridge of her nose. "What do you plan on doing when you get there?"

"Well . . . we haven't exactly gotten that far yet." Rush looks to the ceiling with a sheepish expression. "We have salt though, which is a good first step."

I snort. "We haven't figured out how we're going to get there either." This journey will not go very well if Rush has to carry me the whole way. And I can't face the skin-stealing witch while being held like a fair maiden.

"That might be something I can help you with." The Elder Mother nods her head.

"How?" I ask.

"We'll ask the trees."

I share a confused look with Rush. Once again, the Elder Mother rises from her chair, moaning as her joints pop. "I'm getting older by the second. We best hurry."

The wheels in my head try to turn, but something feels stuck. What's the Elder Mother's incentive? "I'm sorry, and I mean this with respect, but why would you help us?"

She studies me, searching for something. Her round lips flatten out into a line before she bends down to gaze deep into my eyes. The scent of elderflowers rolls off of her in waves. The Elder Mother pokes me in the chest. "I sense great life inside of you."

Then she turns on a slippered foot and shuffles toward the front door. She passes under rows of herbs hanging low from the beams holding up her roof, sending the bundles of sage and rosemary swinging.

"Come on then, goblin boy, scoop her up." She gestures toward me.

Rush peers back at the ceiling. I think he's having a hard time being patient with this puzzling woman. He stands from his slouch against the table and meets my eyes. I give him a small, encouraging smile, letting him know he has the permission he's looking for. He bends to pick me up and lifts me with a slight twirl. Grinning, I loop my arm around his neck. Rush tilts his head toward mine. "Where to?"

My eyes track the woman walking toward the door. "Follow the Elder Mother, I suppose."

"I don't have all night, you two," she calls. "My magic is reaching its peak. I can hear the trees calling for you, dear Sparrow. They're getting impatient." The woman steps outside, leaving Rush and me perplexed by her cryptic words.

As we move to follow her, I whisper, "Did you know she had magic?"

"I've heard stories. I don't know if it's witchcraft or good-natured though."

We share wary expressions and step back out into the night. The Elder Mother is up ahead in a grove of thick trees, and when we reach her, we see she has her frail hands pressed against a tree's gray bark. Her two-toned eyes are closed in concentration. Where her hands meet the elder tree, a faint purple-hued glimmer shines through her fingers.

"The trees are willing to help you." She opens her eyes to glance at Rush and me.

Rush's broad shoulders tense under me. I can feel how leery he is of the old woman by how his hands clutch hard at the side of my ribs and knees. And I wonder if we've unknowingly walked into the home of a witch.

"What do you mean?" I ask.

The woman in question pats the tree beneath her hand. "They've agreed to contribute their body to your cause."

"You'll have to forgive me," Rush entreats. "But I don't understand what's happening right now."

"Goblins." The Elder Mother rolls her eyes.

"I agree with Rush," I interject. "What exactly have the trees agreed to?"

The old woman beams. "Magic, my dear." Then she waves a pointer through the air and says, "Just watch."

With no further explanation, the Elder Mother steps back from the tree, the purple glow under her fingers disappearing. She draws in a deep breath and lets her veined eyelids slip closed.

I hear wood creaking.

The branches of the elder tree shudder in the air as the Elder Mother raises her hands to the trunk. Then the branches start to bend toward the ground. The wood pops as it warps and twists itself lower and lower.

Rush and I gasp in unison as the branches slither to the ground, writhing and groaning. When the tips meet the earth, they slide along the dirt, curving into a circular wheel form. Limbs of the tree branch off and mold themselves into various shapes. I see an image of a bird in flight with a sprig of elderberries hanging from its beak form in the spokes of a wheel. Pictures of elderflower bushels grace the edges of the scene.

Right before my eyes, a wheelchair takes shape. I can see the dip of the seat and the arch of the back growing. It appears to be the perfect size for my lean body.

It's enchanting, watching the tree move like a living creature. With a final groan, the wood grinds together as the remaining branches form into elegant twists for the handles. Then, as everything stills, the elder tree sets in its new shape, and the wood shifts in color. Its body, once dry and gray, slowly blackens. It looks like honey made of pure dusk with starlight poured over top. The chair is an ebony so deep and glossy it resembles a raven's wing.

It's breathtaking.

Every bow of the wood is elegant and refined—the embodiment of raw magic, just like the trees it came from. I gape at the Elder Mother in awe. "It's so . . . beautiful."

She gives me a weak smile, making me wonder if the magic she used has taken a toll on her. The Elder Mother looks drained and weary, as if she's aged years just in the last hour. Her skin has become sallow and papery. I can't help feeling concerned. "Are you okay?"

"Just old, dear." She waves a hand to dismiss my concern. "Go on now, goblin boy, set her in the chair. Let her try it out."

He shakes his head, a mixture of astonishment and fear on his face. "That was witchcraft."

The Elder Mother gives a tired chuckle. "Witchcraft? That, my boy, was elemental magic. I care for the trees as they care for me. The only magic I have is what the trees give me." She spreads her arms wide. "Are you saying these trees are witches?"

Rush stays silent.

"I thought not. Now then, set dear Sparrow in her new chair."

With a petulant grumble, Rush moves to place me in the wheelchair. As he sets me down, I give the back of his neck a reassuring squeeze and catch his reflective silver eyes. I know he's suspicious of the old woman and her magic, especially after what we witnessed with Black Annis. But I have a feeling, deep in my heart, that the Elder Mother is safe, and that maybe she'll even be able to help us figure out a way to get our families back.

As soon as I settle into the chair, I sense the magic humming inside. It sends a warm feeling flooding through my chest.

The chair shifts beneath me.

It bends itself to the shape of my body, contouring to the dips and curves of my bones. It cradles me like a babe in the arms of its mother, softening beneath me so as to not bruise my thin frame.

A laugh bubbles past my lips. I have never experienced magic like this before, and now I can't believe I have a wheelchair like this to call my own.

I lean in to run my fingers over the grooves of the bird and flowers pictured in the wheels. I have a sneaking suspicion the trees purposely portrayed a sparrow after my namesake. I turn to the Elder Mother. "Thank you so much. How can I repay you for your kindness?"

"No need. The trees like you." She shrugs. "They wouldn't have given a piece of themselves to you if they hadn't felt a kinship."

"Well, it's extremely kind." I brush my fingertips over the chair and whisper a thank you, just loud enough for the elder trees to hear. Then I gaze up at Rush to see he's already staring back at me. His arms are crossed over his chest, but he has an endearing smile on his face. "Looks like you found yourself some new friends." He waves at the moonlit grove around us.

The corners of my lips tilt upward. "Are you jealous?"

Rush chuckles. "I'm trying not to be, but . . . think they'd make me a sword or something?"

"I highly doubt it."

Rush snaps his fingers. "It was worth a shot."

"Let's go back inside." The Elder Mother's voice sounds more than tired now. "It's time for these old bones to rearrange themselves."

I grab the wheels of my chair and am just starting to push myself when they're jerked from my grip. The wheelchair has begun to move itself forward. My eyes widen as I scramble to pull the wheels to a stop. The chair immediately freezes, and a yelp escapes me before I say, "What in the world was that?"

"Magic," the Elder Mother calls over her shoulder as she stoops into her cottage.

When I seek him out again, I find Rush looking as stunned as I feel. But as I gently push the chair forward again, it moves itself at leisure. "This is incredible. Rush, look! It moves on its own."

Rush chases after me until he's walking at my side. "I see that." He seems just as mystified as I am.

I rest my hands on the wheels to nudge the wheelchair in the direction I want it to go. I steer it left and right, marveling at the ease with which it changes course. "I can't believe this."

"I still think it's witchcraft," Rush jokes.

Amazement spills out of me. "Can you imagine how much easier this is going to be? I won't get tired from pushing myself anymore."

"And I can walk next to you now." Rush shoves his hands into his pockets. "No more talking to the back of your head."

I glance at him again, but he just stares straight ahead with a happy slant to his mouth.

The chair finally reaches the doorway of the Elder Mother's house, where the old woman is waiting. "I went in and set up a couple of pallets for you to sleep on for the night, and left out some biscuits if you're hungry. There's also a needle and thread on the table to fix those trousers of yours, dear."

My stomach growls.

"You better try to get a full night's rest." The Elder Mother hesitates before adding, "You never know what surprises tomorrow might hold."

-

AFTER FILLING our bellies with shortbread and tea, Rush and I settle onto our pallets. We sit side by side with our backs against the wall and our legs stretched out in front of us. We talk about the spectacular show of magic we witnessed, the strangeness of the old woman, and the impossible creature that chased us through the forest. Neither of us can begin to imagine what it was or why it pursued us only to disappear in a flurry of smoke.

"I still can't believe you threw my book at it." I laugh.

Rush's cheeks flush with a green hue. "In my defense, it was the only available weapon."

My ribs cramp with the force of trying to shove down my laughter so I don't wake the Elder Mother. "What kind of damage could a book of fairytales possibly do against a monster like that? You might've just made it angrier before it ate us."

"It's a pretty hefty book, Sparrow, and lucky for us, the big bad monster was terrified of 'happily ever afters.'" His shoulders shake as he clamps his teeth over his lower lip.

I shake my head with a smile, running a finger over the exposed strip of my knee. "You're ridiculous."

"Ah, here." Rush shuffles over to the table to retrieve the needle and thread the old woman left out. "Let's fix that for you."

"Right. Um, I don't know how to sew. It's always been something my mother likes to do at night to relax." I wince.

Rush gives a mocking gasp. "A woman who doesn't know how to sew? How ever will you find a husband?"

I shove at his shoulder. "Don't be a ninny." I tried once to sew a button back onto a blouse of mine, but somehow, I ended up sewing my shirt closed. My mother never lets me live it down, though I know she secretly finds joy in the fact I still need her. She loves that despite my independence, I'll always come to her when I need socks darned, shirts hemmed, or buttons reattached.

"It's a good thing I know how to sew," Rush says as he scoots over to me. With nimble fingers, he unspools a length of black string, cuts it with his teeth, and begins to thread it through the tiny eye of the needle.

"Where'd you learn how to sew?"

"You know the fishing village I told you about?" he asks.

I nod.

"Well, I stayed with this old fisherman there in return for work. He would fish off his back porch with these big nets, and they often got holes in them. He taught me how to knit them back together. This led me to learn how to patch up his old clothes. After figuring out I didn't want to live around the smell of fish guts the rest of my life, I moved on to the cities and came across a seamstress." Rush knots the thread onto the needle as he approaches my knee. The he carefully pinches the fabric together and lifts it away from my skin so as not to poke me. "I apprenticed with her as payment for staying in the back room. I worked for her for almost six months. It was the longest I'd stayed anywhere."

I lean my head back against the wall. "Why'd you leave? It sounds like you enjoyed being there."

"I did, but it wasn't home. Just didn't feel quite right, like it was missing something." In and out, Rush weaves the thread over the hole. It starts to close before my eyes as he continues. "Not too long after, I ended up back at the glade. Then all this happened . . ." He trails off.

After a moment of silence, I open my mouth and ask the question that's been swirling around my mind since we left the glade. "How are we going to do this, Rush?"

He finishes off his clean stitching with a knot. "Do what?"

"Get everyone back to the glade. How are we going to get through Black Annis?" I can't fathom how a disabled human and a half-goblin are going to face a powerful, poisonous witch in her own territory—we are no match for her.

Rush looks down at the needle still attached to the tied-off thread. "I've sort of been assuming we'd find some way or another to kill her. Maybe use your bag of salt?"

Though no one would blame me for wanting to kill the witch, especially after she took my mother from me, the thought alone sends my skin crawling. No one has ever tried to take Black Annis down before. If they failed, the retaliation would be too great of a risk.

"Fight fire with fire? How would we be any better than her?" After witnessing the massacre in the glade, I don't want to stoop to her level. And even just imagining the witch's blood coating my hands makes my stomach turn. There must be another way.

Finally, Rush looks up at me again. He clearly sees the anxiety on my face, because he squeezes my knee and says, "Hey, we'll figure it out. Maybe the Elder Mother knows something that can help us? She might have some really strong witch repellent stashed away somewhere."

"Repellent would definitely come in handy." I smile, then look down at the sharp metal still attached to me. "Would you get the needle away from my knee so I can go to sleep?"

"Oh, uh—" Shears would've been helpful, but those weren't given to us. Rush must notice this too, because he hesitates, tugging gently at the needle. He meets my eyes once before leaning down and clipping the remaining thread with his teeth. I can feel his warm breath on my leg through my trousers. When he looks up again, the needle is dangling from the side of his full lips, lips I can't help staring at. Heat spreads across my face like wildfire. Clearing my throat, hoping once again that he didn't notice my blush, I shift my pallet away from the wall and fold back the corner of the blanket. I fully intend to crawl beneath it and pretend to fall asleep, because there's no way my racing heart is going to calm down enough to nod off anytime soon. "Thanks," I choke out.

Rush rubs at the back of his neck. "Of course." He puts the needle and thread back on the table and moves to his own pallet. Lying on his back with his hands laced over his stomach, he stares at the ceiling. "Goodnight, Sparrow."

"Goodnight . . . goblin boy." The bubble of awkwardness pops and we dissolve back into hushed laughter, the kind of giggles we used to share as kids. And, ever so slowly, my heart settles. Tomorrow, a new day awaits, and hopefully I'll be that much closer to bringing my mother home.

HAZEL

The sun shining through the Elder Mother's cottage windows paints the backs of my eyelids red. Shaking off the last dregs of sleep, I peek at Rush still sleeping beside me on his pallet. He's on his stomach with his head pillowed in the crook of his arm, and his blanket is tucked up tight beneath his chin. The way the morning light hits him gives him an entirely emerald glow, just like his full-blooded goblin sisters. There's not a trace of his human mother's rich skin tone in sight. In this quiet moment, I want to reach out and see what the scalloped edges of his ears feel like, but my wandering thoughts are interrupted by a small giggle from across the room. I whip my head up to the side and see a young girl sitting on the Elder Mother's kitchen table, her legs kicking back and forth. I sit up from my straw mattress as a pixie-like grin lights up the girl's soft oval face. She gazes at me from her perch and plays with the end of her tawny-brown braid. "Hello!" she crows.

"Hello," I echo as I reach over to jostle Rush awake, not taking my eyes off the child. I hear him sit up behind me.

"What's your name?" I ask.

"You can call me Hazel."

"Hazel, what a pretty name." I place my hand against my

chest. "I'm Sparrow, and this is Rush." I hook my thumb in his direction.

"Oh, I know, silly."

I turn to look back at Rush. He's awake now and appears to share my confusion. When I glance back at the girl, she smiles at me, showing a gap between her front teeth. I scan the open room and see it's empty except for the three of us.

"Hazel, have you seen the Elder Mother? Are you her granddaughter?" Rush questions the young girl.

Hazel covers her mouth with her small hands as she snickers, shaking her head and kicking her legs higher. I take note of the ill-fitting familiar black dress flying around her legs. The material goes over her bare feet and hangs loosely around the chest and shoulders. Something about her is making my brain itch. I study her closely until I catch her eyes: one brown and one blue.

"Rush," I say out of the corner of my mouth, "I don't know how it's possible, but I think Hazel is the Elder Mother."

"I'm sorry, what?" he sputters.

"You're the Elder Mother, aren't you, Hazel?"

"You guessed it! It usually takes people a lot longer than that."

I remember the cryptic comment the Elder Mother made last night, the one about what surprises today might hold. And this is a surprise, indeed.

"What happened to you?" Rush gapes at her.

A pout finds Hazel's rosebud lips. "Nothing happened to me. This is how I always am."

Rush sends me a flat look before facing Hazel again. "When we met you yesterday, you were an old woman."

"Well, yeah." She states this like it's obvious. "That's what I always look like at nighttime."

I knit my eyebrows together. "You turn into an elderly woman at night? Like some twisted version of a werewolf?"

Rush coughs to smother his laughter.

"Sparrow!" Hazel pushes herself off the table and sits in front of my pallet, staring at me with wide, multicolored eyes. "I grow up during the day. Just really, really fast. Then I go backward until I look like me again." She gestures to her childish frame.

"Hold on," Rush cuts in. "Let me get this straight. You start the day off like, what? A ten-year-old? Then age until you hit your eighties?"

Hazel nods her head with vigor.

"Then you age backward until you're a kid again?" I add.

Hazel nods once more.

Rush and I share skeptical glances. "How long does it take for you to reach your oldest?" he asks.

Hazel scrunches up her face and begins to count on her fingers. When she runs out of fingers, she uses her toes. "Twelve hours," she says, clearly pleased with herself. I'll admit, I'm impressed too—mental math has never been my strong suit. Even at eighteen years old, I still find myself resorting to using my fingers when it comes to measurements while baking.

"So, twelve hours to age and twelve to *de-age*. Wow." Rush scrubs his hands over his face. "That means you age about six years every hour." There's a long pause before he turns to me. "I told you it's witchcraft."

"You're not being very nice, goblin boy. It's just magic." Hazel pouts, her upturned nose high in the air.

"Do you know why that happens, Hazel?" I attempt to wrap my head around the way her magic works. The Elder Mother lives in a twenty-four-hour cycle, metamorphosing like a caterpillar crawling into a chrysalis and emerging a butterfly, only to return to her chrysalis and emerge as a caterpillar again. It must be exhausting.

"Kind of." She starts to play with her braid once more. I think this child version of the Elder Mother has grown bored with our questions. In a lapse of silence, I remember how I once asked my mother why none of the faeries living in our glade could use their abilities to fix my heart. She told me that all magic has its limits. Everything and everyone has to be equally balanced. If one creature is more powerful than the other, they won't be able to coexist peacefully. I wonder if this is a rule Hazel's magic follows. I imagine the elder trees contain an endless reservoir of natural power, and the way Hazel's magic grows and diminishes with her age might be the way to keep this balance intact.

I know some humans are bestowed with magic, just like the Elder Mother said she received hers from the trees, while others like Black Annis seek out witchcraft in search of a similar reservoir. The imbalance of unnatural power causes people like witches, who steal magic in imbalanced amounts, to become corrupted and malformed. Though their witchcraft has no limit, their bodies do, and they will always be starved and haunted creatures. I suppose it's why Black Annis craves the hunt and something as toxic as belladonna berries. She takes gruesome trophies and consumes poison to try to keep herself sated.

I attempt to pepper the young Elder Mother with more questions, but she ignores me now, playing with this or that around the cottage. I know I'm not going to win this little fight, so I give up with a sigh. "Okay. Well . . ." I take a gander at Rush. "We better pack up and get going. There's no time to waste. We still have a three-day journey ahead of us."

We slept a bit longer than I would've liked. I had planned to set out with Rush before dawn, but my body obviously refused to acknowledge this decision. I slept well, but I'm still laden with fatigue, and remorse. I just want to get to my mother and the rest of the faeries before any more casualties occur. But knowing Black Annis's reputation, I'm almost positive she's already added more skin to her belt by now. I shiver at the thought.

Rush reaches for the vest and boots he discarded during the night. "Thank you for your hospitality, Hazel."

"Hopefully, we'll cross paths again," I add.

"Wait!" Hazel scrambles back toward us, eyes blown wide. "Can I come with?"

"What? No way!" Rush shakes his head.

The little girl begins to beg. "I can help. I promise."

"Hazel—" I start.

"I helped you last night. You might need me again. Please? I'm so bored."

I can't imagine taking a child on this perilous journey. Though, in a handful of hours, she'll be a grown woman. My mind whirs—Hazel has years of wisdom about magic, and she probably even knows things about witches that Rush and I don't. Plus, her magic just might prove useful down the road.

I turn to Rush with a questioning look.

He groans. "You can't be serious."

"She won't be a child forever, Rush. She has knowledge and power we don't have, and if she wants to come, I think we should let her."

Rush gazes back and forth between Hazel and me. The little girl has her hands clasped against her chest, a hopeful expression on her cherubic face.

"Stop looking at me like that." Rush looks away from her. "You can come, but any trouble from you, and we'll send you packing."

"We will do no such thing," I promise, placing a hand on Hazel's shoulder. "You can hold your own, right? You are the Elder Mother, after all."

Hazel beams. "I sure am, just not yet."

Before I can ask exactly what she means, she hops up and spins around the room, grabbing a white shawl strewn over the back of a chair by the hearth.

"Come on, hurry up!" Hazel's small frame is vibrating with

excitement, and I get the impression she doesn't leave her cottage very often.

I shoot Rush a bemused look as I rise to my knees to transfer into the elder-tree wheelchair beside me. It welcomes me by forming to the shape of my body, and despite my exhaustion, I can't wait to see how much easier it is to travel in this compared to my old decrepit chair.

Rush and I finish gathering ourselves and our possessions, then head for the front door. Hazel is already waiting for us, bouncing on her now shoed toes. Today is going to be interesting.

-

WE'VE BEEN TRAVELING for less than two hours, and the difference in Hazel is astonishing. Her dress no longer trips her, and it fits her upper body like a glove. She's lost the childlike roundness in her face and has become a stunning young woman. Even her youthful wonder has sobered into a serene charisma. At this point, she can't be much older than me, so it's easier to talk to her. I didn't have a sibling to grow up with but imagine this is what having a sister would be like, talking about books we've read and the things we have in common.

My wheelchair moves itself over the rocky forest floor with ease as I watch Hazel dance across the earth, whistling and twirling, feet lighter than air. My heart swells with an old longing, and I feel a smile find the bow in my lips. Sensing a heavy gaze on the side of my face, I peer up at Rush walking beside me. "What?" I lift a brow.

Rush continues to walk, tilting his chin in Hazel's direction. "A shilling for your thoughts?"

I huff a laugh. "I just miss it sometimes." Rush seems to be waiting for more. "Walking . . . or dancing, I suppose."

He seems surprised. I realize he doesn't think I can recall how it felt to use my legs before I was bound to my chair. "I still remember what it was like to not use a wheelchair. Granted, I was eight when my heart gave out, but I still remember before. I used to chase the poor gnomes until they burrowed deep enough into their tunnels that my arms couldn't reach them. I would've danced all night with the goblins underneath the moon if my mother had let me." I let out a wistful breath. " Sometimes I'd give anything for just one more night like that."

Rush stuffs his hands in his pockets, shoulders hiked up to his pointed ears. "I didn't know."

I shrug. "You didn't live at the glade then. Besides, even when you did, we were just kids. I didn't have time to miss those things yet."

"I wish I'd been around before." Rush sighs. "I would've danced with you. We could've even gone on wild adventures."

I smile at him. "We're on an adventure now though, right? Not to mention we've made it in one piece so far. That's got to count for something!"

"I would say, besides me breaking your old wheelchair, it was spectacular. I got to feel like a knight when I carried you." Rush puffs out his chest.

"Make no mistake, sir." I plant my hands on my hips. "I am no damsel in distress."

Hazel finds her way back to us and pitches in, "Sparrow, you'd be the queen. Especially now, seated upon your magical throne." She twirls around my chair.

I flourish my hands through the air as if knighting her, like one of the characters from my leatherbound stories. "If that's true, then you're my court mage."

"I can live with that." She giggles.

The day progresses, mostly in content silence. My chair

guiding itself along allows me to conserve my energy, and lets Hazel and Rush walk on either side of me. We split pieces of fruit and bread from Hazel's cottage, eating as we continue through the trees. The flavors of the wheat bread burst over my tongue, making me homesick. I've never been away from the glade this long before, and I've never gone anywhere without my mother. I miss her fresh bread-and-honey scent.

My mood must be catching, because none of us want to stop and rest while we eat—it feels like too much time will be wasted. We seem to decide in silence that it's best to keep moving, like we all know that the sooner we get to Black Annis's, the better.

I notice Hazel, now thirty-odd years or so, fiddling with something out of the corner of my eye. When I sneak a few glances, I see it's a gray wood bracelet, and she's pulling it on and off her wrist. It's a decidedly subconscious action she does as I see her lost in her own thoughts. After a while of watching her mess with the bracelet, I decide to ask about it. I point at the wooden jewelry she seems to hold near and dear to her. "What's that, Hazel?"

"Oh, this?" She holds the bracelet up. "It's part of an elder tree."

The bracelet is woven in a continuous ring made from the branch of a tree, and the inner circle is smooth, so it can lie against Hazel's wrist comfortably. The outer portion is rough with knots, and I can just make out the imprint of a wreath of leaves wrapping around the band. It looks rustic but also elegant.

"The trees let you make them into a piece of jewelry?" Rush sniggers.

"No, goblin boy." Hazel rolls her eyes. "They gave it to me to use as a tool or weapon. Whatever fits my needs."

Rush snorts. "A weapon? How are you going to use a bracelet as a weapon?"

Without warning, Hazel lashes her arm out in Rush's direction, and instead of a bracelet in her hand, she holds a sharp, wooden dagger. Rush's mouth drops open as he flings his hands up in surrender.

"You've made your point, Hazel." I chuckle. "Can I see it?"

She passes the dagger to me, and I hold it, turning it over in my hand as I study its nimble shape. I can see the pattern of leaves that encompassed the bracelet now wraps around the weapon's handle. I touch the tip of the blade and find it very sharp. "How did you do that?" I ask.

"I told you, my magic lies in the elder trees; it allows me to manipulate its shape. I could turn the piece of wood into anything within reason." Hazel gestures to the plant life around us. "I could even create a singular full-grown tree again, but that seems to be the limit. I've found smaller objects are easier to manage, and a bracelet is much easier to travel with than, say, a staff or a loose coin."

"It's amazing." I pass the dagger back to her. With a bit of concentration, Hazel molds it back into a bracelet and slips it onto her wrist.

Rush shakes his head. "Witchcraft."

I shoot my hand out and smack him in the chest, it makes a dull thump across his muscled sternum.

Hazel sticks her tongue out at Rush.

These two are almost as bad as the imps and brownies. Hazel likes to antagonize Rush much like an imp would prank a crabby brownie. Though, Rush isn't any better, accusing her of being a witch. If we're going to make it to Black Annis's cave, they'll need to learn to get along. And, after night falls, I can only hope we'll survive to see the day.

THE HAG AND THE SIMPLETON

The sun is setting on the second day of our journey, and we've yet to stop and rest. We'll need to find somewhere safe for the night, and soon. I can see the exhaustion in the droop of Rush's and Hazel's shoulders, and even though my new chair does make life easier, I can feel it too.

Thankfully, as spring comes to an end, it's temperate enough not to need a fire to stay warm at night. We can make our temporary camp in a sheltered area and sleep on the ground under the stars. It's a vulnerable feeling being out in the open like this, but some peace is restored knowing that Hazel's presence, with her magic and elder bracelet, allows us to save the salt still sitting in my bag for the more dire circumstances ahead. The Elder Mother has aged many decades since this afternoon. Her braid has become threaded with silvery hair and her hands are more weathered. When she speaks, the lines around her lips deepen. Soon, they'll make their permanent home on her face for the night. Even now, close to her sixties, the woman manages to look elegant, and she holds herself with confidence. Every step she takes seems unwavering. I can't help hoping that one day, I'll know my purpose in life well enough to carry myself as she does. Maybe the power running in her veins helps? I wonder if being connected to the trees, and thus to the earth, can make someone feel significant? Just the magic I feel humming inside my chair is thrilling, and I can't help myself. "Hazel, can I ask you a question?"

"Of course, dear."

"Do the laws of magic apply to you?" I hesitate before rephrasing my question. "Did the elder trees give you a limit to your power?"

By the way Rush angles his rippled ears toward us, I can tell he's interested too.

"Everything natural does, my dear Sparrow. When I am at my youngest, I am at my weakest. I can hardly make a leaf shiver. However, when I am at my oldest, the magic radiates through me. That's how I was able to make your new chair—my magic was at its peak." She pats at her chest. "Magic is something of the heart. What the trees give to me is a very powerful thing, so when I'm young and rash I have no magic to influence a sense of hunger for more power. At my oldest, I'm capable of thoughtful decisions and compassion. It's only in those moments that I'm truly the *Elder Mother*, as you call me."

The comment Hazel made this morning as a child finally makes sense. She wasn't the Elder Mother yet, because she didn't have a drop of magic.

Rush joins in on the conversation. "What happens when you start de-aging?'"

The Elder Mother tilts her head toward him. "The magic begins to drain out of me. It's like soil soaking up the rain. The water returns to the earth until it's time for me to tap into the well again."

"So, it would be best if we confront Black Annis at night when you're at your strongest?" I pause as it occurs to me I haven't asked Hazel how far she's willing to go in this journey. I just assumed she'd help put an end to this. "You are facing her with us . . . right?"

Hazel pins me with an incredulous stare. "I'm not here to enjoy a long walk, dear. The scenery may be nice, but my feet are aching, so I better get to kill a witch after all of this."

I fight the urge to bite at my nails. The time for aimless conversations about what's ahead is over—we need to face this terrifying problem head on and make a plan. "About that. I've been wondering how we're going to rescue everyone. I want to spare the witch if we can, maybe by setting her aside permanently instead of attacking and risking further fury from her? I can only think of laying some sort of trap for Black Annis. That way, we can get everyone out without her trying to stop us. I just don't know what kind of prison can hold her and keep her from enacting some form of vengeance."

"Anything you've got up your sleeve?" Rush asks Hazel.

"There's nothing my magic can do to imprison her. Our best bet is salt. It's the only thing, besides sunlight, that's purifying enough to keep evil away. If we use it right, we could *seal* her away."

Rush points at Hazel and then taps the side of his nose. "We could line every entry into her home, go in, trap her in a ring, then get everyone out, and she won't be able to move a muscle. I heard about a village way up north that fixed their problem with these creatures called the Trow with salt." At looks of confusion from Hazel and me, he continues. "These ugly things would rise from their underground mounds and break into homes in the dead of night to warm themselves by fires and keep the human occupants trapped. They weren't too dangerous, but the Trow got nasty when they got vacated. I heard the people were so terrified of retaliation, they salted their land, and not a single Trow has risen since."

"If we have the same luck as that village, Black Annis would never come to the glade ever again," I realize aloud.

Rush reaches out and brushes a hand over my arm. We both take comfort in the thought that this could be the end of Black

Annis's hunting. The glade would no longer have to live in fear. Hazel will always have the protection of her elder trees, but at least she'll be able to look out her window and know the witch is locked away in her home. This gets me thinking more. "How long have you been aging back and forth?" I ask.

Hazel shrugs her shawl-covered shoulders. "For as long as the elder trees have been around, I suppose. I don't remember anything but this. I like to think Fate or maybe even Death called upon me for this job instead of having me return to the earth just to become worm food."

"Didn't you have a family? A mother? Or father?" Sorrow nestles in my chest at the thought of Hazel being alone for years on end and never remembering the life she might have had before.

I can see a deep sadness brewing in her duo-toned eyes. "If I did, I don't remember them." She pauses. "It would've been so long ago."

Rush makes a sympathetic noise but has no further comment. It seems like the three of us are all missing a parent or two.

"I never knew my father," I say. "My mother never talks about him. I asked the trolls about him once, and they told me he was just a human who passed through. He didn't stay more than two nights."

"His loss," Rush comments.

I offer him a grateful smile.

"Some people aren't meant to stay in our lives. But just because they float on by doesn't mean they weren't important. Your mother and your glade will forever be blessed with your presence because of those two nights. It was just meant to be." Hazel squeezes my shoulder.

I squeeze her wrinkled hand in return. Then I glance at Rush and see him walking with his hands in his pockets again, his eyes on his feet. Over the years, I've noticed that he tends to cover his hands, like it will hide his emotions. It does a pretty good job, too, because I'd give anything to know what's going through his mind right now.

After a few moments, I get my wish.

"My mom couldn't handle a life of faeries. She fell in love with my pop against her folks' wishes and had me." He draws in a long breath. "But she missed being around other humans and went back to her family in the villages. Living in a house with just goblins wasn't right for her, I guess, so she left Pop and me high and dry. Years later, Pop settled down in your glade with a goblin and had the girls. I was happy for him, but once I was old enough, I just couldn't stick around. She wasn't my mom . . . I tried to be here more after my stepmother passed, but I didn't feel like I was much of a comfort. I think my pop just sees my mom, his first love, when he looks at me." Rush's shoulders hunch. "It was just better to stay gone."

A lump forms in my throat. "I know for a fact your father loves you very much," I say after swallowing. "Whenever we cross paths, he talks about you. He's proud you're going out and discovering the world for yourself, but I also know he misses you when you're gone."

Rush gnaws on his bottom lip as I lean over to tug his hand out of his pocket. He has nothing to be embarrassed about. Gazing into his eyes, I see he understands the sentiment. He takes his other hand out and lets his arms swing as he walks.

"Black Annis captured your father?" Hazel asks Rush.

"My sisters as well."

She casts her eyes down. "What are their names?"

"Posy, Primrose, and Poppy." Rush's face lights up as he speaks their names. It's obvious how much he loves them.

"How pretty." Hazel smiles. It sounds to me like she's trying to extend an olive branch out to Rush.

"They're quite the mischievous bunch." I laugh. "They steal the flowers I plant all the time."

"Well, we'll just have to return them to your glade," Hazel says. "Sounds like the girls will have some summer blooms to pocket."

"They would love that," Rush agrees.

The bits of the sky we can see as we wade through the forest are painted in shades of raspberry and gold. My mother always called this the magic hour. The way the sky glows with the kind of brilliant hues we only find in our dreams, it's like it's been washed across the heavens by the Sun's expert hand. My wheelchair passes smoothly over the dirt, catching the flaxen rays of light filtering through the leaves. They bounce off the black-lacquered wood and set my pale skin shimmering. I soak in this moment of warmth and peace as best as I can, closing my eyes and feeling my lashes brush the tops of my cheeks. They feel like the butterfly kisses my mother used to pepper my face with on my sickest days. My heart starts to ache—I'm so tired.

I miss my mother.

I even miss Bramwell and the way the trolls said and did everything in a synchronized manner. I wouldn't even mind being around the gnomes and their messenger tunnels right now. There have been countless times when the wheels of my old chair fell into the holes as I tried to navigate through the garden, but right now, even getting stuck in one sounds nice.

I just need to make it two more days, and then I can start heading back to my old life and routine. Hopefully.

-

It's dark when we decide to stop, but we find a small clearing under a canopy of trees where the ground is flat. There are no large rocks or logs to poke us in the back when we lie down for the night, and I'm more than ready to stretch out my achy legs. But with my body being in a perpetual state of unease, I find it hard to uncoil my muscles.

With a groan, Rush drops into the grass. Hazel, on the other hand, delicate and proper, lowers her now-elderly body onto the ground. Swinging my bag off the back of my chair, I crawl out of my seat to join them. Opening my bag, I pass around well-deserved sweet pastries and the hunks of sharp cheese, making sure everyone gets enough to eat.

Hazel hums in delight as she eats, scanning the tree line between bits of pastry. "This is by far the best thing I have ever tasted. After all of this is over, Sparrow, I will require you to deliver these to my cottage every week."

Even days old, the treat is still deliciously flaky. The buttery pastry melts in layers on the tongue, and the blackberry jam gives it the perfect zing. Though I prefer them fresh out of the hearth, the taste makes me miss home that much more. The food hardens into a solid lump in my throat as I remember we're only in this situation because of me—I still haven't told Rush his father and sisters are in danger because I made a mistake. If only I'd checked the salt behind me after my wheels fell off the path. Instead, I fled in terror like a child, and I put my own fear of a bogeyman above the safety of the whole glade.

I decide to gather my courage. I have to tell Rush the truth, but before I can speak, a smoky mist descends on our camp. I feel it settle in my lungs as I tune in to the bickering. It seems my companions' earlier truce is at an end.

"I'm just saying, maybe someone should stay up and keep watch." Rush purses his lips.

Hazel scoffs. "Keep watch? For what? There's probably nothing but tiny sprites out here right now. My magic will protect us."

Rush crosses his arms. "How do you know that, Elder Mother?"

"Don't be a simpleton, goblin boy." The Elder Mother rolls her eyes.

Rush throws his hands up. "Are you kidding me? I'm stupid because I'm worried about our safety?"

"Hey, you two," I try to interject, but they ignore me.

"No, you're just stupid in general." Hazel smirks.

"You're acting like children." I know they're not listening to me.

"I'm just trying to be helpful, old hag."

I'm surprised by Rush's words, but before I can try and interject again, Hazel says, "Old hag? Bite your tongue, you motherless mutt." Her arm whips out with her elder-tree dagger transforming inside her hand. The mist swirling in the air seems to roil with her outburst.

"That's enough!" I'm angry too now, and I sound like a harried single mother.

Rush is seething and hurt. He jumps to his feet with his hands clenched into fists. I can see how tightly coiled he is, trying not to explode in anger or tears, maybe both. He flickers in and out of sight, losing control of his ability to conceal himself. Then, with a frustrated cry, he starts to walk to the edge of the clearing, a tendril of mist leading the way.

My own anger dulls. "Rush, where are you going?"

"Anywhere but here." He grits out. The farther away he gets, the longer he stays concealed. Then he disappears and his stomping fades into the pitch-black forest.

I look at the old woman sitting prim on the ground. "Really?"

"It's not my fault he's so sensitive, dear," the Elder Mother replies with a smug look.

"He told you about his mother in confidence."

Hazel tosses her dagger into the air. By the time she catches it, she's formed it back into a bracelet.

"I just like to see his green blood boil," she says in a petulant tone after taking in another lungful of mist.

I start to pull my book out of my bag. I'm considering throwing it at her. "You wouldn't have said anything about my father. Neither of us would've thought to say anything about your family."

Hazel's back arcs with guilt. She picks off the leaves and stray twigs sticking to the hem of her black dress. And even though she appears to be an old woman, I can still see the young girl Rush and I met this morning.

The mists begin to clear, and I decide to read my book instead of throwing it. I fall into my story. The clearing is just barely lit by the Moon, but she allows her face to shine bright enough for me to read. Leaves on the ground rustle from the small animals scampering in the shadows. Owls hoot in the distance, and crickets chirp their evening songs. My eyes droop, the words on the pages blurring, I want nothing more than to lie down and drift off to the symphony around me, but I'm worried about Rush.

Almost an hour has passed since Rush stormed off. The mist has dissipated completely now, and with the haze gone, a terrible feeling is gnawing at my gut. Hazel seems concerned too, her warm olive fingers tugging at the end of her braid. I expected Rush to go cool off for a little while and then come right back, but that hasn't happened. And I know him well enough to know he wouldn't just leave us to make this journey alone. Especially not while his father's and half-sisters' lives hang in the balance.

Something isn't right, and for some reason, I think the mist had something to do with it.

Once I point it out to Hazel, she's quick to agree with me. "I'm pretty sure what we were breathing in is responsible for our little squabble," she says. "Someone wants our attention."

THE POOKA

"Hazel, I think we need to go find Rush." I put my book aside, anxiously brushing the dirt from my gray trousers. "He's been gone for too long. I'm worried something happened to him." The Moon only knows what's lurking out there, and the fact that he doesn't have the Elder Mother with him for protection worries me even more. I pick at a stray thread sticking up from the seam Rush stitched over my knee. If I don't get up soon, I'm afraid I might reopen the hole.

"Do you think the sprites got him?" Hazel's voice wavers. Any other time and I might have laughed at her joke.

Giving her a wry look, I scoot back across the ground until my back hits the edge of my wheelchair. I place my hands on the seat behind me, using all my upper body strength and a slight push from my weakened legs to lift myself back into my chair. My heart pleads for rest. "I think if anything got him, it would be much bigger than a sprite. Nothing that small could fell Rush."

"He is quite muscular." She nods.

I feel my brows rise toward my hairline. Did the Elder Mother just pay Rush a compliment on his looks?

"What?" The pitch of Hazel's voice rises. "I notice these things too."

I grin. "No offense, Elder Mother, but ninety percent of the time, you're either too young or too old for him."

"You just want to keep Rush to yourself." She winks.

The smile melts off my face, and I try to hide how her words affect me, but there's no way to disguise my blush. "Right now, what I want to do is find Rush and make sure he's okay," I counter.

Hazel just hums with a smile. Gingerly, she stands from her spot where she was lounging on the grass and tucks her white shawl tighter around her shoulders.

"Well come on, dear." She strolls toward the edge of the clearing, where we last saw Rush flicker in and out of sight. "Let's go find your goblin boy."

Leaving my bag behind, I nudge my wheels in Hazel's direction, and the chair takes off after her. Without having to push my wheelchair myself, and knowing the Elder Mother has my back, I'm able to focus on surveying the darkness for any sign of the half-goblin.

The forest is so dense, almost no light from the moonlit sky can brighten our surroundings. The only glimmers to be found are the fireflies zipping around our heads. Everything else is soaked in shades of indigo and pearly fog. The silhouettes of the trees stretch into murky pools, threatening to devour us. Icy sweat trickles down my neck.

It's dead silent except for the sounds of branches snapping and leaves crunching under my wheels. Hazel's soft footsteps barely disturb a blade of grass, and it seems like even the owls and crickets have nothing to say.

"Why do I have a hunch something terrible is about to happen?" I wonder aloud.

"Maybe because it appears the whole forest is holding its breath?"

"How comforting." I wring my hands in my lap.

We carry on into the gloom with Hazel now leading the way, wading through the thick foliage, searching for clues that might lead us to Rush. There isn't a footprint or a scrap of loose fabric in sight. My heart pounds now. What if we never find him? What if he doesn't want to be found? No, that's ridiculous, Rush would never leave me behind. He never did when we were kids, even though I got around slower in my chair; our squabbling outburst wouldn't change that.

As if she senses my distress, Hazel glances back at me, eyes darting to my chest. I didn't notice I was trying to rub at my heart through the layers of skin and bone.

"Sparrow? Are you okay, dear?" She stops walking until my chair catches up to her and then strolls at my side.

My flesh feels tender where I've been digging my fingers in. "Just a bit anxious."

"You're too young to be this troubled. You don't want to end up with gray hairs like me." Hazel tugs at my short locks.

I give her a tight-lipped smile, and she offers a knowing grin in return. "I guarantee you we'll find Rush in one piece."

Images of Copsewood's torn body sprawled on my bloody doorstep flash across my eyes. I swallow hard and wave off her comforting words. "You can't promise me that."

Before Hazel can reply, we hear a sound echo throughout the forest, and despite the mild air, a shiver finds its way down my back, making my skin prickle into little bumps. I latch onto Hazel's arm. "What was that?" I whisper.

"It sounded like—"

The clattering of metal drifts toward us. Hazel and I share a look before creeping toward the noise. The harder I listen, the more it sounds like the rattling of chains. Something familiar.

Blind, we follow the jarring sound. This is the only lead we have on where Rush might be, and I don't intend to let it go. One way or another, I will find that infuriating, yet charming faerie boy. In just a couple of days, he's become one of the most important people in my life again. And I can't imagine going on the rest of this journey without him.

The rattling grows louder, and another shiver works its way from my scalp to the tips of my numbing toes. This sounds a lot like the collar the giant dog wore. If it is the hound, I'll need to prepare myself for the state I might find Rush in.

Hazel and I break through a thick grove of trees and approach the base of a dark, rugged cliff hanging over the forest. The sound of Rush's voice comes from around the corner. My heart picks up speed. We found him.

The Elder Mother and I have just finished skirting the rocky wall of the moss-covered crag when we see them in an open clearing. Rush stands plastered up against the rocks in front of us, his silvery eyes flickering in the moonlight as he talks to the creature blocking him from escape.

Before him stands a ghastly beast, but not the hound I was expecting. This creature is easily the largest horse I've ever seen, and its inky coat absorbs any light surrounding it. The mane around its head floats as if it were underwater, and I find the source of the rattling noise draped across the horse's colossal body. Phantom chains covered in smoky mist hang in heavy ribbons over its ribs and neck, swinging with every breath.

"Rush found himself a Pooka," Hazel breathes, her voice dripping with awe.

"A what?"

The Pooka turns its head toward our voices. I meet its glowing sulfur-yellow eyes—the same eyes that led to the destruction of my old chair. I don't know where my bravery comes from, but I urge my chair forward over the rough terrain. "Hi, Rush." I don't take my eyes off the Pooka. "Seems like you're the one who found a friend this time."

"Looks like it," he chokes out. "We were just talking about you. This is the creature who followed us earlier."

The Pooka lets out a grating nicker. Followed? More like hunted us. But how is this horse before us also the dog we encountered before?

"Really? How nice." Hazel grabs onto my shoulder to still my chair from moving any closer to the creature. My only thought is to get the half-goblin out of there. "I think it's about time to go back to the camp and get some sleep. Don't you think, Rush?" My voice is low now.

"Sounds great, but I think the Pooka has something it wants to say to you, Sparrow. I guess it tried to talk to us in a more *welcoming* form earlier, but uh, the book happened . . ." Rush's eyes flick between Hazel and me like he's looking for a way over to us. "I'm sorry about that, by the way." He gives the Pooka a grim smile before trying to skirt away from the wall. The horse turns back on him, pinning him in place with a snort.

"The hybrid is correct," whispers a deep, gravelly voice that seems to be coming from every direction at once.

The Pooka turns back toward Hazel and me, taking a step closer with its massive hooves.

"I sense great remorse in you, child. It lures me, traps me. Just as I lured you here with my mist and your anger." The haunting voice speaks again, bouncing off the trees around us and sweeping through our ears.

It takes me a second to register that the whispers are coming from the Pooka. I feel my muscles lock up, and whatever bravery I had moments before dissolves fast. For some reason, I know what it's sensing, and all I can think about are the lines I made in the salt, the gap allowing Black Annis to slink into the glade . . .

"It writhes under your skin. So strong, I can taste its bitterness," the Pooka purrs.

I avoid looking at Rush. I can't bear to meet the questioning gaze I feel on my face. "I don't know what you're talking about." I wrap my arms around my stomach as if I can keep in the truth.

The Pooka stomps a hoof. "The oil of your lie coats my tongue. I don't care for it." The mist wrapped around its chains swirls like a swarm of angry hornets.

"Please stop," I beg. "What do you want from me?"

"You have nothing of worth to me. I, however, hold something you might desire. Let me give it to you, and then I shall be free of this vision. I will leave you in peace."

Hazel's fingers twitch against my skin.

"What do you want to give me?" I ask.

"I possess valuable knowledge of your futures."

I finally meet Rush's stare. His jaw is tight as he gives me a small shrug.

The Pooka scuffs his hoof along the ground. "Do you accept?"

I hesitate. I'm afraid to hear what it's glimpsed. If the Pooka knows the role I played in the destruction of the glade, what else does it know? Will its next words lead me onto the path of redemption, or will it tell me of things I do not want to hear—like the failure of our quest, or worse, my mother's death?

"Go on, dear. The Pooka needs your permission, and he seems to want his freedom." Hazel's voice is low.

I watch the creature's muscled body quiver in anger, misty chains rattling more as it throws another aggressive glance toward Rush.

I need to save my friend.

"Yes—yes, you have permission." My voice cracks.

The Pooka dips its head, ambling closer to Hazel and me until I feel its ghostlike breath on my face. It smells of withering straw and anise. Hazel's leathery hand tightens on my shoulder, her elderwood bracelet digging into my flesh.

"Beware, travelers, guard your heart. Listen for Death's weeping, for she'll mourn the hour she'll embrace a daughter of the trolls. Only an elder can hope to restore her."

My heart staggers. It feels like it'll stop beating at any

moment. I scramble to piece my thoughts together, as the warning creeps into my bones. The Pooka backs away.

"Wait! What does that mean?" I plead.

The creature rears up on its back legs and lets out a thundering whinny, front legs kicking in the air. When its limbs crash back to the ground, it races straight for Hazel and me.

This is it—this is the end.

Then, right before the creature is about to trample us, it dissipates into a swirling mass of misted smoke. The smoke blasts over our faces and out into the night air. I cough and wave a hand in front of my nose. Well, that was terrifying. All we're missing is some flashes of lightning and claps of thunder, and we'd have a picture-perfect nightmare.

"Goodbye to you too!" Rush shouts after it, relaxing his rigid stance.

Hazel chuckles. "A Pooka never says goodbye."

"Did that just happen?" I feel dazed and unsure as my mind circles back to what it said about a daughter of the trolls. Was the Pooka talking about my mother?

Rush comes toward us. "Considering I spent the last hour chatting with it, trying to bide my time, I would say it indeed happen. I tried to slip away while concealing myself, but I swear it could see me since it tried to bite me for my troubles." He brushes his hand against the back of my head, cupping it as he moves to lean against the handles of my chair. He folds his arms and braces his weight on the twisted wood.

"What was that creature, Hazel? Do you have any more Elder Mother wisdom up your sleeve?" I twist in my chair to gaze at her, still standing behind me.

"A Pooka is considered a spirit in this neck of the woods. They can appear to people in many forms, whatever best suits the situation."

"What do you think its intentions were? Good, or bad?" Rush asks her.

"They're known to be both malevolent and benevolent, depending on who you talk to. Everyone will tell you the Pooka are drawn to people for varying reasons, and they are gifted in prophecy." The Elder Mother looks at me like I might confess to why the Pooka sought me and my remorse.

I ignore her look. "So, whatever it just said is true?"

Hazel eyes me but doesn't press any further. "Very much so. Pookas are truthful creatures, but unfortunately, their prophecies tend to be cryptic and hard to follow in terms of Fate. Once upon a time, I heard we would've also had Fortune on our side, allowing us to make paths out of our own freewill. History doesn't recount what happened to her, but all we know now is there's only Fate to choose our destiny, and her prophetic creatures to lead us through life while Time and Death wait along the edges and the Sun and Moon watch from above us."

I press the heels of my palms into my eyes until I see stars. This is all too much to take in, Time and Fate and this supposed Fortune. I need to focus.

The prophecy the Pooka gave us crashes over me in an overwhelming wave. I have good reason to believe it's forewarning my mother's death. And all I want to do is get back to our safe little clearing so we can all put our heads together and unravel this puzzle.

"I'm sorry, Rush." Hazel apologizes over my head. "What I said under the Pooka's misty influence was out of line. It fed our frustrations, hoping to lure us out into the forest and into its grasp."

Rush shifts against my handles. "That was a pretty low blow, but I understand. The wrath I felt was unparalleled. I'm just surprised we didn't flat-out murder each other."

"Still, you have my sincerest apologies. You know I don't remember my mother or father. You can have a shot at me if you'd like," Hazel offers.

"There's no need. I'm just ready to lie down." Rush laughs,

his breath sweeping across my neck and ruffling my hair. He still smells like cinnamon, which seems impossible after days of traveling.

"I think that's what we all need." Hazel reaches out to rub at my back.

With a sigh, I sit up straight and pull myself together. Now is not the time to crumble under pressure. If the Pooka truly saw my mother's impending death, we need get to Black Annis's cave, fast. Making progress these next two days is going to be crucial.

"I'm glad you're okay, Rush. Please, no more running off into dark forests. Either of you," I plead.

"I think we can manage that." Rush offers Hazel a friendly smile.

The woman gives one of his jagged ears a tug. "I believe so too."

With a roll of my eyes, I coax my chair back in the direction we came from, letting Rush stumble to catch himself since I'm no longer holding him up. We all need to rest, but I already know I'm going to have a sleepless night—the Pooka's prophecy isn't going to pick itself apart.

THE TRUTH

As we find our way back to the clearing, Hazel and Rush are dragging their feet. I was able to sink into my chair and let it follow my two companions. My fragile heart often makes me exhausted by the end of the day, but I know Hazel and Rush are worse for having walked all day long.

The three of us slump to the ground and try to get comfortable for the remainder of the night. With the nerves I'm riding on, I know this won't be an easy task.

I can see some of the wrinkles in Hazel's face beginning to smooth out under the waning moon. She's making the transition from the Elder Mother into her younger self again. It's a curious thing to see after having watched her grow older and older by the hour.

Rush, on the other hand, looks drained but as striking as ever. He moves to tug off his scuffed brown boots and vest before getting comfortable. With his every movement, his skin shifts in color like the wings of a dragonfly.

"If I were you, I'd keep your boots on," I suggest. "You won't want to wake up to a critter making its new home in the toes."

I laugh as Rush scrunches his nose and pulls them back on. Then he balls up his vest to use as a pillow and flops onto his back. I would've thought after all the time he's spent out in the world traveling, he'd have learned that lesson by now.

I can't help but remember how when I was younger, during Christmastide, I would set my shoes outside the house at night in hopes of finding little gifts inside them in the morning. When I was older, I found out the trolls would come along and leave things like tiny figures made of twigs and the best date plums from the garden. Sometimes my mother would even leave recipes she picked up from the village in the soles.

I love new baking recipes.

I'll never forget the time I woke up to find a seemingly empty shoe. I remember being *very* disappointed, but when I tried to put my foot inside, I felt a sharp nip at my toes. The imps had replaced my treats with a mouse. Afterward, I shook out my shoes every day, just in case.

Soon, I hear the sound of hushed breaths. When I glance at Hazel, I see her laid out on the soft earth with her shawl draped over her body like a blanket. Brown streaks have started to weave throughout her gray braid. So much for putting our heads together to figure out what the Pooka's prophecy meant.

I try to lie down and close my eyes against the sounds of nocturnal animals coming to life around us. I keep an ear out for anything out of the ordinary, anything bogey-like. What this would sound like, I'm not sure, but I listen hard enough to hear the clicks of bats as they hunt the prey skittering along the trees. I can even hear the distant yips coming from foxes tumbling through the underbrush. No matter how hard I try, I can't push the noise out of my head. I turn onto my side, open my eyes, and come face-to-face with Rush. His luminescent eyes are already staring back at me.

"Hi," I whisper.

"Hi." He smiles.

My heart skips a beat. "I can't sleep."

"I can't either. This forest is particularly loud."

I shift around, trying to get comfortable on the ground. "Your goblin senses are probably going crazy."

"It's a blessing and a curse." Rush sighs.

I reach out to poke at his slightly pointed nose. "What can you smell?"

"What? Seriously?"

I fold my arm underneath my head. "Come on, humor me."

"Alright." He closes his eyes and inhales deeply. "It smells damp, mostly. It rained days ago, but I can still smell it under the soil. There's a richness to it, even under the decaying leaves. You get past the musty layer and it's crisp."

"Sniff me out something specific, not just the whole forest."

Rush rolls his eyes with a grin. "Of course, Your Highness. Let's see, there's some trees to the left of us brimming with sap. It reeks of sugar, almost to a cloying level. I think some of it's even crystallized. About a quarter-mile away there's a bush full of berries—"

"Oh!" I interrupt him. "Maybe we can pick some on our way out tomorrow." Fresh berries would be a nice change from our dwindling fare.

Rush holds up a hand to stop me. "Absolutely not."

"What? Why?"

"They smell sour, like vinegar. I'm pretty sure the berries are rancid." Rush's dimples make an appearance. I want to bury my finger into one of his cheeks so bad it's embarrassing.

"Okay, never mind then." I frown.

He adjusts the crumpled vest under his head and chuckles. "It's for the best."

"You're probably right." I know he is—I've grown to trust his nose.

We lie there, quiet, facing each other and listening to the wildlife around us. My mind wanders back to our encounter with the Pooka. From what I've put together, the future it saw included the death of my mother. It sounded like the Pooka told us how to prevent that from happening, too, but I just don't understand how.

"What are you thinking about? You've got this cute frown on your face," Rush says.

Said frown turns into a shy smile, but it's quick to dissolve as I think about the reason for it in the first place. "I was thinking about the Pooka's prophecy."

"It was quite obscure, wasn't it?"

"I think it was talking about my mother." I run my fingers through the grass under me.

"Your mom? What makes you think that?" He scoots closer to me.

"The Pooka said, 'a daughter of the trolls.'"

Rush squints. "Couldn't it be talking about a changeling?"

I shake my head as best I can while it's pillowed against my arm. "I don't think so. There hasn't been a changeling in the glade for years. It has to be my mother. The trolls think of her as their daughter."

Rush hesitates for a moment before he says, "I've always wondered about that—her being their daughter."

"Ah. Yeah. It's a story not often shared." My heart wrenches at the thought of my mother's past. She only told me the story once and never mentioned it again. It's as sensitive of a topic as my father.

"You don't have to tell me." He reaches out and touches the hand still playing with the grass.

"It's okay, I want to." I clear my throat, swallowing before I continue. "My mother was a human baby the trolls took."

I hear Rush draw in a sharp breath through his teeth. He has an accusatory look on his face. I know exactly what he's thinking about the trolls.

"They didn't kidnap her—they saved her. Her parents were awful drunks. They neglected her to the point of starvation. When the trolls found her, she was filthy and wailing in her crib, and her parents weren't home. The trolls guessed they had been gone for almost a full day. Maybe passed out somewhere from drinking at the local pub all night long." I can't fathom giving life to a child and not providing it with unconditional love. My father doesn't know I exist in the first place, but after the love and care I received growing up, I couldn't imagine a present parent neglecting their child. My mother did everything in her power to make sure I was happy even when I wasn't healthy. She was always there for me, no matter what. It's why I need to be there for her now. No matter what happens, I will return my mother to the glade.

"Oh, Sparrow," Rush whispers, lacing his long fingers through mine.

I continue my tale. "The trolls couldn't even bear to leave a changeling in her place. They took my mother back to the glade and raised her. No one came looking for her. Despite the blood in her veins, the trolls are her true parents." I give Rush a watery smile. "They love each other so much. It doesn't surprise me that my mother went to find Bramwell and the others when Black Annis came."

Rush studies our hands. "I saw the trolls that morning before Black Annis disappeared. They were frozen, floating right next to your mom. They're together in the witch's cave right now. I bet they're protecting each other."

"Most definitely. I know my mother is defending every faerie in that cave. Your family included." My remorse is starting to resurface, thinking about Rush's family. I'm responsible for them being among the captured.

Rush brushes his thumb over my knuckles. "I bet my sisters are terrified. Black Annis is their worst nightmare."

"Mine too. But your father is with them. I'm sure he's keeping them as safe as possible." I'm not sure I can invest in any of my own words. When Rush gives me a dismal smile, I'm not sure he can either, but I try again anyway. "Posy, Primrose, and

Poppy are resilient girls. They'll be okay. Just picture how happy they'll be to see their big brother coming to their rescue. You'll be their knight in shining armor."

This earns me a real smile.

"Your father will be pretty proud of you, too," I add.

"I'm sure he'll give me a hard smack to the head for putting myself in danger, but if it all ends well, he'll be happy."

I laugh. "There's something to look forward to."

Another quiet moment passes, and I try again to shove my shame down. We soak in each other's nearness, hands still cradled between us. This close, I can smell Rush's natural spicy scent, and I just want to curl into him. But my thoughts drift, and I circle back to thinking about the Pooka seeing through my shame and proclaiming his vision. "What do you think the Pooka meant by 'guard your heart'?" I ask Rush.

"I'm not sure. Maybe just be prepared?" He shrugs a shoulder.

"Or to be careful? We *are* walking into a witch's lair . . ."

"It's definitely possible." Rush shudders. "The bit about Death's weeping was creepy."

"It was probably just a way for the Pooka to instill fear and urgency. A prophecy isn't a prophecy without a little theatrics." I try to laugh at my own joke, but it comes out more like a croak.

Rush enjoys it though, his eyes crinkling as his large frame vibrates with silent laughter. I can tell he's finding it hard to keep it together and not wake Hazel sleeping a couple of feet away.

I shush him. "Don't wake the Elder Mother."

We both turn to peer at Hazel. Her hair is almost entirely brown now; she appears less and less like the infamous Elder Mother, and more like just Hazel.

"Elder . . ." Rush muses.

I tug at his fingers. "What?"

Rush taps his thumb on my hand. "The Pooka mentioned

something about an elder restoring the daughter. Maybe Hazel is going to be the one to save your mom."

I roll the idea around. It is plausible. The word elder could mean an elderly person or an elder tree, and Hazel has connections to both options. I peek back over at her, and somehow I know, deep down, she's going to be the answer. "I think you're right. I've felt like Hazel's going to be important to our journey from the beginning, but not this important." I squeeze his hand again. "Are you glad she came with us now?"

"The Elder Mother has been a thorn in my side, but she's helped you in so many ways. I couldn't be more grateful for it." Rush beams at me.

He unlaces our fingers and reaches for my face, tucking my hair behind my ear before he swipes his thumb over my cheekbone. He studies every inch of my face, from my green, almond-shaped eyes to my button nose and, finally, my bow-shaped lips. I think I know what's coming, but just as Rush leans toward my face, guilt flattens me. I can't keep the truth to myself for another second.

"I have something to tell you," I gasp, clawing my fingers into the grass until I reach the cold dirt.

Rush's brows furrow. "What is it?"

"It's my fault."

His thumb stills against my cheek.

"What is?"

"Black Annis. It's my fault she got into the glade."

Rush shakes his head. "What are you talking about, Sparrow?"

"It was my job to check the barrier before nightfall. My chair fell off the path, and it was already dark. I was too scared to check behind me, but my wheels had dragged through the salt." A tear drips down my cheek. "It's my fault Black Annis got inside. I was a coward. I'm the reason everyone was either murdered or taken." My body begins to tremble.

Rush slowly removes his hand from my face, shaking his head more. His mouth opens and closes, like he's at a loss for words. Then, he breaks his silence, but what he whispers next is an arrow to my heart. "What have you done?"

"Rush, I'm so sorry." I continue to weep. "I wish I could take it back."

"All you had to do was look behind you, and none of this would've happened?" His voice is numb, despondent—I think he's gone into shock.

"I know. I was childish. I thought I would see the witch behind me, and I couldn't bear it."

"All of that blood . . . it's on your hands, Sparrow." His face is a mask of sorrow. I can almost see his heart cracking.

Tears pour in rivers over my cheeks now. The private guilt was hard to bear, but now I feel even worse having told the truth.

I don't know what type of reaction I expected from Rush, but his sullen response is breaking my heart. And I deserve every bit of his disappointment, even if it shatters me.

With a final shake of his head, the half-goblin scoots away, giving me a melancholy look before turning his back to me. I feel all the potential between us fizzle like smothered ashes.

I turn away so I can't see the pain rolling off his back as he slips in and out of sight, and clamp my hands over my mouth. Silent sobs rack my body.

I feel my fingers throb with rushing blood as an anxiety attack builds inside of me. My chest feels like it's caving, and guilt feasts on my bones. I've truly lost everyone I love, and it's *all* my fault.

THE SILENT TREATMENT

The next morning, Rush refuses to speak to me. No matter how much I plead with him, he just looks at me with sad eyes, then ignores me. He even goes so far as to use his ability to conceal himself when I won't leave him alone. His message is begrudgingly received.

I can't fault him for being childish—I wouldn't want to talk to me either right now—but even though I deserve it, we need to get along, somehow. At this point, I don't think he'll ever forgive me, but the road ahead is perilous. We have to stick together. Maybe he'll come around later this afternoon.

Even as a ten-year-old, Hazel senses the tension when she wakes, but thankfully, she doesn't pester either of us with awkward questions. We just gather our belongings in silence and set out before the waking sun.

Morning dew collects on every surface, and the surrounding foliage shines like glass baubles in the dawn light. The birds flit through the air warbling their songs, coaxing the rest of the forest to life. Hazel joins them, whistling mesmerizing harmonies through the gap in her square teeth. When she isn't whistling, she fills the silence with enough conversation for the three of us. I'm almost convinced everything is okay, that nothing looms ahead of us, or between us.

"One time, a man came to my cottage and tried to cut down an elder tree without asking," Hazel says, her animation bright and cheerful. "Everyone knows you have to ask the Elder Mother first. It was so silly."

This sparks a question I hadn't thought about before. "Even the trolls ask permission for scraps of wood, right?"

"Well yeah, of course." She stares at me like I've grown two heads before dismissing me. "Anyways, I turned the wood he'd splintered into snakes and chased him off! I let the little twigs haunt him for a whole year." Hazel giggles.

"That's a bit cruel, don't you think?"

She shrugs. "He had it coming."

The child skips at the side of my roaming wheelchair while Rush walks ahead of us with his hands balled in his trouser pockets. He has a forlorn stoop to his back as he trudges forward.

I let out a long exhale before turning back to Hazel. At least conversation with her took my mind off things. "Why do you let the trolls take elder twigs?"

"They're using them to give life. It's better than letting someone ruin a tree just for a dumb chair."

"Makes sense. Do the elder trees always want to help humans and faeries?"

Hazel flicks her braid over her shoulder and sticks her nose in the air. "As long as the cause is worthy." She changes the tone of her voice to imitate her older self before bursting into giggles again.

I laugh with her. Rush glances over his shoulder. The silent suffering I see in his eyes sobers me, fast.

"I still don't understand why they felt my situation warranted their sacrifice." I say this to Hazel while gesturing at my wheelchair, moving itself along the uneven ground. It ripples under my body almost in acknowledgment, like it knows I'm talking about its life source.

Hazel puffs out her round cheeks, and her mixed eyes dart to glimpse me sideways before turning to her dirty slippers. "Maybe they like you because you're friends with the trolls. Their magic is all over you."

I raise my brows at her. "It is?"

Hazel squints at me and wiggles her fingers in front of my nose. "You've got little golden specks all over you." She gives me a toothy grin. "It looks like you rolled around in pollen."

"Wonderful," I grumble. Self-conscious, I scratch at my skin, wondering if I can rub the remnants of the troll charms off my body. Maybe little bits of their magic cling to me from being around them for eighteen years?

"Stop doing that, you look funny," Hazel teases.

I stick my tongue out at her, sending her into hysterics.

"So, little miss Elder Mother, you can see residual magic as well?"

"Yep! It's the only magical thing I can do when I'm this young," Hazel answers.

"It doesn't seem very useful."

She frowns. "I don't know. I knew you weren't an evil witch when you and goblin boy showed up. I could've killed you if you were."

"Hazel!" I bleat out a laugh.

At least she has the nerve to appear bashful. "What? I'm just saying."

Rueful, I shake my head. "Can you see your own magic, violent child?"

"Well, it's not really mine, but to me at this age, it's only visible on the inside." She holds her wrist up in the air, so her elderwood bracelet is on full display. "The elder trees' magic is the color of summer lavenders. It's very pretty." She gazes at my chair. "The wheelchair has a purple glow to it too. It's very queen-ish."

I peer down at the wheelchair, hoping I can catch a glimpse at the magic only she can see. I thought I'd seen a faint purple glimmer coming from the Elder Mother's hands the night she made my chair. I figured it was coming from her, but I suppose it was the elder tree giving its magic to Hazel. The Elder Mother is still full of many secrets.

"Black Annis's witchcraft covered my mother and the faeries in a blue glow. Do you think you'll be able to see traces of it to help us find her cave? All we know is her home is in a cave somewhere surrounded by the banshee trees." That would sure make her little trick useful.

Hazel wrinkles her nose. "I should be able to. Her magic will be like a trail of rotten breadcrumbs to follow."

"How charming," I say, though my pulse races at the thought.

-

THE DAY WEARS ON. Summer is fast approaching, and the temperature is beginning to reflect it. My skin feels tacky in the direct sun, and the ends of my hair stick to the back of my neck. My bodice's bones poke into my ribs, making the tunic underneath cling to my back with sweat.

To everyone's relief, Rush sniffs out a brook under a shady grove of trees. It burbles over smooth sun-soaked stones and stretches for what seems like miles through the forest. When we stop along its edge, Rush takes his and Hazel's waterskins and crouches to refill them, leaving me to fill my own. I try not to be hurt by his neglect, but I fail. This endless cold shoulder seems so out of character for him. Then again, he is fueled by the agony of knowing this is my fault. The girl he was going to kiss just the night before set a witch loose on his family. If I were him, I'd feel the same. In the end, his silence is a kindness.

Since it takes some effort to transfer out of my wheelchair, I try to just bend in my chair as far as possible, so I can submerge the waterskin into the brook. I can't reach. I bend as much as my wheelchair permits me to. I fold my body, knees pushing into my chest, but the way the water recedes into the earth makes it too far for me to reach without sitting on the ground. With a groan, I slide myself to the edge of my chair, ready to shift myself onto the grass. Before I can make my move, Hazel comes up behind me and stops me with a gentle hand on my arm.

Studying her at this time of day, I'd say she's in her forties. She could even be the same age as my mother. She takes my skin and kneels by the stream to refill it. Her black dress fans out around her in a stunning way. Without even trying, she's a graceful woman. Once it's filled, Hazel caps the top and hands it back to me with a smile.

"Thank you."

"My pleasure, dear." Hazel takes off her bracelet and holds it in between her palms, concentrating on transforming the wood with her temporarily limited magic. When she unfolds her hands, she holds a shallow wooden dish. Leaning over the brook, she dips the bowl into the water, filling it to its sloped edges. Taking care not to spill, Hazel hands it to me. "Here, Sparrow, drink up."

I didn't realize how thirsty I was, and I drink the water with vigor. It slops over the sides and runs down my chin. Hazel refills it for me numerous times before I feel sated.

I turn in my chair to put away my full waterskin and dig around inside my bag until I find the parcel of dried meat. While Hazel drinks her fill from her elderwood bowl, I unwrap the meat and portion it out for the three of us.

Rush sits a few feet away, still kneeling in front of the brook. He cups the water in his hands and washes his skin of the grime and dirt that's built up over the last few days. When he stands up, I hold out his portion of meat between us. He glances from my offering to my face, water dripping from the tip of his nose, and turns away.

My stomach sinks. Mortified by his blatant rejection, I snatch back my hand and set the food into my lap.

"Rush!" Hazel snaps.

"What?"

"Don't be petty. With how little there is left, you're in no position to turn away food," she scolds.

Rush furrows his brow. Hazel quirks her own at him. She's acting so much like my mother right now, it sends a pang through my heart. The half-goblin thrusts out his arm and I meet his gaze as he waits for me to place the strips of meat into his palm. Water from the brook slides down his cheeks like tears. There's so much pain in his eyes. As soon as I give him the food, he turns away again.

"Would it kill you to say thank you?" Hazel chastises him.

"Thanks," Rush mumbles, and walks farther down the stream to eat alone.

I hang my head. "It's okay, Hazel."

"No, my dear, it's not," she counters.

I wrap an arm around my stomach as I tear into the stale meat. "I deserve the silent treatment."

I caught Hazel up on our fight earlier when Rush disappeared to relieve himself. Her then-youthful face crumpled with sorrow, and she folded me into a hug. Hazel didn't blame me when I told her the attack was my fault. She understood my fear, even as she let me own up to my mistake. Her reaction was exactly what I had hoped to receive from Rush.

"No you don't, dear. No one deserves to be shunned, no matter what mistake they make. You're hurting just as badly."

"I have blood on my hands. Rush's father and sisters are in danger because of me. They could be dead already for all we know. He's grieving them."

Hazel frowns. "You'll have to shoulder this burden your whole life, but there's no need for him to kick you while you're down."

I wring my hands. "His actions are justifiable. He has every right to ignore me, and I have to respect that."

Hazel opens her mouth to argue, but Rush approaches us.

"Let's go." He sighs.

We follow him in silence.

-

THE THREE OF us exchange few words for the rest of the day. Rush continues to stew in his sadness, Hazel remains indifferent, and I sit soggy with self-condemnation. I let my wheelchair trail behind Hazel and try to lose myself to the environment around us. To ease my anxiety, I name all the flora and fauna I recognize, give new titles to the things I don't, and count the wildlife crossing our path. I name a perplexing-looking flower a Bumfuzzle and count about thirteen and a half animals.

Eventually I lose interest, slumping in my chair in a very unladylike position, but when a flash of color catches my eye, I struggle to put myself upright again.

With a gasp, I nudge my chair toward what I think I briefly saw.

At the base of a great elm tree, just a foot wide, is a gnome hole with the top of a red mushroom-capped head peeking out, and I know I've just spied a messenger.

THE MESSENGER

"Excuse me," I call out to the gnome.

Hazel and Rush stop in their tracks to swing back and look at me. When they see me peering into a hole in the ground, they exchange confused expressions and come to huddle around my shoulders, squinting in with me.

"Hello?" I holler into the tunnel. "My name is Sparrow; we could really use your help."

"Sparrow?" a gruff voice echoes from the hole.

The gnome's mushroom hat is the first thing to pop out, the fleshy toadstool resembling a flaming ruby speckled with white stars. Next, a set of creased eyes and a freckled hooknose appears, and under his nose flourishes a puffy white mustache that curls at the ends to tickle the corners of his blue eyes.

"Fern? Is that you?" I ask.

The gnome's spotted hands curl around the edge of the hole. He pulls the rest of his stout body out of the tunnel and stands in the grass before me.

"It is you!" I cry.

Fern is one of the gnomes I befriended when I was a child. He taught me how to tend to the garden and sow the soil for the next season's bounty. We'd spend hours picking berries while he described the gnomes' semi-secret tunneling systems. Fern even told me all about the humans and creatures he'd met while delivering letters. And he was there the day my heart gave out, the day I collapsed among the gourds. He stayed with me, stroking my hair while he sent some of his brothers to find my mother.

"Little Sparrow! You're alive," he crows.

Fern brushes off his dusty patchwork clothes before coming closer to hug my leg. The top of his cap just reaches my knee. I lean down to pat his back while he clutches at my loose calf muscle.

"I thought you were a goner, my girl!"

My hand stills. "Why would you think that?"

He peers up at me.

"I narrowly made it out of the glade with my life." Fern shudders. "Black Annis came in through the garden and butchered the gnomes to pieces. There's only a handful of us couriers left."

I hear sympathetic noises behind me.

"That afternoon, I decided to go back and search for survivors." Fern tugs on the leg of my trousers. "All the people who were left were just bodies. Everyone was gone. I tried to find you and your momma, but there was no trace of you. I've been in the tunnels exchanging messages with the others, trying to figure out what happened. I was worried sick." The gnome buries his face into my leg.

"Hey, it's okay, I'm alright." I try to comfort him, rubbing at his knobby back.

With a sigh, Fern steps back and straightens out his shirt. He runs his hands through his mustache and loops his pointer fingers through the ends, tightening the curls. Once he puts himself back together, the gnome clears his throat. "What are you doing all the way out here? You're days away from the glade —did you escape from the witch's home?"

Hazel steps forward, wrapping her shawl over her shoulders

and pulling her graying braid from underneath the thin white material. "Actually, Mr. Fern, we're heading toward Black Annis's cave."

The gnome gapes. "Are you all muttonheaded? Why in the Elder Mother's name would you do such a thing?"

A grin spreads across Hazel's wrinkled lips. Fern has no clue who he's talking to.

"The glade was empty because Black Annis took everyone. She has my mother." I peer over my shoulder at the half-goblin giving me the silent treatment. "And Rush's father and sisters."

Rush purses his downturned lips and moves to place his hands in his pockets. I take a risk and put a hand on his wrist to stop him. He has no reason to hide his emotions right now. And despite how upset he is with me, I see Rush's posture soften. When he meets my eyes, there's a little less despair in them.

I turn back to Fern and fold my hands in my lap. "I'm responsible for all of this. I left a crack in the salt barrier around the glade because I was too afraid to double check, and now I'm trying to make things right by saving everyone who's left. Nothing I say or do will really make up for what I've done, but at least I can try."

"Oh, my girl." Fern gazes at me with damp eyes.

"I don't expect you to forgive me—" I start to say before Fern interrupts me with a small hand on my shin.

"What's done is done, Sparrow. All we can do is move on and be better. You're doing the right thing." He pats my shin and straightens out my trouser leg.

Having the gnome's forgiveness patches one of the holes in my heart. I can almost feel a layer of my guilt slough off and dissipate like smoke. I smile down at my friend. "Fern, can I introduce you to someone?"

He peers up at Hazel, who's beaming down at him. I can see how pleased she is the gnome knew of her.

I motion to the older woman. "This is Hazel. She's also known as *the* Elder Mother."

Fern is wonderstruck. His robin's-egg-colored eyes widen, and his jaw drops. He's staring at Hazel as if she's hung the moon. Recovering from his reverence, Fern clears his throat again and takes his mushroom cap off. "It's a pleasure to meet you, ma'am." He bows his wispy, balding head.

Hazel chuckles. "I believe the pleasure is mine."

"My brothers and I grew up hearing stories of the all-powerful Elder Mother. We treat anything that comes from your elder trees like rare jewels," Fern declares, eager to please.

"For that, I thank you." Hazel dips her chin.

The gnome sneaks a glance at my wheelchair, running his gaze along the picture in the spokes. He studies the bird frozen in flight with its beak clutching an elderberry sprig. "Is this your handiwork, ma'am?"

"It sure is, Mr. Fern. Sparrow was in desperate need of a new chair. It was lucky she and Rush found me when they did."

"Mighty kind of you. It's glorious." Fern fiddles with the edge of his hat. "May I ask, why are you going on such a journey with these two?" He glances at Rush and me. "No offense."

"None taken." Rush laughs. It's like music to my ears to hear him sound so caught off guard with happiness. I just wish it were because of something I said.

"Well," Hazel muses, "I've come to accept they're my friends." She looks between Rush and me with a twinkle in her eye. "Between you and me, I think they're going to need a lot of help when we reach the witch." She winks at Fern.

This sends him into bashful mumbles, and he fans his rosy face with his mushroom hat.

Looking back at the hole behind him, I think of all the tunnels underneath us. An idea strikes. "I'm sorry to ask, Fern, but I need a favor."

The gnome plunks the toadstool back on his head. "What is it, my girl?"

"Would you be able to send a message for me?" I ask.

"Well, of course!"

"I don't ask this lightly. I'll be sending you out into dangerous territory."

I hear Rush snort behind me.

Fern puffs out his chest. "Anything you need, I'll do it."

This is either going to be an excellent idea or exceptionally stupid. I pluck at the loose thread again, the one at my knee that bothered me the night before. "I need you to send a message to my mother."

"What?" Rush and Hazel say in unison.

"What about the witch?" Hazel is quick to ask.

Rush parrots her concern. "What about our families, the faeries?"

I feel a headache start to form between my brows. This could be a terrible idea, but we need to take advantage of this one shot at communication while we have it. "I know, I know. It's a risk, but I think it's one we should take. Don't you two agree?"

Hazel and Rush pass glances back and forth, having a silent conversation. Rush gives a firm nod of his head, which makes Hazel's lips thin. But in the end, she looks to me in agreeance.

Fern's chest deflates. "What do you need me to say?"

As the thread comes free, my request spills from my lips. "Tell my mother I'm coming for her and the faeries. We'll be there tomorrow night—tell her to be ready."

Fern meets each of our eyes and nods.

I hold out a finger, and the gnome grabs on to it. "Thank you. This means more than you will ever know."

Fern releases me and turns to the Elder Mother as she speaks. "Please be careful, Mr. Fern."

The words seem to embolden him, and he puffs out his chest as he says, "Yes, ma'am."

"Good luck," Rush adds. "And watch your back. Don't let anyone in that cave fall into any further danger."

The gnome walks back toward his hole. When he reaches the edge, he gives us a salute and jumps, disappearing. I feel terrible putting him in danger, but my mother must know we're coming. The faeries need hope—maybe it'll help them hold on for one more day. If they're still alive, that is--I just have to have faith we'll make it in time.

-

WE TRAVEL WELL into the night before we stop. Rush tells Hazel he feels we've covered enough ground to make it to Black Annis's cave tomorrow around when Hazel's magic is at its strongest. And I feel a small amount of victory knowing he's speaking loud enough that I can still hear him. I pray this means his disappointment in me is beginning to dull.

None of us know *exactly* how we're going to trap Black Annis, and rescue my mother, Rush's family, and the rest of the faeries, but I do know the witch won't be willing to hand over anyone. With any luck, having the Elder Mother on our side is going to give us the upper hand. If something goes wrong with building a salt barrier and there's a fight with Black Annis, hopefully Hazel can make sure the casualties are few.

My shoulders slump. At least Hazel has magic, and Rush is strong and has goblin abilities. They both have useful things to contribute to this possible skirmish. I, on the other hand, am about as useful as a sack of wheat. The most I can do is roll over Black Annis's toes, hard. And I'm not sure it would be helpful when it comes down to battling a witch with endless magic and poisonous kisses.

The three of us settle on the ground for the night. Rush falls asleep as soon as his head touches the grass. But I'm having a hard time sleeping—in the next twenty-four hours, I will face the witch who haunted my childhood dreams. The thought makes me sit up with my arms wrapped around my legs and my chin on my knees. We're going into a bogeyman's home, and we're going in blind.

"Sparrow?" Hazel sits up next to me.

"Yeah?"

"Are you okay, my dear?" She reaches out and touches my spine.

I shrug. "When I set out on this journey, with the intention of saving everyone, I had no plan, and here I am approaching the end, with a half-baked idea. It was childish to think I could be some sort of hero."

"If it makes you feel better, none of us truly know what we're getting into." She pokes my back. "But that's why we're together. We'll figure this out as a team."

"Two-thirds of the team can't even talk to each other."

"Rush will come around," Hazel tries to reassure me.

"You don't know that." At this point, I feel like whatever was between Rush and me has crumbled and blown away in the wind. Though I still feel a pull toward him, I don't know if he'll ever feel the same.

Hazel pokes at me again. "I do. That boy still looks at you like you're his destiny."

I give her a disbelieving stare. She rolls her eyes and takes off her bracelet. I watch as the gray wood warps and stretches. The next thing I know, Hazel holds an ornate hairbrush.

"May I?" she motions toward my head.

"Oh. Um, sure."

It's been a long time since someone else brushed my hair.

Hazel works the knots out of my waves. She smooths my hair for almost five minutes before she speaks again.

"I once heard an ancient proverb about Fate. It said two people who are destined for each other are connected by an invisible red thread. The thread will never stretch, tangle, or break—regardless of the time, place, or circumstances."

The pass of the brush over my head slows as Hazel falls into her memories.

"I remember once a couple came to me asking for a blessing of wood for a crib, one that would keep their baby safe. But first I made them tell me their tale. It seemed like one of missed connections at first. They grew up in the same village and their parents were the best of friends, so they always thought their children would grow to marry each other. The children had childlike love for each other, but much like the tide, they drifted apart. Then, one day, the boy became a man and went to work on a boat somewhere hundreds of miles away from home. When he came back a couple years later, bearded and salted by the sea and thinking of his childhood love, the girl had become a woman and was being courted by another."

"The man didn't give up, did he?" I ask.

"Ah, he did. But not because she decided to marry this other man. Because she decided to go live a life of her own. She left with all of her possessions, looking for an adventure."

"Well, then what happened? How did they find each other again?"

"By Fate. She tugged at the man's string once almost five years had passed and made him desire to leave his little village in search of a home by the ocean. After a while, he found himself far, far away, with houses made of limestone and black-sanded beaches. He'd lived there for a couple months when he strolled into town and a certain something caught his eye."

"What was it?"

"It was a little store. One where the owner ground her own paints from the things she collected by the sea and constructed brushes of horsetail. She even stretched her own linen for her canvases."

"It was the woman's store, wasn't it?"

"It was, my dear. Time helped Fate by leading them to each other after many years of adventures and self-discovery. They fell madly in love and got married with their feet wet by the shore. In the end, I was moved by their story and gave them all the wood they could carry so they could build the crib for their first-born child. I've always believed in Fate and her siblings, but never her string, not until that story and not fully until I met you and Rush."

"Really?" I ask, turning my head.

Hazel places her weathered hand on top of my head and makes me face forward so she can continue to comb my hair. With each pass of the brush, it rasps against the back of my neck, and I feel some of the tension leaving my body.

"Those two people could have been chance, but you two . . . I don't believe in coincidences. I have never met anyone with more kismet than the two of you, not since that couple. Your thread will not break, my dear. You'll get through this trial, together. I can feel it." Hazel taps my skull with the back of the brush. "You have to listen to me. I'm your elder."

I turn to face her again. "Thank you, Hazel."

She pats my cheek and refashions the brush in her hand back into a bracelet. She slips it onto her wrist and pats the ground. "To sleep you go."

"Yes, Elder *Mother.*"

I curl on my side with my bag under my head, letting my eyes fall closed as I try to ignore what could be lurking around us in the darkness. I force myself to focus on the possible positives—tomorrow evening I *will* see my mother.

TO BE CAPABLE OF MURDER

We leave camp the next morning so early, Hazel hasn't even finished de-aging yet. She's irritable in the way all children are when they're woken up too soon. It takes a lot of willpower not to laugh when she sits up with a scowl.

She rubs at her eyes with fists and tries to flatten out her mussed hair as she walks. After she eased my mind last night, the least I can do is pay her back in kind and make her a little happier this morning.

"Here, Hazel." I pat my lap.

She gives me a disoriented look as she continues to rub her one brown eye.

"I can do your hair for you," I offer.

She yawns as I help her into my wheelchair. It continues to push itself after Rush, who repeats Hazel's yawn while stretching out his brawny frame.

I plait Hazel's hair, starting at her forehead. My fingers weave through her silky locks, crossing the three strands over each other, going straight back in a sharp line until I reach her ends. I secure the braid with a leather strip and let it fall between her birdlike shoulder blades. It's a slight change from the loose braid that usually starts behind her ear.

Noticing I've finished, Hazel feels the top of her head and gives me a dazzling smile. Now she can start her day with a more chipper attitude.

"Rush, look!" Hazel yells.

She hops from my lap and chases after Rush so he can see her hair. She almost trips on the temporarily too-long hem of her dress. When she reaches him, she grabs onto his hand and gives it a tug. The grin Rush offers makes my chest throb. It's only been a day, but I've missed seeing his pearl-like teeth.

Rush lifts his arm and twirls Hazel. Her baggy gown spins around her like a black cloud, sending the girl into gales of laughter. My heart soars, seeing the two of them finally getting along. Rush lets her hand go and reaches out to pull on at her fawn-colored braid. "Very nice." He beams.

He glances over his shoulder and gives me a tight smile. Dumbstruck that he's acknowledging me, I give him an awkward grin in return. Then I urge my chair to pick up the pace so I can roll beside Hazel and Rush instead of trailing behind. I feel like the Elder Mother could be right—maybe Rush will forgive me after all.

I wonder if seeing Fern's forgiveness yesterday is what's softening his heart. I study Rush for the first time since he started giving me the cold shoulder; he looks exhausted, and I can see dark green smudges under his eyes. His once-white shirt has turned a dingy brown color from sleeping on the ground, and even his tan vest has stains from sliding under his head in his sleep. I reach out and pluck a blade of grass off his vest. Part of me wants to be helpful, but the other part of me just really wants an excuse to touch him. Rush gazes at me in surprise.

"Sorry, you just had some grass on you." I retract my hand.

"Oh." He hesitates. "Thanks, I guess."

"No problem."

On the inside, I'm screaming with joy. I'm thrilled we're on speaking terms now. I can only hope that, as the day progresses, we'll have an actual conversation. We'll be forced to if we want to form a solid plan for how to trap Black Annis.

To keep the camaraderie going, I try to scrounge up a meager breakfast for the three of us from what little food we have left. All I find inside my bag is my half-full pouch of salt, and some nuts, fruit, and crumbs. I pull out a sack of almonds and dried figs and pass a handful of each to Hazel and Rush. With any luck, we'll procure more food for the journey back to the glade. Black Annis must have food in her cave—she must eat more than poison, right? Thoughts of the witch make me shiver.

Hazel bounces around me and Rush in circles, energetic and talking about a fat squirrel we passed while stuffing her cheeks with food. Rush tries to follow her rambling as he eats, but I notice he keeps glancing at me sideways. I meet his silver eyes as I take a sip from my waterskin. But when I raise my brows at him, he just looks away. I guess we aren't on full speaking terms just yet.

The sun peeks over the rim of the forest base, and by its height I can tell Hazel is about to start her twelve hours of aging into the Elder Mother. From here on out, it's going to be a race against time. We have to reach my mother and the rest of the captives at the perfect moment, right when Hazel is at the peak of her power.

"Is it naive to think we might be able to escape Black Annis without having to kill her as viciously as she gutted the faeries in the glade?" I think out loud.

Hazel stops mid-speech and gapes at Rush with wide eyes, like she's trying to make sure he also heard what I said.

"We need to be prepared for anything, Sparrow. But I think trapping her in a salt barrier is a good plan," Rush answers.

My chest tightens. "But what if it doesn't work? What if we don't have enough salt?"

The half-goblin glances at the Elder Mother. "Then we fight fire with fire."

This reminds me of the conversation Rush and I had before. I fully believe that most of the time there must be another, better way, but if worse comes to worse . . . "I've never hurt anyone on purpose before," I mutter.

"If it came down to it, could you do more than just hurt her?" Rush asks me.

I chew on my thumbnail. "I don't know."

"What if you have to, to save your mom? I know I'd kill to save my sisters."

"I'd do anything to save my mother," I reply.

Rush nods. "Then, there you go."

"But you wouldn't have to, Sparrow!" Hazel pipes up.

Rush gives her a dubious look. "Why do you say that?"

Hazel smirks. "Because I'd do it. If the plan goes awry, I'll kill the witch!"

That's when I learn there's nothing more terrifying than a child saying they're going to murder someone.

Rush lets out a startled laugh. "Oh yeah? How so?"

"With this." Hazel takes off her bracelet and holds it aloft.

I see her hand shake as she concentrates on trying to transform the elderwood. Her eyebrows furrow and she sticks her tongue out the side of her mouth. She's too young to call on the magic of the elder trees yet.

"Don't hurt yourself," Rush teases.

Hazel frowns at him. "I'll turn it into a dagger when I'm older. The dagger will kill the nasty hag."

I push her arm down. "We'll see little miss Elder Mother. Let's just try to get there first."

We continue for a few minutes, each of us in our own

thoughts, until Rush's steps falter. He tilts his head and inhales deep.

I slow my wheelchair to a stop. "What is it?"

"Stagnant water, I think." His nose wrinkles. "It smells like death and algae."

"What a combination." I can hear the disgust oozing from my voice. "Should we keep going this way?"

Rush hikes his shoulders toward the sky. "I don't see why not. It could just be a small pond. We'll walk around it."

With that, we continue.

The closer we get to the water Rush is smelling, the more the trees thin. Some of them even appear sick. The bark is dappled with black patches and covered in a sticky, tar-like fungus. The scent of their decay is putrid and saccharine, as if they're rotting from the inside out. I try my hardest not to gag, but Rush starts to dry-heave.

Hazel pinches her nose closed and starts to noisily breathe through her mouth. She smacks her lips together with a grimace. "The air stinks so bad I can taste it."

Something is wrong with this area, really wrong.

The grove of diseased trees ends and dumps us at the water's edge, where a moldering smell wafts from its surface. What Rush thought would be a pond turns out to be a vast lake, and there will be no simple walk around it. Looking to the left and the right, I can't see the edge—we might have to travel quite a while out of the way just to see where it ends. Even looking across the lake there is no distinct shore. With the duckweed covering the surface, it's hard to tell if the water ends as far as a stone's throw away or many miles farther.

The three of us stare at the revolting duckweed-covered water. The tiny aquatic plants spread across the lake in a thick layer, almost making it seem like a solid marsh. From the smell alone, I imagine the water underneath is polluted.

Rush groans aloud and pinches the bridge of his sensitive nose. "Let's double back and figure out a better route."

Rush lays a wide hand on Hazel's shoulder and steers her back in the direction we just came from. I'm about to urge my chair to follow them when I see the duckweed ripple.

"Hey, wait. I think I just saw something." I'm tipping forward in my seat to inspect the water and see if I can find what caused the movement when a sizzling, mottled green arm shoots out of the lake and grabs the front of my bodice. I hear Hazel let out a blood-curdling scream, and Rush call my name, then the next thing I know, I'm being dragged from my wheelchair and pulled underwater.

JENNY GREENTEETH

Whatever yanks me into the lake, it lets me go just as fast as it grabbed me. But the first thing that hits me isn't panic, it's how hot the lake is. The water is an uncomfortable kind of warm, like a pot that's been placed over a fire to boil. The second thing is how bad the water stings my eyes. I can feel the bacteria breeding inside the murky lake as I kick my weak legs, trying to stop myself from sinking. My attempts are pathetic, and I move only inches upward.

Barely any sunlight breaches the dense layer of duckweed glazing the surface. I can already feel an itch in my lungs because I wasn't able to take in a full breath before I was pulled under. I try to stay calm, but knowing I'm not alone under the water isn't helping.

A ray of light appears not far above my head. I'm able to make out the blurry shape of Rush's arm fumbling through the water, trying to find me. This creates waves on the top of the water, breaking up the sheet of duckweed and letting shafts of sunlight illuminate the filth in the lake. Rush doesn't know how far I've been pulled down; he won't be able to just reach in and pull me out like he hopes. But at least now I can see which direction to swim in. I kick my legs as hard as I can. I haven't been swimming since I was a child. Years before I got sick, my mother taught me how to swim in the stream connected to our watermill. But since then, my muscles have deteriorated, so I don't make much progress.

A spike of pure nervous energy races through my heart, automatically making me nauseous. My heart is already racing with fear and pumping extra hard now that I'm holding my breath, a dangerous combination that could lead to me passing out sooner rather than later. The energy is useless. One might think it would help me achieve great feats and get out of this disgusting lake, but it does much the opposite.

I fight against the fire now burning in my lungs and try to propel myself up with my arms. I already feel exhaustion consuming me. My tall boots and clothes make my body feel leaden. Part of me wants to give in to the fatigue, but my mother's face flashes in my mind. Surrender isn't an option. It wasn't when my heart gave out, and my life crumbled in my hands, and it is no different now.

With a final thrust of my arms, I break through the layer of duckweed with a gasp. The tiny pellet-like plants stick to my skin, coating my face and hair in a slimy film. I shake myself in disgust.

Hazel stands close to the trees, crying with her small hands clutching the handles of my wheelchair. She's pulled it away from the water and back to a safe distance. With her lack of power, there's nothing she can do to help. She's just a child. The fear and anguish of seeing me in trouble and knowing she can't do a thing about it makes her little face pasty. All of her earlier bravado has fled from her like the tears on her cheeks.

Rush is only a few feet ahead, lying on his stomach on the shore with his arm shoulder-deep in the water, still trying to feel around for me. His face is a mask of pure terror when he meets my eyes.

"Sparrow!" he yells.

Just as I take in a large breath to call back to him, I feel a sharp claw wrap around my leg, pulling me back under, and this time, my attacker doesn't let go. Instead, I'm caged in a pair of long, sinewy arms. I thrash, trying to break the creature's bony grip, but it's almost impossible with my hands pinned to my sides. All I can do is kick back at its body.

As we sink farther in the water, the creature spins me around in its grasp. The first thing I see is the witch's sharp, mildewy teeth pulled into a monstrous smile, and she snaps at my face like a child playing with her food. I continue to writhe against her hold, watching the bubbles slipping past my lips rise to the surface. But the more I fight back against the hag, the more determined she gets. Her arms tighten, making it feel like my ribs are grinding together.

Using what little strength I have left, I slip one of my arms free, forcing my palm against the water witch's blotchy green face in an attempt to push her away. She nips at my fingertips until I shift my grip and dig my fingers into her milky eyes. I must hit a nerve, because she shoves me away and glares. I try to paddle backward, out of her reach, but I'm a second too late. The hag swipes a black claw at my face, nails catching my forehead. I feel my skin split from my hairline straight down through my left brow, and the rest of the breath in my lungs escapes when I scream. My mouth floods with bloody water as I clamp my hand over my face. I try to swim for the surface again, but I'm out of energy, and out of air. I look at the leering creature before me—she is death incarnate.

Far above me, the weeds part.

I whip my head up as I begin to choke.

Rush has dived into the water.

The closer he gets, the better I can see him, squinting against the sting. I'm quickly becoming lightheaded, but I reach a desperate hand up to him, hoping he can see me in the gloom.

Just as my eyes start to flutter closed, Rush wrenches my arm, dragging me upward. When we break through the surface, Rush wraps an arm over my shoulders and swims to shore for the both of us. I sputter and cough, grateful for the air, but feeling like we got away too easy. From my short encounter with the witch in the water, I can tell she likes to toy with her victims. She gave me a false sense of hope the first time, letting me go above the water to take in a gulp of air. But when she pulled me back under, she taunted me with her control and strength.

Glancing over my shoulder, I see her floating behind us, her eyes just above the water. Her wild hair hovers on top of the lake like sheets of seaweed. In the morning light, I can see black veins spreading out underneath her steaming, patchy skin like toxic spiderwebs. She starts to bubble in the purifying exposure of the sun. I have no doubt this bogey is the reason the water and surrounding trees are infected and rotting.

"Hurry!" Hazel screams, scrambling out from behind my chair. She runs toward us as we reach the bank. Rush plops my upper body on the soggy ground and clambers out to drag me from the water. When he grabs onto my duckweed-covered hands, I feel clawed fingers grab at my ankle, yet again.

As Rush tugs, the hag tugs. I'm being pulled between the two of them, one set on saving me and the other presumably on eating me. I hear Hazel sobbing as she scurries back to the safety of my chair. There's nothing she can do besides get herself hurt, and I can see she knows the best thing she can do for us is stay out of danger.

The witch's hand reaches higher up on my leg, then her other hand extends farther than the first. She's using my body as leverage to climb out of the water and out into the sun even though it's lethal to her. Her bubbling, skeletal arms wrap around my torso, and I feel myself sliding back into the lake.

Rush grunts as he digs his heels into the soft earth, his slippery hands grasping my elbows to yank. My bones cry out with me in protest. Blood from my forehead and eyebrow drip into my eye, sending my world into shades of agony.

"Hazel! Your knife!" Rush is still pulling hard.

Hazel weeps. "I can't! I'm too young, the magic is gone!"

Rush roars in frustration.

The hag digs her claws into my sides, and I let out a shrill scream. My whole body is alight with pain. I just want it to stop, but this water witch won't give up until one of us is dead.

That's when I get a terrible idea.

"The salt! Get the salt from my bag," I yell to Hazel.

She hesitates for a heartbeat before rooting around in my bag. Once she finds the half-full pouch, she clutches it to her chest and runs for the three of us grappling on the ground.

"Rush, grab the witch!" I yelp.

Without question, Rush lets go of my arms and throws himself on top of the hag. If this creature is going to act like a witch, it'll die like a witch. I figure if a ring of salt is enough to deter hags, then it might kill them as well.

I twist in the creature's arms, and Rush latches onto her back. She shrieks in confusion and panic now that we aren't trying to escape, now that we're fighting back. We've trapped her in the sun, and she's boiling.

Hazel reaches us, her body wracked with tremors and her face stained with tears. She jerks a shaky hand toward me, offering up my salt pouch. I wipe the blood from my eye and take it from her while deflecting a flying claw from the hag. Hazel falls back to the ground and crawls out of reach.

"Open her mouth," I command Rush.

Our eyes meet, and a morose sense of understanding passes between us. Our plan to trap Black Annis with the salt is about to go out the window, and our only option if we survive this is going to be a violent one.

I let out one single sob as I set out on the most gruesome

thing I have ever done. Clamping my lips together, I keep in the strangled concoction of screaming and sobbing that chokes me. Then, I begin to commit a murder.

Sun save my soul.

Limbs are flying everywhere. Sharp elbows jab into soft skin, and teeth gnash at anything they can reach. After receiving a punch to his cheekbone from the hag, Rush hooks his hands inside her mouth, grabbing her fetid teeth to pry open her jaws. She flops around like a dying fish, letting me go to fight off Rush.

I climb onto my knees, bones grinding into the ground as I untie my pouch. I steady one hand on top of the creature's lurching shoulders and pour the salt into her mouth. I watch it run down her throat like the sand inside an hourglass. I continue to pour until the salt fills her throat and starts pooling inside her mouth. Her tongue blisters and sizzles like her sun-purified skin as it disappears under the last trickle of salt. She chokes as her body starts to seize and smoke, but Rush doesn't let go. He holds her melting mouth open and tilts back her head so she can't spit the salt out, and I use my body weight to hold down her flailing legs until they start to slow. Only when she stops twitching do I let go.

I was right—salt does kill a witch.

As I pull away from the corpse, some of the skin comes away from her legs and sticks to my hands. We've burned her from the inside out. Trying to suppress a manic laugh, I flick my hands, watching the green bits of skin and duckweed fly off my arms.

Climbing out from underneath the body, Rush lays her head on the ground. The edge of the lake laps at one of her lifeless eyes. He shakes the flesh and tiny plants from his hands and stands behind me to put them under my armpits and haul me backward. Hazel sits on the ground by my chair in shock, her face frozen with horror.

Rush stops dragging me and comes around to crouch before me. Then, without warning, he wraps me up in a hug. Our skin and clothes squelch as he pushes our bodies together. He tucks his bruising face into my neck and sighs, the tip of one long, jagged ear brushing against my cheek. Even under the scum from the lake, he still smells like warm cinnamon. It makes me want to punch him.

"I'm sorry," he mumbles into my mucky skin.

I pull away from him, bewildered. "What?"

"I'm sorry," he repeats.

Plants fall from my hair as I shake my head. "What for?"

"Everything. For the way I treated you. For not being an adult and talking to you. For being upset."

"Rush," I breathe. "You deserve to be upset with me."

He clutches my hands. "No, Sparrow. You made a mistake. You've unleashed something beyond terrifying, but you're doing everything in your power to fix it. You're owning up to these mistakes and doing your best. I can't be upset about that anymore. We're going to figure this out, together."

I open my mouth to argue, but Rush moves to cup my cheeks. He wipes a trickle of blood from the corner of my eye. I hear Hazel shift away as if it will give us privacy.

"I thought I almost lost you. You have no clue how sick I felt when I realized you would die thinking I hated you. Everything I was feeling before seemed so pointless. I'm done with being upset; I physically can't be. You showed me yesterday that you know me better than anyone else, and I can't let that go." He pauses. "Can you forgive me?"

"I forgave you a long time ago."

Rush beams at me and pushes all my sopping hair behind my ears. With his hands cupping my jaw, he pulls my head forward till our foreheads rest against each other. I flinch back with a hiss and touch my tender skin. Rush wipes my blood from his skin, a sheepish look on his face.

"That's definitely going to leave a scar," Hazel remarks from her new spot. "Your eyebrow is so split, I could put my pinkie inside it."

My stomach rolls.

"Real nice, Hazel." Rush palms his face.

"What?" She shrugs. "I thought she should know. Jenny Greenteeth got her good."

Rush's jaw drops along with his hand as he glances at the body lying behind him.

"The water hag was Jenny Greenteeth?"

Hazel gives him a childish grin. "As she lived and breathed."

From her twisted human appearance, I was able to identify her as a witch as soon as she turned me around in her arms. But had I known who she truly was, I might have been too afraid to fight back.

Jenny Greenteeth was the bogeyman every child who wandered too close to a body of water was warned about. Despite being secluded in the glade, I grew up hearing cautionary tales from the gnomes.

Jenny had once been a human, who sold her soul like any other witch to gain magic. I see now, by looking at her corpse, the price her body paid to house so much witchcraft. And her malignant nature had poisoned everything around her as well, including the surrounding forest.

Like Black Annis, Jenny Greenteeth craved the hunt. The gnomes told me stories they heard while delivering messages. They said the villages were swarming with rumors about people disappearing beside lakes and ponds. It rapidly spread through the towns that a witch lived under the water, transporting herself from lakes to ponds to wells, sniffing out her prone victims—much like Black Annis's ability to appear out of thin air, swooping from one place to another. But Jenny Greenteeth was known to pull unsuspecting humans into the depths of her watery home to play with them before making her kill. Her hunger was never satisfied. If anyone could help it, they stayed away from deep water and warned the next generations of children and grandchildren about the bogeyman. I remember I was even hesitant to learn how to swim in the stream at the glade because of everything the gnomes told me.

A shiver runs through my frame. Rush and I just slew this legendary hag. On the outside, he doesn't seem affected by his part in Jenny's death, but his silver eyes tell a different story. They look haunted.

Jenny Greenteeth was the first thing I've ever intentionally harmed, besides a stray spider here and there—but that's not the point. I feel shame prickle at my skin like goosebumps. Not even an hour ago, Rush asked me if I could kill Black Annis, and in the moment, I didn't think myself able-bodied enough to kill anything, much less a powerful witch. I tried to convince myself I'd be able to do it if my mother's life was on the line, but even then, I had my doubts.

Now, I know I'm more than capable.

I ended Jenny Greenteeth's life in such a slow, cruel way, and I did it to save my own skin. I can't help but feel mortified. I didn't know I was able to do something so ruthless. Even though I rid the world of someone evil, I still feel guilty for the loss of life at my hands.

I hear a murmur of conversation between Hazel and Rush, but I can't focus enough to understand what they're saying. The skin around my eye, all the way to my hairline, is throbbing. Before I became wheelchair-bound, I only ever suffered from a couple of scraped knees. After that, I received an occasional bruise while learning to pilot my chair—I bumped into more walls than I care to admit—but this injury, it is severe. I reach for my head just as someone lays a hand on my back. "Are you okay?" Hazel asks.

I jolt myself out of a daze. "I will be, eventually." I give her a wry smile and notice her aging process is finally visibly starting. "I just want to find some clean water to rinse off in."

"I second that." Rush shoots his slimy fingers into the air.

Hazel pulls her hand away and not-so-subtly wipes it on the skirt of her black dress. "Great, because you guys stink."

"Hey Hazel, how would you feel about a hug?" Rush says.

Hazel narrows her eyes. "You wouldn't dare, goblin boy."

Rush smirks. "But wouldn't I?"

Hazel hops up from her seat on the ground and darts away, far enough to be out of Rush's reach.

"Alright, you two." Despite everything we just endured, I laugh. "Let's get a move on. We have a journey to finish and family to save."

I reach back for my wheelchair, preparing to transfer my sore body.

"Here, let me help you." Rush moves to lift me from the ground.

"No, I got it," I say, stopping him. I start the ascent into my chair, but Rush grabs my bicep, trying to help pull me up. It throws me off balance, and I land back on the ground. "Rush, really, I got it. I'm okay."

He folds his hands into his pockets.

After I get into my wheelchair, and it molds to the shape of my body, we backtrack through the trees, leaving the sight and scent of decay far behind us. As my chair pushes itself along, I try to scoop the duckweed and slime from my skin, but it's stubborn and sticks like honey and feathers. Peeking over at Rush, I see he's having the same trouble.

"Let me know when you can smell fresh water," I tell him.

Rush scrunches and wriggles his nose. "I think my sense of smell is forever damaged by that moldy lake."

-

It takes us another hour until we find a stream, and I still haven't dried off. All that's changed is the amount of stress rising up inside me again.

We're running out of time.

My hair continues to drip, and when I try to run my fingers through the short strands, I'm horrified by its gummy texture. Rush's tightly coiled hair is odd and shiny, like it's coated in syrup. Little bits of plant life thread themselves into his curls and seem to take root there.

Hazel walks along the stream with our three empty water-skins, trying to give Rush and me privacy by leaving to refill the containers. For someone only now approaching sixteen, she's perceptive.

I waste no time sliding out of my chair and onto the edge of the stream. The clear water is shallow enough that I can sit in it, and it'll just reach my chest. Rush steps into the water and turns to me. I know he's going to try and lift me before he even reaches for me. I hold up a hand and smile. "I can get in myself."

"I just thought it would be easier if I—"

"No, it's okay. I can do it. Nothing got hurt besides my face," I reassure him. I love his willingness to help, but since he's forgiven me, he's adopted a mother hen attitude.

I slip into the stream and sit on its rocky bottom. The water is shockingly cold, but a welcome change from Jenny's sweltering lake. I scrub my skin of slime and watch the pieces of duckweed clinging to my body wash away with the gentle current. I tip my head back and swish around my hair, knocking any algae loose. But I hesitate before cupping water in my hands and splashing my face, and I suck in a sharp breath from the pain tingling across my skin. I swear I can feel individual drops of water sliding through the slash in my skin. If we had the time and instruments right now, I'd need to get stitches, but unfortunately, we have neither.

As quick as I can, I pull myself from the stream and back into my wheelchair. I cross one foot over my knee and pull my boot from my leg. Since I wore them into the stream to clean them, they're filled with water. With a grunt, I wrestle them off and pour their contents onto the ground. We need to get moving, and *soon*.

Rush is just walking out of the stream when I start to pull the squishy boots back on. He bends down on one knee. "Let me do that. You must be tired."

"I appreciate you trying to be helpful, but I can do these things by myself. I'm a big girl," I say with slight exasperation. He's treating me like I'm helpless.

"You've been through a lot, just let me—"

I break. "Stop! Stop treating me like a child. I'm not something broken in need of fixing." My chest heaves. "I love how caring you are, I really do, but I am not any less capable than you are right now.

Rush and I both went through the physical trauma of murdering Jenny Greenteeth. We each have our bumps, bruises, and scrapes, but being disabled doesn't make mine worse. I'm not about to fall apart on him, and being treated as such makes me feel useless.

This"—I gesture to my wheelchair—"means nothing. Just because I can't move around on my own two feet doesn't mean I'm in constant need of help." I close my eyes and take a deep breath. I feel petty for being so worked up, and I can see Rush is still shaken by our fight with the water witch. And I know he's just worried about the state I'm in after my near-death experience and act of unholy violence. I could be falling all over Rush worried about his mental health, but I know him. I know he's strong, but if he were feeling a little broken he'd ask for help.

I may feel broken later, but the blood oozing from me is

filling these cracks for now. There are more important things to focus on, like saving our families.

I temper my tone, speaking more gently. "One way or another, we're going to make it to Black Annis's cave today. I would drag myself through the dirt to get there if it meant saving my mother. The Pooka's prophecy has been ringing in my ears nonstop, and if we're going to prevent its visions from becoming true, I need to ask you to stop underestimating me and what my body is capable of. Let me feel strong enough for right now. Let me get your family back." I let out a long, shuddering breath. "Please."

I place a hand on Rush's cheek, bending my head to gaze into his eyes. "You have such a soft heart, and I am so grateful you've made space in it to worry about me. But my disability doesn't make me any less capable of great things. I didn't realize it till just now, so don't look so surprised—I wasn't hiding this revelation." I laugh at the half-goblin's raised brows. "We defeated Jenny Greenteeth together, Rush. I need you to believe in me. I'm okay."

"I believe in you." Rush lays his hand over mine. "You could get in a fight with the Moon, and I still believe you'd win." He peers at the sky before whispering, "I've heard she's really tough, but I bet you're tougher."

I throw my head back and laugh. This ridiculous boy is stealing my heart.

Hazel picks this time to rejoin us with our full waterskins. "Looks like all your threads have straightened out, Sparrow." Her duo-toned eyes sparkle. "I told you so."

Rush gives me a questioning look, but I just shake my head. Someday I'll tell him what the Elder Mother told me about the red thread of Fate tying us together, but not today. We need to get moving.

Almost like Hazel heard my thought, she says, "Enough besotted glances, let's get moving."

I remove my hand from Rush's cheek and tuck my clean hair behind my ear. Hazel's right—we've lost enough time.

Gazing to the horizon, I see the white banshee trees guarding Black Annis's home. They can't be more than a handful of hours away. I hope Fern was able to find my mother and tell her we're coming, because nothing is going to stop me from reaching her.

JUST A SCRATCH

I feel sick. I can't tell if it's from the anxiety still corroding my stomach or the sluggish blood leaking from my head. Either way, all I want to do is stop and heave my breakfast into the bushes.

Both Rush and Hazel give me worried glances as we travel. I try my best to smile at them, but my lips feel numb and bloodless. The overload of constant worry and exhaustion is sinking into my bones. I will never be more thankful for my enchanted chair pushing itself than I am at this moment. What if I'm just a second too late? What if I'm way late? But even if I'm not too late at all, how am I going to get mother and everyone else out?

If only the Pooka's prophecy were clearer.

Black Annis isn't going to wave us inside, offer us tea and biscuits, then let everyone go home. The witch keeps people, plays with them, then skins them alive so she can wear their hides around her belt. Hospitality is the very last thing we should ever expect. My body slumps in my chair, and I tilt my head back to gaze at the sky. In just a few more hours, we'll confront the witch who's terrorized my home. The thought that we might not make it back to the glade makes my heart stutter. Every single one of us could lose our lives today.

I blink away tears as a murder of crows flies over my head. I count eight of them, their feathers dripping with shades of night.

The trolls used to tell me crows are either a good sign or a bad one—it all depends on how many are flocked together. Two crows means good news, whereas five means disease or pain. Eight, on the other hand, means impending grief and sorrow. A chill spreads through my body as pieces of the Pooka's prophecy echo in my head.

Beware, travelers, guard your heart . . .

Does it mean to protect myself against the grief of possibly losing my mother? Against my welling anxiety? I'll never understand why faeries have to be so cryptic. I'd be a lot less anxious if the Pooka had just been straightforward and told me how to fix everything.

At least one thing I know for sure is Hazel will play a part. The Pooka told us, *only the elder can hope to restore her,* and there's no doubt in my mind now that it's referring to the Elder Mother. I haven't shared my suspicions with her yet, but I have an inkling Hazel knows more than she says she does. From the moment I met her, she's been tight-lipped and mysterious about certain things. When the Elder Mother stares at me, I sometimes think she knows all my secrets. Like she can see right through me, see what makes me tick. And yet, though it's disconcerting, I trust her.

My other worry is the safety of whatever faeries might remain. I've torn apart parents and children, siblings and lovers. The amount of guilt I have thinking about the families I might have had a hand in destroying is immeasurable.

Then I think about Posy, Primrose, Poppy, and Rush's father. I will never be able to forgive myself if something happens to the goblins. Rush might have forgiven me now, trusting they're all still alive, but if they're not? There's no way he won't blame me. Even if he claimed he didn't, I think he'd always harbor resentment toward me.

And I'm pretty sure my heart can't handle that. The feelings I've developed for the charming half-goblin boy are strong. I've known him since I was eight, but I haven't truly come to know him as an adult until now. During these last four days of traveling, we've bared our souls to each other. I've seen his soaked by both stars and sunlight, and I'd never seen anything so beautiful. I've seen his shame and sorrow, but I've also witnessed his humility and strength. If Hazel is right, and we do have a fated red thread connecting us, I never want it to snap. Once again, I can only hold on to the faith that we'll make it through today and return to the glade so I can tell him all of this.

I sigh.

I want nothing more than to return to my everyday life. I've missed my mundane routine. I would give up a kidney right now just for a day picking sun-warmed fruit in the garden while I reek of perspiration. Or chasing the ever-pranking imps around the glade and running over my own toes with my wheelchair as I try to catch them. It's the simple, irritating things I crave like never before. If we all survive our encounter with Black Annis, I would even let the trolls make a changeling. And I'd sit with Bramwell and the others so they can teach me how to weave one of their children's elder-twig hearts. I even want to watch the golden glow of a troll charm give the heart life. At this point, I would even put up with the human babe they take in the changeling's place.

I just want the opportunity to encourage all the faeries' mischief if only to see them alive and happy once more.

Tonight is going to be the end of everything or the start of something new. Only time will tell.

At the pace we're going, the three of us have made a lot of progress. We should reach Black Annis's home just a moment before nightfall, and Hazel will be brimming with elder-tree magic—

My thoughts are interrupted by a sharp gasp from Hazel. Her multicolored eyes are blown wide, staring at the forest floor as she covers her mouth with a trembling hand. I search the ground for the source of her shock. Emerging on wobbly legs from a gnome hole partially hidden by brambles is Fern. He clutches his left arm to his chest. It's tightly wrapped with fabric torn from the hem of his brown patchwork shirt. Even from where I'm sitting, I can see the fabric is soaked in fresh blood.

Fern's lips are pallid, his skin beaded with sweat. The mushroom hat sits askew on the top of his head. Something ghastly has taken place on his quest to deliver my message.

"Fern!" I roll closer. "What happened? Are you okay?"

"I'm so sorry, my girl." He stumbles.

Hazel leaps forward to catch the tiny man before he falls on his face. She props him up against the base of a tree and moves to sit on the ground beside him.

"Your arm, Mr. Fern?" Hazel motions to his soiled dressings.

"It's just a scratch, Elder Mother."

From the dark blood dripping from his makeshift bandage, we can all tell it's more than just a scratch.

"Let's see it then," Rush says.

Fern waves us off. "Oh, don't worry yourself over this old gnome."

"Mr. Fern," Hazel scolds.

A pink hue spreads across the gnome's pale face. He holds out his arm toward Hazel and turns his head away. She cradles his arm and begins untangling the knot in the fabric, unwinding it.

This time, all three of us gasp.

"I told you." Fern shrugs a shoulder. "It's not so bad."

He's missing a slice of skin from wrist to elbow. It's been peeled from the back of his arm in a perfect, even strip by something very sharp. Under the oozing blood, I can see the soft pink-and-white marbling of his muscle tissue. No wonder it's still bleeding so much.

"What happened?" I ask Fern again.

His white mustache droops. "Black Annis caught me."

"How?" My brows start to scrunch together, but I'm rewarded with a searing pain spreading across my forehead. Jenny Greenteeth's parting gift is going to take some time to heal.

I've come to know gnomes as being the slyest of the faeries, especially with their tunneling system. And I'm surprised the witch was able to get her hands on Fern.

"You're telling us she caught you, skinned you, and let you go?" Rush sputters.

Fern peers up at me with glazed eyes. "I'm sorry, Sparrow."

My heart sinks. "What for?"

He rolls his eyes to the heavens as if asking the Sun or Moon for forgiveness. "Black Annis knows you're coming for your momma."

All I can hear is a dull buzzing in my ears—we no longer have the element of surprise. The witch is expecting our arrival.

We all considered the risk sending the message would be, but I feared more for Fern's life or capture. The possibility of the witch thinking he was there to rescue them and then maiming him for that was what was most prevalent in my mind. It might be naïve, but Black Annis knowing that there's more of us coming wasn't high on my list. This was supposed to be a quick, secret mission.

"It will be alright, dear," Hazel reassures me.

Rush addresses the messenger. "Tell us exactly what happened, Fern."

The gnome worries at the ends of his mustache with his free hand. Hazel takes the breezy shawl draped around her elbows and starts to tear it into strips to bind his arm. Fern is about to protest her ruining her shawl, but Hazel gives him a stern, though not unkind, look.

With a sigh, he begins to tell his tale. "We gnomes have a tunnel that leads right outside the border of the banshee trees. Some of us thought it was lamebrained to have a hole by a witch's home, but we made it just in case. Times like these, it sure came in handy. Anyways, I poked around and found her cave." Fern shudders. "It was like a bedeviled labyrinth in there. It took me a few shakes, but I found the center." Fern wavers.

"What did you find?" I push for more information, feeling my nerves running down my back like sweat. Maybe it is sweat? I feel nauseous.

"Black Annis had your momma and the faeries caged like animals. All stuffed together like a slaughterhouse." He sounds apologetic. "It was barbaric."

Rush reaches out to push my hair aside and lay a hand on the back of my neck. I can see him glancing at me with concern from the corner of my eye when he realizes how clammy I am. Despite my sticky skin, he doesn't remove his soothing hand.

"They were all alone in the room at first, so I was able to go to your momma and tell her you and your friends were on the way. She looked so heartbroken, but she told me how proud she was. Her little bird finally going out into the world."

I let out a tearful laugh. Hazel, still wrapping Fern's arm in careful layers, peers up at me with a solemn grin.

"Then the hag showed up, waltzing in out of nowhere, smiling at me with her belladonna-stained lips. I nearly wet myself." Despite his pain, a self-deprecating chortle slips from underneath Fern's mustache. "The next thing I knew, I was frozen and shining blue!"

"Witchcraft," Rush mumbles.

"She tormented me until I told her why I was there. I tried to hold out." Fern shakes his head. "I really did, but once she started relieving me of my flesh, I couldn't help it." Fern stares into my eyes. "I told her you were coming, Sparrow, and she let me go to spite you. She wanted me to find you so you would know she's waiting. I'm so sorry."

I reach down to clutch his little hand in my own. "It's okay, Fern. I feel terrible. I'm the one responsible for you getting hurt. I shouldn't have sent you—I'm just glad she didn't take more than skin."

"I'd sneak into a witch's lair for you any day, my girl." The gnome beams at me, then winces as Hazel ties off his bandages and pats his narrow shoulder.

"Thank you, Elder Mother." Fern's face is full of dreamy gratitude.

She rights his crooked mushroom cap and gives him an appraising nod. "My pleasure, Mr. Fern."

Fern clears his throat as another blush graces his wrinkled skin. "I did leave out one thing though."

Rush shifts behind me, leaning in close to the gnome. "What's that?"

"Black Annis doesn't know that Sparrow isn't alone. I never told her about you or the Elder Mother."

"Well, this sure works in our favor." Hazel gives Fern a commending smile.

Rush chuckles. "We'll be Queen Sparrow's secret weapons."

"My knight and my mage. The aces up my sleeve." Now I truly feel like a character from the books I love so much. I have my court, a deadly mission, and my kingdom to save.

Hazel pats the gnome again. "You did well, Mr. Fern. Thank you for your help."

"And for your sacrifice." I add. "You should find all the gnomes you can gather and head back to the glade. Get your arm treated, and prepare for the rest of the faeries' arrival. We should be back in four days if everything goes well."

"Do you feel well enough to travel?" Hazel asks him, laying the back of her hand against his head to feel for a fever.

"Nothing a little nibble of food can't fix."

Rush slides his hand from my neck and crouches behind my chair to dig around inside my bag. He emits a hoot of triumph and produces the sack of remaining dried figs. Rush then hunkers down in front of Fern and presents him with the fruit.

The gnome's blue eyes glitter with desire as he holds out his hands in supplication. As soon as Rush deposits the sack in his palms, he tears open the wrapping and devours the figs. Healthy color soon returns to his lips.

"Better?" I ask.

"Better," he sighs with a happy look on his freckled face.

Fern climbs to his feet and turns to Hazel, still sitting on the ground beneath the tree. He takes one of her olive hands and plants a whiskery kiss on her knuckles. Then, he goes to Rush and holds out his good arm. Rush takes Fern's wee hand between his large pointer finger and thumb and gives it a tender shake. Finally, Fern comes to me and takes in my face for the first time. "Oh, Sparrow." He frowns. "Your poor head."

"I'll be okay. It's just a scratch." I touch my forehead as I hold back a wince.

Fern titters. "At least when it heals up, you'll look real rugged. No one will mess with my girl." He wraps my leg in a hug, the same way he did a day ago, as he says, "You be careful, you hear? You and I have a garden to tend to back home. Those fruits and vegetables won't plant themselves."

"Yes, sir."

I refuse to think this is goodbye, but I'm also realistic—there's always a chance we won't make it back. We don't have any salt left, we have no real plan now . . . and Black Annis may just kill us all before we even set foot inside her cave. I glance over at Hazel. The only trick we have up our sleeve is the Elder Mother and her magic. Hopefully it's enough to keep the witch at bay while we get everyone out.

With a final pat to my leg, Fern turns back to his hole. He

sits on the edge and swings his legs inside. He glances over his shoulder at us. "Good luck, everyone." Then he drops out of sight, and we hear the padding of his scurrying feet fade away.

I wipe the sweat off the unscathed side of my head and let out a long breath.

"Are you alright, dear? You're looking a little peaky," Hazel says.

I brush aside her worry. "I'm fine. We should go, there's still ground to cover."

Hazel presses her lips together and hesitates, glancing at Rush. She nods. Her stiffening joints pop as she stands up. Once she brushes off her dress and deems herself ready, we continue our journey.

My queasiness is getting worse.

I still can't decide if I should chalk it up to blood loss or nerves. Nevertheless, I'm in trouble. I imagine finally coming face-to-face with Black Annis and emptying my anxious stomach all over her feet. That will surely dazzle the witch into giving up my mother.

I wish this feeling would go away. I can't be a hero tonight if I wheel around all woozy like a drunkard. I retrieve my waterskin from my bag and take sparing sips. "Anyone else feel a little unstable?" I ask after swallowing.

Rush laughs. "You could say that."

Hazel gives me a sideways glance. "You're a fretful little thing, aren't you? Present situation excluded, you tear up your insides with worry, don't you?"

I dodge her inquisitive glance.

"I've had this all-consuming feeling, this anxiety, since I was a child. It developed just after my heart gave up on me." I clear my throat. "My mother took me to village doctors, and they tried to diagnose me with hysteria. They wanted to pump me full of herbs and serums I didn't need just so they could say they had the treatment for something that 'plagues womankind.' All the more coin in their pockets, right?" I choke out a flat laugh. "One doctor was bold enough to call me a witch because of it."

Rush sucks in a sharp breath. "You were just eight years old."

"I don't have much faith in doctors and their practice anymore. I haven't gone back to the village since."

Hazel shakes her head in revulsion. "The nerve of those men."

"I trust you know there's nothing wrong with you, Sparrow," Rush says. "You do know that, don't you?"

My palms start to sweat. Admitting my anxiety exists makes it swell—it puffs up its chest and preens its worry-slick feathers, taking up all the room inside my torso.

"It's perfectly normal. Especially with everything you've gone through," Rush assures me after his question goes unanswered.

Hazel hums in agreement.

I waver for a moment before changing the subject. "We're going to make it through this, right?"

Hazel's expression is guarded, but I see wariness in her hooded eyes. "I sure hope so, dear."

I look up at Rush as he strides by the side of my wheelchair. I stretch my clammy hand out and hook my pinkie through his. Touching him like this grounds me. And if I close my eyes, I can visualize a thin red bow attached to each of our pinkie fingers. I nearly feel the thread coil around our hands and trail up our arms like veins.

Rush could be my destiny.

Just as it was my destiny for my heart to fail me, or for Hazel to save my mother, perhaps? Everything happens for a reason, or at least that's what mother always says. I pray whatever happens next leads to a destiny that includes a happy ending.

THE MAGIC HOUR

We enter the magic hour just before we make it to the banshee trees. The dwindling rays of warm sunlight glaze the forest around us in gold.

The Sun and his beams soften the contours of the grim trees in front of us. The bone-white bark is hazy, and less intimating in this light. The magic hour can make almost anything lovely.

But it's deceivingly peaceful.

Once we set foot past the border of trees, we'll be inside Black Annis's domain. Glancing between Rush and Hazel, I can tell they aren't ready.

Rush stands with his hands in his pockets. I see a curve to his shoulders as he stares at the banshee trees. His deep skin shines like a coin in the sinking sun, and I can just make out the barest hint of goblin glimmer on the high points of his face. A dark bruise blossoms amid the green of his cheekbone, courtesy of Jenny Greenteeth. I watch his mouth quirk to the side as he chews on the thin skin of his inner cheek. Trying to soothe his tension—or maybe to soothe mine—I let my hand fall to the back of his leg and rest there. He gazes down at me with a silken smile and brushes my jaw with the back of a finger.

Keeping my hand on Rush's leg, I glance at Hazel.

A fretful groove creases her forehead, her graying brows low over her blue and brown eyes. I notice her wrinkling mouth pinch as she fiddles with the end of her braid. She still wears the tight plait I created for her earlier this morning when she was young enough to sit on my lap. The sleepy dawn feels like a lifetime ago. I can see our day's journey weigh on her through the silver in her hair and the loose strands that have escaped by her neck.

Rush shifts to stand behind me and bends over to rest his elbows on my chair's twisted handles. I feel his spiced breath on the back of my ear.

"Looks like we made it," he rumbles.

I try to exhale the stress in my body and tilt my head back to rest against his unbruised cheek. "It's been a long four days."

Hazel lets out a snort. "You can say that again."

She transfers most of her weight to one leg, so her hip is propped up against the side of my wheelchair. As she crosses her arms, her calming, velvety elderflower scent washes over me.

The three of us huddle together, grasping this quiet moment as tight as we can. I'm not quite sure if we pause this long just to let Hazel's magic crest, or if we're stalling. With as many times as Death and her cold fingertips have crossed my mind, I'm sure Rush and Hazel have thought about her as well. There's a possibility the three of us might not walk out of these woods together, and we all know it. So, we stare straight ahead and watch the low light of the evening sun sink between the trees. The gloaming brings a faint breeze whispering at our backs, and I feel a shadow of foreboding hang over us, threatening to descend.

This is the calm before the storm.

The swirl of moths and butterflies in my stomach begs the

return of my nausea. The slit in my forehead has crusted itself over with dried blood, but I can still feel the skin of my eyebrow letting loose a languid bead of blood every now and then. Judging by the warmth I feel around the wound, I know my skin is angry and red. At the very least, I no longer fear bleeding out. Sweat slips down my lower back as my frail heart flutters. Four days of overwhelming anxiety has done a number on my already-weak body. Not to mention, my legs ache from sitting all day and then sleeping on the ground all night.

Rush turns his face against my head, making my spiraling thoughts crumble like fragile ruins.

"How are you feeling?" he asks.

"I'm quaking in my boots." I tap the toes of my tall black boots together to accentuate my statement. "We're about to stare into the mouth of a beast and dare her not to bite us."

Rush's rich laughter reverberates through my skull.

"A beast, indeed." Hazel tuts. "Black Annis may have fearsome teeth, but we've learned even monsters can be vanquished, dear." She rolls the elderwood bracelet on her wrist over the back of her folded arm. It could be a trick of the dwindling light, but I swear I see it pulse with a lavender gleam.

"I don't know what I should be more afraid of, her bite or her talons." Rush says.

"Her talons," Hazel and I answer in unison.

My eyebrow gives a throb in consensus. Jenny Greenteeth's claws hurt plenty. "I don't feel prepared. I knew today was coming, but now that the sun is going down and this is all becoming much more real, I'm terrified," I admit. "I have nothing but this wheelchair under me and a new battle scar. How am I supposed to face the witch like this?"

"You have us," Rush says. "The Elder Mother and I are your secret weapons, remember? This gives us a leg up."

"I know," I sigh. "But I've feared Black Annis my whole life. I prayed every night growing up I'd never meet her, that she'd never sense weakness in the barrier. Yet here I am, rolling into her home without a plan besides some stabbing. I can't imagine we'll be able to negotiate with her."

"No matter what, you can't trust a thing she says," Hazel warns. "Black Annis will lie through her pointed teeth."

I groan and bury my face in my hands. "This is going to be impossible."

Rush straightens behind me and puts his broad palms on my shoulders.

"It'll be okay Sparrow; we'll be with you every step of the way."

"There will be no *stepping* on my part." I smirk beneath my hands. "I might just have to *sit* this one out."

Rush jostles my shoulders. "That's not what I meant."

Hazel laughs beside me. "You *walked* into that one, goblin boy."

Rush pinches my shoulder and leans sideways to see my face. "You guys got jokes, huh?"

"Trust me." I peer up at him. "After a decade of being disabled, I've got plenty of wheelchair jokes on hand. You've just got to stick around long enough to hear them."

His gaze seems to drill right into me. "I think I can manage that."

I turn to Hazel before Rush can see the scarlet blooming on my cheeks as I flounder for something to say. "Magic?" I blurt. "See any?"

Hazel gives me a knowing grin before sweeping the trees before us. "Some. I only see a handful of tiny blue orbs floating around like dust motes. I can't discern an obvious trail."

I squint into the blanched forest. "I'm sure once we go deeper into the trees, you'll find a more concentrated path."

Rush looks between us. "Hang on, did I miss something?"

"Ah, you eluded the conversation when you were giving Sparrow the silent treatment."

Rush gives me a remorseful smile, a blush of his own staining his face emerald.

"Hazel can see remnants of other creatures' magic. It's like when my mother and the faeries were enrobed in blue when Black Annis used her witchcraft on them. Except Hazel can see what lingers behind, invisible to our eyes."

Rush raises his brows and gives Hazel an impressed look.

I scrunch my nose. "Apparently, I'm covered in the trolls' golden magic dander."

Rush convulses into gleeful laughter.

"Yeah, yeah, laugh it up."

I persuade my wheelchair to roll backward, trying to catch Rush's toes. He jumps out of the way and holds his stomach as he continues to laugh. "I'm sorry, but it makes you sound fuzzy and adorable."

"I'll show you adorable." I urge my chair to chase Rush in a circle around Hazel, trying to clip his heels as he dances away. The Elder Mother only shakes her head at our antics. My wheels just catch on the back of Rush's boot, making him stumble forward when Hazel grabs onto my elder-tree chair's handles. It obeys her by gliding to a stop. I give her a playful glare for stopping me without permission.

"Alright." She chuckles. "That's enough, children."

Rush sticks his tongue out at me behind the Elder Mother's shoulder. I don't have time to retaliate before Hazel speaks again. Her face is somber now. "It's time."

Twilight has officially fallen.

The magic hour and its warmth no longer grace the forest, and the banshee trees in front of us are haunting in the setting sun. Their branches don't sway; they shudder in the swelling breeze. Once again, this dead forest reminds me of a giant's finger bones reaching into the sky. I imagine what it would look like if their colossal skeletons were buried in the earth under our feet, their hands the only thing rising out of the ground, begging for light. I try to swallow my nerves. And the three of us hold our breath as we move closer to the barrier of trees.

It's now or never.

THE BANSHEE TREES

Just moments after we step into the grove, the wind picks up more, brushing over our skin like icy fingertips and leaving a chill in its wake. The gusts tangle my short hair into knots while bitter air creeps its way beneath my clothes, slipping in through my tunic's loose arms.

Ominous howls echo around us.

I share a distressed look with Rush and Hazel. The gale blowing through the bare branches of the banshee trees produces a sound akin to screaming. And I see now that the trees do bear a resemblance to the faeries they're named after.

The gnomes once told me about the wailing women, the banshees, when I was just nine years old. Over the years, I've found the small men's best and most fearsome tales are told in the garden during a hard day's work. I was picking our winter garden, wrapped in layers of woolen scarves, when I heard Fern's brothers talking about the frost-tipped trees that surround Black Annis's home. They spoke of the weeping that could be heard coming from the frosty, bone-colored forest.

I remember my tiny heart thumping with fear when I rolled over with frozen fingers to ask them what was causing those cries. They huddled around my creaky chair and told me about the creatures who would haunt my dreams for weeks. They said banshees are faeries who herald Death. Their keening can be heard far and wide when someone is about to die. They're known to predict death with such accuracy that some village people believe banshees are actually Death herself, disguised as bewitching, ivory-skinned women. Now I've experienced first-hand how the trees before us, imitating their screams, have received their name.

The cold wind rips a gasp from my lungs as something dawns on me. And I hear the Pooka's gravelly voice in my head. *Listen for Death's weeping, for she'll mourn the hour she'll embrace a daughter of the trolls.*

These cries we hear drifting through the spindly branches are no coincidence. They're warning me of my mother's impending death, just like the Pooka prophesied. Maybe my mother doesn't have much time left . . .

"We need to move faster," I alert my companions, turning my face toward the Elder Mother. "Hazel, do you see any more of Black Annis's magic?"

She presses her round lips together and squints into the distance. "Just barely, dear." She points a knobby finger to my right. "There's a subtle shift in density over there. I think it's our best chance."

I nod and nudge my wheelchair in the direction she's suggested. It takes off at a steady pace, smoothly rolling over the barren ground. I sink my thumbnail in between my teeth and gnaw. Dizziness and nausea are building up like an inescapable tower inside my body now, and I feel my anxiety fill its surrounding moat to the brim.

Sensing my unease, Rush walks beside me and trails his warm hand over my shoulder blades. I take in a deep, shuddering breath to calm my stomach. The closer we get to finding

Black Annis's cave, the more afraid I am, and I can only hope, once I face her, I won't tremble like a newborn fawn.

I wish I were more like the Elder Mother. Her footsteps rarely hesitant, she walks, quiet but assertive, with even the blades of grass around her feet bending to her will.

I wish I was strong like Rush. I could never be physically Herculean like him, but I desire his strength in faith and determination. This whole journey, he's maintained his resolve and never let doubt lead him astray.

I want to be unshakable like my mother. Never once have I seen her unsteady. Not even the night Black Annis crept into the glade. I'll straighten my spine and push my shoulders back with poise when I meet the witch.

Confident. Strong. Poised.

I can be these things too. I've let my disability lead me into a life of constant apprehension. I've always said being wheelchair-bound didn't mean I couldn't do great things; I even just told Rush this after Jenny Greenteeth. Yet, I always turn around and belittle my ability to cope with anything difficult for someone like me. Anxiety has been my jailkeeper, but tonight I will be brave and take back the keys. No longer will my fear lord over me. I'll be my mother's little bird and fly free.

"There," Hazel declares, making me jump in my seat, my assertive thoughts blowing away in the howling wind.

"I see a path up ahead. It leads straight through there." She jerks her chin toward the tightly packed trees before us, then takes the lead while Rush and I trail after her. With guidance, my wheelchair weaves through the narrow gaps between the tree trunks, reminding me of a fox bending its nimble body through the underbrush. I love this chair. I glance down at the wheels of my ebony elder-tree chair and watch the hypnotizing spin of the images curling in the spokes. The wooden sparrow with the sprig of elderberries in its beak flies in a continuous circle. The bundles of elderflowers around the edges of the image dance with every turn of the wheel. The faster my wheels spin, the more blurred the pictures become, almost to the point they disappear.

This strikes an idea.

"I know how to play the ace up my sleeve!"

Hazel stops walking until the three of us gather in a triangle beneath the banshee boughs.

I glance up at Rush. "You need to disappear."

He bleats a surprised laugh. "I'm sorry, what?"

I shake my head to straighten my jumbled thoughts. "When we approach Black Annis's cave, you need to use your ability and conceal yourself. But you'll have to remain unseen the whole time."

"Aha!" Hazel nods. "Brilliant, Sparrow." She turns to Rush. "The witch will never even know you are there."

Rush rubs at the back of his neck. "How exactly does staying hidden the *whole* time help us? I can see the use in a sneak attack, but even just entering the cave?"

"We use you as our true hidden advantage. If Black Annis doesn't know you're there in the first place, you can get close to your family and my mother," I explain.

"This way, you won't end up like Mr. Fern and get skinned for your trouble," Hazel adds.

Rush shudders and drops his arm to his side. "I would like to avoid that for sure." He pauses. "But what about Hazel?"

I glanced at the woman in question. "What about her?"

"What part will she play?"

"Well, I'm here to throw the witch off balance. She already thinks Sparrow is going to show up alone. Once she sees me, she'll have to reevaluate everything she has planned. She'll be able to sense my growing magic."

"Like a bloodthirsty hound assessing a threat," I say.

"Exactly." Hazel dips her head.

"We can use your feud to our advantage," Rush supplies.

I tilt my head. "How so?"

"Maybe Black Annis will be so focused on the Elder Mother and her power, she won't even notice me trying to open the cage Fern mentioned."

I mull over Rush's idea. It's risky, but if Rush could do this while staying concealed, it might be possible. But there are still so many flaws. "What do we do afterwards? You spring the cage, and the faeries are free . . . then what?"

Rush frowns. "I hadn't gotten that far yet."

"Black Annis would surely notice you then." Hazel scrubs at her wrinkled forehead. "Our only option is to kill the witch. Especially now that we're out of salt. She won't have any in her home. Nor can we wait and try to trick her into the sun—she's too smart to be purified like that."

My body jolts as my heart misses a beat. Deep down, after our encounter with Jenny Greenteeth, I knew we'd have to murder Black Annis, but now it's becoming so real, and I can't breathe. I don't want to go through this all over again.

"How do you propose we kill her then?" Rush asks.

Hazel shrugs. "Elder-tree magic?"

"You don't sound very sure about that." I groan.

"It will be just like I said when I was younger and more excitable—I'll use my dagger."

Rush strokes his chin. "This will require you to get very close."

I don't like the thought one bit.

Hazel quirks a thin brow at him. "Are you worried about me, goblin boy?"

Rush rolls his eyes skyward. "Heaven help me, but I am. If you're within arm's reach of her, you're in danger. I saw how fast she killed Copsewood back at the glade."

"Well, isn't that nice. But you needn't worry about me, handsome. These old bones are more agile than you'd think." She smiles, a twinkle in her duo-toned eyes.

Rush blanches.

I swallow my laughter, pressing my hand to my lips. "Rush is right though, Hazel," I mumble from between my fingers. "You're taking a huge risk."

"Seems like we don't have much of a choice, my dear." Hazel's voice sounds rough now.

We all take a moment to let this sink in. Hazel is right. We all know Black Annis won't let us leave, and she's cruel enough to slaughter anyone who tries.

It's us, or her.

"I'll have to create an opportunity that allows you to get close enough. She'll be suspicious of you from the get-go," I note.

Rush lets out a gruff noise. "What we really need to do is be open to improvisation. We don't know what'll happen once we step inside the cave."

"I can try to use my dagger to hold the witch at bay, but if she uses witchcraft instead of her talons, we're in trouble. I can try to use my tree magic as pure energy instead of manipulation, but I've never attempted that before. If worse comes to worse, we'll play it by ear," Hazel concludes.

What a grim plan we've concocted.

We all share a dour look before returning to our literal witch hunt. Hazel scans the forest as we continue along the trail only she can see. The descending twilight paints the forest around us in gloomy shades of plum and navy. It reminds me of a deep, ugly bruise.

The hairs on the back of my neck rise as I roll through the long banshee-tree shadows. They stretch out like malformed claws, resembling the nails that cleaved open the skin of my brow. I imagine one of them coming to life, trying to pluck me out of my chair. I continue to survey our surroundings while paranoia crawls across my skin. My eyes drift toward the sky when I spot something in the distance. Straining to see in the dark, I can only make out indistinct shapes fluttering in the tree branches.

"What are those?" I point to the swaying silhouettes.

"Flags?" Rush's skeptical voice answers.

The closer we get, the more they appear to be heavy cuts of fabric draped over the limbs.

Hazel shuffles to a stop. "Those are not flags."

My mouth drops open, and all of my blood follows its path by draining to my legs.

Hanging in the lowest branches of the banshee trees are sheets of skin. Black Annis has hung her recent trophies out to tan like leather hides.

My tired heart hammers against my chest. It hurts so much that I have to press a hand into my sternum.

We're all stock-still, paralyzed by the atrocity. The skin is scattered among all the trees ahead of us, stretching on as far as we can see in the dark. We're staring at twenty lost lives.

I choke as I watch the flesh wave in the wind like a macabre version of a greeting. Tears well in my eyes. This image will forever be seared in my brain, and the deaths of these faeries will always be my burden to bear. I'll carry them with me forever. Even though it sickens me, I must know if any of the skins are human or goblin. It's horrid, but I know I'll be able to tell if a square of the dangling flesh is my mother's. I'd recognize her sun-drenched, freckled skin anywhere.

I coax my chair forward until I sit beneath the branches. I prepare my curdling stomach with a deep breath before I peer up. With the drying pelts suspended over my head, I can see that the flesh ranges in size and color. It's easier to figure out what kind of creature each trimming of skin once belonged to from this close.

Some of the smaller, dark brown, furry pieces belonged to an imp. I see a smear of sticky honey in the hair, telling me the poor creature's last meal was one of the elderberry cakes I delivered to the barn the day of the attack.

I swallow.

Then I gaze at the tree to my left and guess the creamy, crepe-paper-textured slices I see came from either a brownie or a gnome. Both kinds of little faeries resemble wizened old men. The only thing that tells them apart is the difference in attitude. Brownies are grumpy and secretive, whereas gnomes are jovial and natural social butterflies. There's no trace of personality in this butchered flay of skin.

My brimming tears overflow when I scan the tree on my right. The large, moss-covered slabs bending the branches with their weight undoubtedly came from a troll. My heart squeezes at the thought of my mother witnessing the death of this faerie. She saw all the trolls as parental figures, but I know her softest spot is for Bramwell. I can't imagine my mother's grief if this flesh came from him.

I turn away from the gruesome scene with tears pouring down my face as I check to see what state Hazel and Rush are in.

The Elder Mother stands in the middle of the carnage with tears of her own sinking into the grooves of her face. She's become whey-faced, the color draining from her olive skin. Hazel tugs at the end of her braid as she mutters what sounds like prayers.

At first glance, I can't find Rush, and a trickle of panic fills me as I twist in my seat, searching for him. A loud sniffle leads me farther into the trees where Hazel and I haven't yet dared to venture.

He stands beneath the bare boughs of a thin banshee tree

with his arm outstretched. When I roll up to his side, I see he's rubbing a piece of dried skin hanging from the tree between his thumb and forefinger. The skin shifts between his fingers, catching a sliver of moonlight. It's a vivid goblin green.

All the air vacates my lungs.

"Rush," I gasp. "Please tell me that's not what I think it is."

"I can't lie to you," he croaks.

"Do you think—" I cut myself off before a sob can break loose.

Rush gazes down at me with bloodshot eyes. He lets go of the brittle skin and drops to his knees. I lurch forward in my chair to try and catch him out of instinct. But Rush isn't physically falling, he's just falling apart. His body withers like a dying flower as he drapes his large frame over my bony knees. He wraps his arms around my legs and lays his cheek against my thin thigh. I hesitate before reaching out to put my hand over the back of his neck. My fingers sink into his short curly hair.

I clear the tears from my throat before trying to verbally console Rush. "It might not be them."

Rush's shoulders heave. His weight is making my atrophied legs go numb, but I don't say a word. I rub at his back as I wait for him to gather his thoughts. We sit like this for many minutes before he props his chin up on my knee and looks up at me through his dark lashes. "But it could be. That could be one of my sisters up there."

My fingers tighten in his hair. "Don't say that, not when we don't know for sure. We can try and figure out how long it's been drying, it could be old, too old."

Rush looks up at me with doubt.

"Let me take a look, okay?"

With a slight squeeze to my legs, Rush releases me and stands up, brushing dirt from his olive-colored trousers.

My chair glides forward until the skin is just above my nose. I study its iridescence in the light of the moon. It's undeniably goblin flesh. My stomach gives a turn of protest as I reach out to rub it. The skin feels dull and stiff against the smooth pads of my fingertips, and it occurs to me that this skin feels dry and crispy, like the pages of an ancient book. The corners of my mouth turn down as I backtrack to where Hazel still stands mourning beneath the night sky. I turn to the closest cut of flesh and press it between my fingers. It has give to it, unlike the frailness of the goblin skin.

"Rush," I call. "Come feel this."

"What are you doing, Sparrow?" Hazel hisses, horrified I'm touching the hanging flesh.

"Rush found goblin skin."

Hazel looks stricken. "Not his family . . ."

"No, it can't be," I reassure her.

Rush comes to my side and grasps at the chunk of skin, desperate. "It's squishy. Still feels like leather, though."

"Right, to still be supple, it could have only been out for at most two days. This is what meat feels like after a couple days when my mother and I dry it out at the glade to make jerky."

Rush wrinkles his nose. "So that means?"

"The goblin skin you found is way more than four days old."

"It couldn't possibly be your father or your sisters," Hazel realizes.

I see the emotional agony leave Rush's body at hearing this news, and I'm beyond relieved. I don't know if I could shoulder the guilt if his family's death was on my hands. Rush forgave me for putting their lives in danger, but I'm sure the forgiveness would've been revoked had we concluded the skin to be theirs. At least, this is what my anxiety whispers to me.

"These poor souls." Hazel's voice is full of sorrow.

"The best thing we can do right now is make sure the rest of the faeries make it out with their lives," Rush says.

I nod in agreement.

Hazel exhales and glares deep into the forest, staring in the direction Rush and I just came from. "I can see puddles of Black Annis's magic through there. I'm guessing we're not far from her home."

I swear I hear Rush gulp.

"There's no time to waste," I rasp. "Let's go find us a witch."

THE LABYRINTH

Rush and I follow Hazel like a pair of ducklings as we wade through the trees. She's homed in on the invisible trail of remnant magic Black Annis left behind. The way Hazel hunches her shoulders as her elderly body stalks through the night reminds me of an animal tracking its prey. I notice her toy with the wooden bracelet around her wrist to keep her hands busy, and I can almost see the power building up beneath her thinning skin, ready to be released out into the world.

The elder trees gave a great deal of magic to the Elder Mother. With any luck, she won't have to wait much longer to dip into the well. She's just a couple of hours away from reaching the peak of her magic—it's the perfect timing.

Large stones and boulders litter the ground as the terrain beneath us starts changing. We're entering a new part of the forest, where rocky outcroppings become as common as the banshee trees. We have to be getting close now.

Hazel lets out a grunt and comes to an abrupt stop, and Rush runs right into her back. He catches the Elder Mother as she starts to tip forward, thrown off balance by his muscled build.

She spins on her slippered heel with a glare, breaking Rush's stabilizing grip.

"That was my bad." He holds his palms up in defense.

Hazel huffs. Tonight, it seems like she's getting crankier the older she gets, and I have an inkling the horrid scene we left behind has something to do with it. Even I'm having a hard time sifting through my emotions.

"Do you see something?" I ask her.

The Elder Mother's mismatched eyes sweep over our surroundings. Her face twists in distaste at what she sees. "It's everywhere. The whole forest is steeped in her witchcraft. It looks like a blue grime has settled over everything."

Rush sniffs at the air. "I think I can smell something. It's sweet but kind of disgusting."

Hazel taps the side of her nose. "That would be belladonna you're smelling."

I shiver at the thought of the witch's poison as I inch my wheelchair closer to where Hazel stands. "Where's the cave?"

"On the other side of these trees," she answers.

Rush blows out a long breath as he runs his hands over his short hair. I see the nervousness taking root in his body. "This is it, huh?" He puts his hands down to shove them in his pockets. "Is it too late to back out?" The corners of his lips quirk, making his dimples sink into his cheeks.

I give a soft laugh. "You never had the option to back out. Someone has to be the knight in shining armor."

His silver eyes flash as he cocks his head. "I suppose you're right. Hazel definitely couldn't pull off chain mail."

"I think I'd look quite dashing," Hazel deadpans.

I take in the two of their faces, and pray I get to see them happy and playful like this again.

A gust of wind at our backs blows in a distant scream. I feel as if a cold pail of water is being poured over my head. Death is weeping again.

"Sparrow? Are you okay, my dear?" Hazel's voice rings with concern.

"The Pooka's prophecy. The weeping it mentioned is about the banshee trees. My mother's running out of time."

Hazel and Rush pause for a heartbeat to interpret my brisk answer. Once they grasp the meaning of my rambling, they jump into action.

"Let's go then."

Rush gently shoves at the handles of my chair until it pushes itself forward. I eyeball him for pushing my chair, and he gives me an abashed look. Then the three of us rupture through the line of colorless trees and come face-to-face with the yawning mouth of a cave. The way the moon illuminates the outside makes the entry resemble an endless black hole. The rocks around the opening are coated in a dense layer of moss and lichen, and I'm surprised anything full of life can grow here.

"Now would be a good time for you to disappear, goblin boy," Hazel whispers.

Rush gives a bleak nod. "I'll be with you two right up to the bitter end, even if you can't see or hear me. I'm there."

I reach out and grasp his hand, and I'm automatically enveloped in warmth. I give Rush the most dazzling smile I can muster, even though I'm scratched up and covered in dried blood. "I'll see your face when this is all over. It'll be a very welcome sight."

Hazel gazes at Rush with crinkles at the edges of her hooded eyes. "Good luck, handsome."

The last thing I see of Rush is a blush spreading to the tips of his pointed ears, but I can still feel my hand wrapped in his, and he squeezes it before letting go.

"It's now or never," his bodiless voice remarks.

My heart starts to pick up again, my moat of anxiety threatening to flood. I scramble for any thought that might calm me down.

Confident. Strong. Poised.

I can do this.

"I'm ready." I let out a breath.

Hazel twists the bracelet around her wrist. "Onward."

-

WE'RE all blind as we enter the cave. I widen my eyes as if it will magically help me see better in the dark, but it's useless—the cave is pitch black. All we can do is shuffle forward, sightless.

I hear Rush hiss as he trips over a rock, and it goes skittering somewhere ahead of us, bouncing off the wall. Hazel stifles a cough. My lips twitch with the start of a smile but I keep silent, unlike my companions.

Desperate, I search for any speck of light, but as my wheelchair crunches along the rough cave floor, a bright light explodes before us. Out of instinct, I throw my hands up in front of my face and squeeze my eyes shut, expecting an attack.

Seconds pass.

Nothing happens.

I lower my arms and peek one eye open to see a vast cavern washed in blue. Hovering far overhead is an enormous globe of cobalt light, easily the size of a house. It crackles with energy and blots of magic as it floods the cave with an eerie phosphorescence.

Black Annis knows I've arrived.

I stare at Hazel with gaping eyes—her whole body is bathed in the blue light. It makes the wrinkles in her face appear etched deep in her skin, like carved stone. She swivels her head in my direction to return my mystified gaze. Black Annis sure has a flair for the dramatic. I turn to see Rush's reaction. Of course, he's concealed, but I do receive a reassuring pat on my shoulder.

The cave we've entered turns out to be less of a cave and more of a giant chamber. The room stretches on for miles. And high above us, the vaulted ceilings are hung with giant stalactites. The fluttering of bat wings coming from the icicle-like structures floats down to my ears. The anxious part of me can feel their beady eyes leering. The most harrowing part of the cave, the bats notwithstanding, is the labyrinth waiting ahead. I didn't think Fern was being literal when he told us Black Annis's home was a labyrinth. I expected a few tunnels that might seem confusing to a small gnome, maybe even some twists and turns to get easily lost in . . .

Not this.

This is something out of the legends. It reminds me of a gilded book I have sitting on my crowded bedroom shelves back at the glade. It's a made-up story about a callous king who orders a craftsman and his young son to construct a maze that can hold a bull-like beast at its center. The king feeds the monster human offerings to keep it satiated. Eventually, a hero comes along, enters the labyrinth, and slays the beast, putting a stop to the ruthless murders. I suppose if this were an ancient fantasy story, Rush, Hazel, and I would be the heroes; my mother and the faeries the offerings; and Black Annis the beast in need of slaying.

The maze greeting us is obscene in height. The slabs of wet stone making up its walls must be as tall as the towers I've read about in fairytales. There's no way to climb the slick rock and find a shortcut, so we'll just have to find the middle of the labyrinth the old-fashioned way.

I see the first problem we'll encounter staring us right in the face. "There are three starting points," I drawl.

"Of course there are." Hazel groans.

I hear the slight scuff of Rush's boot. Knowing him, he's

silently screaming. Maybe even pinching the bridge of his nose like he does when he's annoyed.

My heart rate picks up. "We can't just guess which way to go. We'll waste too much time."

"What do you suggest we do, dear?"

I sit and weigh our options. If we all travel together through each starting point, it could take hours. I don't want to risk giving Black Annis one more moment to harm my mother or the faeries. Nor can we let Hazel's magic dwindle.

The decision seems to be made for us when a scream comes from the middle entrance. We jolt forward, ready to take on the labyrinth together. I make it through the opening first and then hear a loud grunt behind me.

When I spin around, I see that a clear blue wall of witchcraft has sealed off the entrance. Hazel is on the other side, with imprints of Rush's hands against the wall next to her.

I'm trapped without them, separated.

A second scream comes from the third entrance. Hazel and I look at each other through the wall with eyes blown wide.

A piercing wail comes from the first entrance. Then, like a haunted chorus, screaming and yelling and crying echo throughout the cavern, coming from every direction. It's deafening.

"We need to split up," I shout over the noise.

"What?" Hazel yells. Rush's ghostly hand beats against the witchcraft wall in objection.

"It's insane, I know, but there's no other alternative. Black Annis already knows I'm trapped in here—we're on borrowed time now. Please tell me the other entrances are still open?"

Hazel purses her lips and nods.

I put a protective hand over a ringing ear. "I don't like this either, but it'll give us our best shot at finding the center faster. Hopefully, one way or another, we'll each make it there. Then we'll just have to stall the witch until we're ready." I dart my eyes in Rush's direction. I'm afraid of acknowledging him or his existence in case Black Annis is close enough to hear us over this cacophony. The thought makes my blood freeze.

Hazel follows my eyes to where Rush is standing concealed next to her and nods in understanding. If Rush makes it to the center first, he can wait, safe and invisible, until Hazel and I arrive, but if one of us beats him there, we'll have to bide our time by distracting the witch until we're all together again.

Rush flattens his hands on the wall again.

I tilt my chin in his direction, so he knows I'm talking to him. "We don't have a choice."

His fingers twitch before he gives the blue surface a couple pats.

I have his blessing.

Once Rush's touch leaves the wall, I turn to face the looming labyrinth. I haven't even seen much of the inside yet, but its towering height is enough to intimidate, and its pitted slate walls drip with the water from the stalactites growing out of the ceiling.

The screaming stops. Only a trail of agony lingers in the air. Black Annis is playing with us. We might be giving in to her game, but that doesn't mean we can't beat her.

I gulp before guiding my wheelchair farther into the middle entrance of the maze. The wheels bump along the uneven ground, splashing through shallow, grime-riddled puddles. In the back of my mind, I hope my beautiful black-lacquered chair won't be corroded in the suspicious water.

Being by myself makes my heart palpitate hard. I'm terrified to go in alone, but my mother needs me. The Pooka's prophecy is on an endless loop inside my head.

I won't let her die.

Glancing behind me, I see Hazel walking toward her entrance. Her head is tilted back, studying the globe suspended above us. The Elder Mother is stiff, but she still looks confident.

I try to peek to the right, even though I know I won't be able to see Rush. I just have to picture him there, standing with his hands in his pockets.

"Ready?" I call out to my companions.

"As I'll ever be," Hazel grumbles back.

With that, Hazel steps out of my sight into her entrance. A split second later, I hear Rush's light footsteps fade into the maze as well.

Now, they're trapped in here too.

I straighten my spine and narrow my eyes, quelling my fear. I encourage my wheelchair forward through the baleful labyrinth.

THE FEARSOME BUMFUZZLE

I can't tell which place I've traveled through is worse, the grove of banshee trees or Black Annis's cave. Each has its own sinister charms. One was a shady forest haunted by disturbing disembodied screams, foretelling the death of someone I loved. The other is a damp labyrinth in the home of a witch with a craving for other people's skin.

I take the time to consider my options as I weave my way through the dank maze. I conclude that Black Annis having my mother in her possession might make the labyrinth just a bit worse.

Ludicrous thoughts such as these are the only things keeping me sane in this dreary cave. My brain is playing tricks on me, turning every shadow into a monster.

Unfortunately, Black Annis's massive orb of light floating above the labyrinth can't dispel the darkness from every corner. Each nook and cranny being diffused in the color of her venomous magic doesn't help its already eldritch nature, and the maze's deepest edges house the worst of the imaginary shadow monsters. From the corners of my eyes, it seems like the fiends are reaching out to drag me into the darkness with them. I imagine razor-sharp claws and needle teeth hooking into my pliable skin like Jenny Greenteeth's did so easily. Except this time, instead of drowning in water, I'll be choking on pure gloom.

To push down my surging anxiety, I wrap my arms around my stomach, protecting my softest and most vital parts. If only it were enough to keep my fear at bay. Every time I come across a fork in the maze, the pressure on my chest grows heavier, and the choice between right and left feels too important. Too vital.

If I don't get out of this labyrinth soon, my heart just might give out all over again.

To my dismay, I stumble upon yet another crossroads. My wheelchair slows itself to a stop and sits still in front of the dewy wall that branches off into two passages. I have to choose which direction to go, quick. I sit there and resist the urge to chew on my nails.

The labyrinth mocks me in the blue incandescence.

I glare back at it.

Sweat beads on my forehead as I gaze between the two paths. No matter what, there'll be no rhyme or reason to my choice. There's nothing around me to hint at which way I should go. If only Fern had left some form of trail to follow. A long ribbon or train of breadcrumbs would have been nice. I would've even appreciated large charcoal arrows drawn onto the ground. Nothing says *this way to the witch* quite like charcoal arrows.

I must make a decision. Now. My muscles stiffen as I jerk one of my wheels, telling my enchanted chair which path to take.

Left it is.

I nod to the make-believe monsters hidden along the walls as I turn the corner. I think maybe if I acknowledge them, they'll leave me alone and cease to exist in my peripheral vision.

I want to laugh at myself.

Making up nonsense is the only way to stay brave. I decide

that with the next thing that makes me want to panic, I'll give it a different name, just like I did with the plant life in the forest yesterday.

Out of nowhere, the giant light above my head dims. It shines with a very faint blue glow, plunging the labyrinth further into the shadows. I pull my wheels to a stop and sit rigid in my chair. A blanket of foreboding drapes over my shoulders, threatening to smother me. I don't know what the fading blaze means, but I don't like it. Feeling meek, I nudge my chair to continue its path.

I hear a terrible rasping noise.

Much to my embarrassment, I realize it's my own ragged breathing, and I take gulps of moisture-laden air to try and silence my anxious wheezing. This is not the best place for someone with anxiety—well, for anyone really. I strain my ears, listening for even the softest sound. The only thing I can hear besides my wheels' grating is the water dripping from the ceiling. Besides that, it's so quiet I could hear a pin drop.

My chair carries on at a steady pace for a few minutes, nerves making my body vibrate now.

And each new corner my wheelchair takes makes my heart race. I never know what bogey my brain might concoct next. I scour every crevice, searching for any of the shadow monsters I banished from my imagination. I would loath their return to scamper along the walls.

Every few seconds, I get an itch to look over my shoulder. It's an overwhelming sensation I try to fight. Though, the last time I neglected to glance behind me is why we all ended up in this mess.

I finally obey the nagging urge, and just as I expected, the path behind me is empty. There's nothing but tall shadowy walls and dirty puddles.

That's when I hear the slapping of bare feet running on the

wet ground in front of me. I whip my head back around so fast I tweak my neck.

There's no one there.

I let my hands trail over the spokes of my wheels, urging my chair to slow down. I hold my breath, hoping I just imagined the sound. It's dead quiet again. The steady drip-drop of water splashing against the maze floor is the only sound to reach my ears as I smooth the pads of my fingers over the flying sparrow pictured in my wheels. I remind myself to be strong, to be my mother's free little bird. I just need to be brave and get through this Timeforsaken maze.

Shaking myself off, I push at my wheels and let my chair drive me forward again. I attempt to put myself into the shoes of the legendary hero I read about. It's easy to feel like I'm on a quest to slay a bull-like beast while being lost in this labyrinth. The only things I lack are a sword and a ball of thread to help me find my way back home.

Perhaps I do have thread, it's just attached to another person. Instead of leading me back home, it will lead me back to him. I hope Rush is okay—

Footsteps sound again.

This time, they come from behind me.

The fine hairs covering my body stand on end, and as I yank my chair around, I catch the barest glance of blue blur disappearing around the corner. There's no way I imagined this. This is not an anxiety-fueled illusion. Something else is inside the maze with me besides Rush and Hazel.

As though in answer to my thought, a feminine laugh bounces off the wet walls.

It's official—I'm panicked.

My heart thumps in my ears as I roll myself backward. My eyes darting around, trying to catch sight of whatever taunts me.

To preserve my sanity, I name the creature tormenting me a

Bumfuzzle. No one can fear something that sounds so soft. I spin around and thrust my wheelchair forward, pushing as hard and as fast as I can go, willing my elder chair to take over.

The chair seems to sense my distress and quickens beneath me, going at breakneck speed. I've never once gone this fast.

The tread of shoeless feet striking the floor sounds behind me again. I don't dare look over my shoulder this time. I have enough fear flooding my body. But whatever's behind me is getting closer, and I can hear it closing the distance between us with every footfall.

I don't think my wheelchair is fast enough to outpace this creature, and the thought makes me hyperventilate, my eyes filling with tears. I don't know if I'll be able to escape.

Then, a talon-tipped hand grazes the back of my exposed neck. My heart shutters. It feels like claws made of cold metal. I try to spur my wheelchair to go faster. I see the dead end. I cry out, realizing I'm being cornered like a petrified animal.

There's no escape. The Bumfuzzle has caught me.

My chair slows itself to a stop, preventing me from smashing myself into the wall. My body heaves as it racks with sobs. I have no other choice but to face what's been chasing me and hope I survive the encounter. It crushes me to think this could be the end, that I might not reach my mother after all. Hot tears pour down my grimy face as I start to turn my chair around. The edges of my wheels scrape against the stone as I push back into the corner, as far as I can go. My tears blur my vision so much, I can hardly see the creature creeping toward me.

"Hello, pet," a woman's satin voice singsongs.

My chin trembles as I try to clear my eyes.

Confident. Strong. Poised.

I try to take a deep breath to calm myself, but let out a whimper instead. So much for not letting my anxiety lord over me.

"Don't cry," she coos. "There's nothing to be afraid of." The woman pauses, letting mischief seep into her voice. "Yet." She leans down until her hazy face is level with mine, her long hair falling over her shoulders, framing her gaunt face as it brushes over the hands I have bunched in the fabric of my trousers. She extends her skeletal hand toward my face, fingers curling around my chin and tilting it up. Her iron talons prick my skin.

My final tears fall from my eyes, and I know without a doubt Black Annis stands before me.

She's younger than I would have imagined. From far away, before, it was impossible to see what her face looked like. I expected a weathered hag, but instead, I'm greeted by a disturbing, stunning, blue-skinned woman. She's terrible and beautiful, the same way a nightmare might disguise itself as a dream.

Her poison-drenched lips curl up into a lethal smile as she sees my recognition sink in. Her fingers tighten around my chin.

"Let's have some fun, shall we Sparrow?"

Hearing my name fall from her black-rimmed lips makes my blood run cold. I can't help but gasp.

"Hush now, pet. It's time to daydream." The scent of toxic berries wafts from her mouth as she speaks.

I try to rip my chin from her iron grip as she bends her face closer to mine. Her solid black eyes glitter—she's relishing my struggle. She's as cold-hearted as everyone says she is.

Black Annis plants her full lips against the jagged flesh of my torn forehead. Her mouth is shockingly cold against my inflamed skin. The witch lets her touch linger before pulling back to gaze into my dewy eyes.

"A kiss of belladonna, to invite the nightmares to play," she sings.

My head starts to swim, her poison-steeped kiss making my vision distort. The last thing I see is Black Annis's gleaming, pointed teeth pull into a grin before my world goes black.

A DANCE WITH BELLADONNA

When I open my eyes again, everything I see ripples like a mirage. The towering walls of the labyrinth no longer stand still. Instead, they bend and flow like waves in a river. The floor beneath me looks like it's breathing, rising and sinking with its every inhale and exhale.

I hold my breath, trying to stop the spinning in my head, and realize the ground has stopped moving. As I blow out, the floor sinks. I take a deep breath in, and the floor rises.

It's reflecting my breathing.

With a giggle, I draw in rapid breaths just to watch the floor bounce.

Then, I notice the flickering.

The glowing orb overhead is pulsating. It throws the shadows along the walls into a writhing dance as the blue light blinks in and out of sight.

Why am I in this maze again?

The constant motion around me is making me sick.

I try to grab my chair's wheels to ground myself, but I miss them, my depth perception thrown off.

A twinkling laugh mocks me.

I turn my woozy head to find the source of the laughter, but the time between my head turning and my vision is off. Everything feels a few seconds delayed. I have never been so disoriented in my life—at least, I don't think I have.

I try to remember why I feel this way. Something must have happened—how did I get here? Maybe I'm just sick, delusional? My chest does feel funny, almost hollow, and withy. I shake my head. No, not important enough . . . There's something else happening, I can feel it.

Every time I get close to the answer, it drifts away. It's like trying to catch water in your palms with your hands splayed wide. No matter how hard I try, I just can't get them to come together.

All I remember is a smell, something sweet, maybe even a little too sweet. Is it fruit?

Finally, my wandering eyes settle on a long-limbed figure. I can remember the woman's name, but I don't know who she is.

Black Annis stands before me with radiant cerulean skin and smooth charcoal hair, which hangs in a straight curtain down to her slender waist. She looks like a fairytale queen from one of my books. Her face is flawless, from her pointed pixie nose to her stained, pouty lips. Her slim frame is clothed in a gauzy black shift. By society's standards, her dress would be considered immodest, but I think it makes her look daring. Even the thin chain girdle she wears slung around her hips is bold, albeit a bit dated. She's easily the most beautiful creature I've ever seen.

One thing strikes me as odd though—the swaths of what seems to be leather hanging from the side of her belt. They swing in time with the swaying labyrinth walls, and my stomach turns as a memory claws at the back of my mind. There's something unfortunate about the scraps she's embellished herself with. I can't put my finger on what it was, but the detail feels crucial.

Black Annis's doe-like eyes twinkle as she peers down at me.

When I meet her inky stare, her keen teeth pull into an inviting smile, and I can almost imagine a motherly love on her face. I want nothing more than to be cradled in her arms and drift off into a peaceful sleep.

"Sparrow," she croons.

I release a dreamy sigh. The way my name sounds coming from her sweet lips feels like home. It nestles me in warmth and safety. Visions of a luscious, sun-soaked glade with lovingly hand-paved paths floats across my vision. The taste of honey lingers on my tongue as I feel the ghost of a nurturing kiss on the crown of my head.

Maybe Black Annis is my mother?

I glance down and hold out my hands in front of my face. At first, I hit myself in the nose, trying to focus on my shaking arms. Then I squint and pull them away, to where my depth perception isn't as bad. The light above casts the skin on the back of my hands in a wicked blue, but when it flickers out, I see my pale ivory skin shining in the dark. It seems unlikely that this beautiful, blue-skinned woman is my mother.

Then who is my mother? Where is she?

Full of mourning, I peek back up at Black Annis, and I'm sad I don't get to enjoy having this creature as family.

My heart misses a beat, almost as if protesting my thoughts. I frown.

"What's the matter, pet?" she asks. "Aren't you having fun?"

"I don't—I don't think so." My voice wavers like my surroundings. "Have you seen my mother? Is she here with me?"

The pleasant smile slips off her face.

My mind continues to wander. "I believe there's something important I'm supposed to be doing. Do you know what it is?"

Black Annis's gaze grows feral. "What an unruly girl you are, inviting witches into your glade all willy-nilly. Your foolish lines beckoned me to play there, but now you refuse to play with me in my own home? You must obey the rules, pet."

I scrunch my brows together in confusion. The taut skin of my forehead starts to burn.

"Rules?" I echo. "What game are we playing?"

"A Dance with Belladonna. My very favorite game. All you have to do is stop thinking and give in." She reaches forward and taps a nail against my stinging forehead.

"Give in to what?" A starry-eyed quality drenches my voice.

Black Annis smiles a wolfish smile. "The terror."

Then, my thoughts become woolen. The temperature in the labyrinth drops as the globe above me takes on a dark, sinister hue. I rub at my unfocused eyes, trying again to make sense of everything. But when I look back at Black Annis, my trembling heart freezes, turning to ice in my chest. Instead of the heaven-sent creature I'd been admiring, I see the creation of a devil commencing before me.

I choke and try to steady myself by placing my hand on the wall beside me. My skin meets the frosty stone with a wet slap. The wall feels slick, the liquid coating the rock seeming thicker than the water running down it. I pull my arm back, fast, and to my dismay, my hand comes away red.

Blood covers my palm in a sticky layer, shining a rich garnet in the ebb and flow of blue light above. I gag, wiping at my trousers, trying to remove the blood from my skin. It soaks through the gray fabric of my trousers, and as the stains set, I turn to the wall to see it running with red. Rivulets of blood slide down in gory sheets. All around me, the labyrinth is showering blood like grotesque waterfalls.

Mouth open, I gape again at the creature stooped in the darkness. I now know Black Annis is not an angel nor a maternal figure, she's a witch. The arms I'd longed to hold me are now like sharp-edged spindles. And her once-round, innocent eyes look wicked as she drinks in my fright.

Black Annis's features sharpen and make her appear sunken with starvation. The lips I thought were sweet are soaked with poison, and they stretch over sharp teeth matching the ferocity of her curved iron talons. Then I remember the lethal kiss, the one the witch bestowed upon me like a morbid imitation of a gift. And the longer I study her, the more warped she becomes. Her limbs get knobby as they grow long and disjointed, her obsidian eyes multiply over her bony face, spreading in pairs over her cheeks and forehead. She smirks at me through elongating fangs. She's transformed into a giant blue spider.

The venom in my system must be exaggerating her appearance, making her look like the bogeyman of my nightmares, because this—this is impossible. Still, knowing it isn't real doesn't stop my heart from racing. And as the witch inches toward me, I catch sight of the girdle dangling from her waist. The scraps of leather are transforming as well. Obscure shapes bulge along the surface of the material, trying to stretch into something new.

A hand bursts forth from a piece of green-tinted leather. It takes the form of a goblin arm reaching out to me, searching for someone to liberate it. A cry lodges in my throat; I'm too afraid to even move. One after another, arms rupture from the other swaths, and I remember they're Black Annis's past victims, the ones she wears as trophies. These faeries she's killed are begging me for freedom, pleading for me to end their suffering. They hold out their hands, trying to seize me in their fraught grip. The closer the witch gets to me, the closer the arms get to snatching at me. They swipe at anything they can reach. The furry arm of an imp gets so close to my face, I feel the wind it creates as it whizzes past my nose.

Only when Black Annis lurks over me with a web of saliva swinging from her teeth, and the wrinkled arm of a brownie grabs onto the sleeve of my tunic, am I finally able to scream. It rings through the labyrinth, carrying itself over the towering walls as I pray someone will come to save me.

The shrillness of my shriek is enough to send the hag skittering backward in surprise. She snarls at me, fury lighting a fire in her bottomless eyes. She stalks toward me again, when I hear a distant shout.

"Sparrow!"

Black Annis pauses. The leather arms that were desperate to reach me hang limp against her side now. "Your friend is trying to find you, pet, but this is a solo dance."

I ignore her. "Help!" I cry.

"Sparrow! I'm coming for you, dear!" The voice I heard before answers my call.

"Let's play a new game, shall we? How about a little Hide and Seek?" Black Annis's teeth click together. "You're it."

The witch steps back and turns toward the oozing walls of the labyrinth, her spidery limbs sticking to the bloody stone. She ascends. Scuttling along the lofty wall, her emaciated body zigzags through the gore. Once she reaches the top of the tall maze, she gazes down at me. Her eight pairs of eyes blink one after another as she gives me one last razor-sharp grin before disappearing over the edge.

I sink back into my wheelchair and squeeze my eyes shut. I don't want to see anymore.

"Sparrow? Where are you?" the voice calls, this time much closer than before.

At this point, I can tell it's coming from an older woman. Is she my mother?

"Hello?" My voice cracks. "I'm here."

I sit with my eyes closed, too afraid of what I might see if I open them again. The belladonna flooding my senses could make me envision anything. At least sitting in my own world of darkness like a sullen child, I can't see the witch's bitter magic overhead. Or the breathing floors and rippling walls. If it weren't for the paranoia and anxiety nibbling at the tips of my fingers, I could stay here for hours—I could hold out. Although I still can't shake the feeling that I've forgotten something. It's something Black Annis doesn't want me to remember, so that must mean it's important—she was angry when I mentioned my mother. Could that be it?

"Oh, Sparrow." The old woman's soft voice gasps in relief, and I can hear her feet shuffling toward me. "There you are. I thought I'd lost you to this maze forever."

I keep my eyes pinched closed. "Who are you?"

The footsteps stop. "What? Have you lost your mind, dear?"

I shake my head. "I don't know what I've lost, ma'am, but I know it was something great."

I hear the woman shuffle again, and the beat of my heart thunders at a bruising pace.

"What happened to you?"

"I danced with Belladonna," I reply.

I hear her suck a sharp breath through her teeth. "Open your eyes, Sparrow."

I shake my head again, clenching my hands into fists. She pads closer yet. "You'll just have to trust me, dear. I'm here to help you. Let me see those peepers of yours."

I reluctantly crack one eye open. I'm met with a glorious view. This woman is the angel I've been waiting for. She is older, as I thought, but she still maintains an air of grace, and her beauty shines through her, as if the lavender light seeps from her pores. She stands in a halo of benevolent magic with her worn hands tangled at the end of her silver braid. I can see the worry for me in her remarkable, multicolored eyes.

She beams at me, the gap in her front teeth knocking a memory loose. I see a young girl, not more than twelve, dancing through a forest, holding the hand of a handsome, dark-skinned young man.

I study her, tilting my head to the side. "You're not my mother, are you?"

The woman laughs in a sad way. "No, dear, but I am the *Elder* Mother."

My head swirls with the pressure of repressed memories and Black Annis's poison. I press my fingers into my eyes and rub, hard. When I pull my hands away, they're coated with a syrupy substance, almost like the pulp of mashed berries. I yelp, trying to shake the liquid from my hands.

The Elder Mother motions toward my face. "Let's get this fixed, shall we? Green eyes suit you better."

I examine my discolored fingers. "Is this real?"

Her face crumples with sadness now. "Not all of it, but I'm sure it feels real."

I regard her with tears in my eyes.

"I can't imagine the things you've seen," she says before extending her glowing hand out to me. She reminds me of a seraph in a stained-glass window of a cathedral, coming to banish the malignancy infecting me. I reach out to her in kind, wanting to be absolved of the belladonna coursing through me. This angel will be my liberator, the one who will save me from the witch.

MAGICAL SALIVA

I expected my absolution to be a lot more grand. I imagined the sound of angels singing as the heavens part or a divine blessing bestowed upon my head, but I receive neither. Instead, the Elder Mother licks her thumb and scrubs at my tender forehead.

I cringe at the saliva she spreads over my skin, trying to move my head away like a stubborn, muddy child refusing to bathe.

"Hold still, Sparrow," she scolds.

Pulling the long sleeve of her dress over the heel of her hand, she wipes away the remaining spit and inevitable print of Black Annis's berry-stained lips from my face.

My head begins to clear, the labyrinth around me ceases to move, and the floor no longer rises and falls with my breath. Even the blood running down the walls is once again water.

I gaze down at the thigh of my trousers where I wiped my hands, but there are only dark water patches now, not a spot of blood in sight. My fingers, on the other hand, are still stained a deep blue. If I didn't know any better, I would believe they were berry-stained from making jam all day. But this discoloration came from my eyes. Out of nowhere, they start to water profusely. I touch my fingers to my cheeks, and they come away smeared with fresh blue syrup. "What's happening to me?"

The Elder Mother tilts my chin up, searching my sticky eyes. "You're expelling the rest of the belladonna in your system. When you first opened your eyes, they were solid indigo, not a bit of white to be seen." She taps my nose with a wrinkled finger. "I didn't much care for the color on you."

I shudder as I remember Black Annis's ebony spider eyes. I must've looked like a pale imitation of the witch. Hazel continues to use her sleeve to wipe off my face, catching my colored tears before they can leave blue streaks down my face.

Hazel. I remember her. What a silly thing to have forgotten. Then my thoughts topple like a line of dominoes, the memories of the last four days crushing me all over again. My mother, the slaughter at the glade, Rush, the Pooka's prophecy, all of it. The anxiety threatens to drown me with its precarious, full moat, my tower of nausea looking on. I take in calming breaths.

I'll tread these waters until I reach the other side. I'm stronger than my guilt and worry.

"Everything coming back into that noggin of yours yet?" Hazel probes.

I nod. "It hit me all at once. I'm so sorry."

Hazel cocks her head. "For what, dear?"

"For us being forced to split up."

Hazel tuts and taps a knuckle under my chin. "It wasn't your fault, dear. We fell into the witch's trap." Happy with my face's cleanliness, the Elder Mother steps away from me and nods at her handiwork. "Back to normal and as darling as ever. New scars and all."

I give her a small smile. Then I remember the half-goblin in the labyrinth with us. Now that we know Black Annis isn't lurking in the maze anymore, it feels safe enough to whisper about the concealed half-goblin. "Do you think Rush heard me scream?"

Hazel lifts a shoulder. "I'm not sure. It was a good thing I was close enough to hear you and find my way through the maze. It's awful big."

"I'm lucky you were near."

"What happened?"

I lean back in my chair and thread my fingers through my hair, gripping at the roots. "Black Annis happened. I think she planned on messing with me the whole time. Whether to stall me from finding my mother or not, she really does have a taste for games." A shiver runs through me because I know right now she's hiding, waiting for me to play more.

Hazel snorts, disbelief coating her features. "Games?"

"She played with me the whole time. After she kissed me, I was pretty much fallen at her feet. I thought she was an angel. But once I mentioned my mother, she became a living nightmare." Goosebumps ripple over my skin. "I could've sworn she ran across the walls. I think I'll be afraid of spiders for the rest of my life."

Hazel lifts a gray brow.

"Right now, Black Annis and I are playing Hide and Seek." I roll my eyes.

"Sounds like the hag is waiting for you to find her in the center of the labyrinth now."

"Maybe with this game, there'll be no more surprises? Maybe we won't have to worry about bumping into her until we're ready?"

Hazel hums. "Better not jinx it." She raps her knuckles against my elderwood wheelchair.

"So, now what?"

"We try to find the center of the labyrinth, together," she replies.

"What about Rush?"

"We stick to the plan. At some point, we'll all make it there. He could already be waiting for us for all we know." She pats my hand. "Best not to think of too many things while your brain unscrambles itself."

"I suppose . . ."

"*Sparrow.*" A whisper floats over the labyrinth wall in front of us. Is that—no, it can't be.

"*Sparrow, come find me,*" the voice of my mother whispers again, but this time, it comes from another direction. I look at Hazel in alarm before racing off toward my mother's voice.

"Sparrow wait!" The Elder Mother chases after me. "It's not your mother."

"*Sparrow . . .*"

Somewhere in the back of my mind, I know Hazel's right and Black Annis wouldn't let my mother wander free in the labyrinth, but I don't care. I haven't heard her voice in days. I twist around corner after corner, trailing after the witch's cruel trick.

When Hazel catches up to me, she yanks my chair to a stop. I don't even try to fight her. "She's playing with you, my dear. No matter how much you want it to be your mother, it's not real."

"*Follow me,*" the voice echoes, calling again and again, but every time it speaks it's farther away. Just like the trail of bread-crumbs I wished for earlier.

"I know, I know." I tear my fingers through my hair. This maze is making me lose all common sense. We need to get out of here, fast.

"*Follow me.*" The echoes drift away again, almost like they're laying out a path.

"Call me crazy," I sigh. "But I think we need to play 'Follow the Leader.'"

Hazel frowns. "You don't think Black Annis is just leading us on a wild goose chase?"

"*Follow me!*" my mother's voice shrieks. Both of us clamp our hands over our ears. The scream follows the same echoing path as before.

"I think our only option is to wait and see. I don't want to find out what'll happen if we don't participate." I wiggle a finger in my ear, trying to get the ringing to subside.

Hazel's shoulders hike upward as she resigns herself to playing the hag's game. "Tag, you're it," she grumbles before walking past me.

We travel in relative silence, listening for more whispers. The way sound bounces off the tall stone walls makes it hard to tell exactly where the voice is coming from. We must make a wrong turn at one point, because all we hear is my mother's musical laughter. When we turn around and go the other way, it stops.

"Hazel." I break the silence. "How did you know just wiping away the belladonna would work?"

"This way."

"Oh, I didn't. At least not fully." Hazel stops, trying to gauge which direction the voice came from before spinning on her heel and turning left.

"What do you mean, you didn't know?" I exclaim, urging my chair to follow her.

"It's pretty simple, dear. I just did what I thought made sense. I saw in a tome about poisons once that if your skin comes in contact with something that has hallucinogenic properties, the best thing you can do is clean the area immediately to reduce effects. It suggested using fresh water and something with cleansing properties like salt. It's obvious we didn't have that, and my saliva ended up being enough,

so don't get into a tizzy, you would've expelled it yourself anyways. Belladonna wears off quicker when it comes in contact with your skin compared to ingesting it, it just muddles your mind for a while and seeps right out."

She waves a hand at me over her shoulder.

I don't appreciate the simplicity of her answer.

"But why did that work? It was a little too easy if you ask me."

"Maybe so," Hazel agrees. "But that's just the magic of nature."

The light on the path ahead seems to dim, and we come to a crossroads: left, right, or forward. Hazel stands stock still listening for any clue. My chair creaks as I shift my weight.

"This way," comes from the left. *"No, this way,"* comes from the right.

Hazel rolls her eyes. "Oh, very funny."

"What do we do now?" I ask.

"Forward." Hazel marches on. "I'm getting sick and tired of this witch's games."

I hesitate before steering the conversation back to how the older woman saved me from the belladonna. "Do you have magic spit, Hazel?"

The Elder Mother cackles, but she doesn't respond.

"Did the elder trees give you magical saliva? Could you grow a tree if you licked a seedling?"

I continue to follow her through the maze, pestering her with questions she won't answer.

She decisively chooses which way to go every time we reach a crossroads, picking the path with confidence. At this pace, we'll find the center of the labyrinth in no time.

"Follow me."

-

AS WE TRUDGE on through the winding maze, I can't help but rub my sternum. I remember how empty it felt when I was infected with belladonna. A lot of the things I saw ended up being hallucinations, but this felt real. It's unsettling that I can still feel an echo of the hollowness. The heart beating in my chest is the only thing keeping me from spiraling.

I focus on something else.

Having Hazel travel with me through the musty labyrinth is enough to scare my shadow monsters away. I have no need to talk myself down from a cliff of fear. Everything is named as it should be—no more Bumfuzzles to be found. The walls are just stone slabs, and the dark corners are just shaded crevices. Now that I know it was Black Annis chasing me through this cave, I can call her what she is: a witch. A terrible, cruel witch. "I can't believe I called Black Annis a Bumfuzzle," I murmur.

"What was that, dear?"

"Hm? Oh, nothing," I stammer, not realizing I've spoken out loud. I'll take this tomfoolery with me to the grave.

Hazel peers over her shoulder at me.

"How are you feeling?"

I let out a dry laugh. "Like I'm sleep-deprived, half drowned, scratched up, and poisoned."

"Sparrow."

"Fair. Do you feel ready to see your mother?" Hazel asks after hearing her voice whisper to us again.

I honestly haven't thought about it that way. This whole journey has been about rescuing her, yet I've neglected to think of what our reunion will really be like. I don't know what state I'll find her in. I can only hope she's in better shape than I am.

"I'm a little nervous," I admit.

"This way. Hurry!"

Hazel takes us left down a long path in the maze, picking up the pace.

"Why's that?"

I continue to rub at my chest. "I'm not sure. For some reason, I don't feel like the same person I was last time she saw me."

Hazel nods. "You've been through a lot since then. You've met prophesying creatures and slain a legendary hag. Not to mention fallen in love."

I choke on surprise. "Love?"

Hazel gives me a wry grin over her shoulder. "Yes, love. You've grown up, Sparrow—you've battled your inner monsters and are preparing to battle a real-life one again. Your mother will be so proud of who you've become in this short time."

"It's just been one terrible thing after another. What if all this trauma is too much to recover from? I don't want to wind up searching for a semblance of stability and power like Jenny Greenteeth or Black Annis."

The Elder Mother scoffs. "You could never!" Then she stops in the middle of the path and turns to face me. "Sometimes, terrible things change us for the better. I want you to remember that everything happens for a reason, dear. You are who you are right now because it was meant to be."

"Hurry!"

In a rare moment of distraction from following the voice, Hazel mutters under her breath, "I'm sure your mother was the one who ensured that."

Confusion descends over me. "What do you mean my mother ensured who I am?"

Hazel's eyes flicker over my body before turning back around and resuming her brisk walk through the maze.

"I don't know, don't listen to me."

"Hazel—"

"Follow me."

"I'm old. I say weird things, let's move on."

"Hazel, come on. You can't really expect me to drop this, can you?"

The old woman stays silent. I don't know if this 'ensure' business was a slip of the tongue or something Hazel intentionally said. For what purpose she would have to offer this peculiar little statement with no explanation, I can't even begin to grasp, but it's very much something the Elder Mother would do.

But it bothers me. I've gotten the feeling Hazel knows more than she says many times now. She's been cryptic and secretive, even as a child. The night I met her, she pushed at me, trying to glean information about my mother and the trolls. Hazel is without a doubt hiding something from me.

"I hope you know you're not going to get away with that response." I'm answered with silence. "Fine, we'll talk about it after this mess is over."

Hazel begins to whistle a soft tune, filling the silence of the cave with her bird-like song. She may avoid me now, but after my mother and the faeries are safe, I'll harass her nonstop. I think after everything we've been through together, I deserve an explanation for her elusive ways.

I still trust Hazel, though. The Pooka's prophecy more than hints at the Elder Mother being the one to save my mother. And I have to believe anything she's kept from me won't get in the way of this goal.

"Do *you* feel ready?" I ask her.

"Hm?" Hazel seems absentminded as she hums and takes a sharp right onto a new path.

My chair veers to follow her. "To see my mother. According to the Pooka, it saw you save her."

"Who knows what anything the Pooka said means, but perhaps if I kill Black Annis, it'll be considered saving her."

"I didn't think of that."

Hazel trails a hand along a wet wall. "It seems to be the most probable possibility. I can't think of anything else I'd be capable of doing for your mother."

"Well, the Pooka used the word 'restore.' She could be injured." This thought causes my heart to pick up.

"Maybe . . . my magic doesn't apply to humans, though. It's strictly in the manipulation of the trees, you know this. Perhaps using the energy as a weapon to defeat the witch, thus saving your mother, is what the Pooka meant?" Hazel peels her hand from the wall and shakes the water off.

Disappointment crashes into me. "So you don't have healing magic?"

"I could heal an elder tree if it were damaged, but not a human."

I'm about ready to tear my hair out. What had the Pooka meant?

"So, you don't have magical healing spit then. It was just the water and sodium living in your mouth?"

Hazel chuckles. "Yes, dear, I'm afraid so."

"That answers that question, then . . . but you still didn't tell me what would happen if you licked a seedling."

"How about I let you know when I try it?" she offers.

I shrug. "Works for me. But you know what this means, right?"

"What?"

"Black Annis's poison can be dissolved by any old salt-riddled, purifying saliva and a wipe of a sleeve. Makes her seem a little less sinister and a lot more absurd."

"In her defense, even you weren't clever enough to think of wiping her kiss from your brow."

I jut out my lower lip. "It was scary, okay? When you're surrounded by bloody walls and giant spiders, the last thing you think about is wiping away her kiss like your least favorite aunt got ahold of you."

Hazel nods in sympathy, but before she can respond, a clank of iron resonates through the labyrinth.

"Sparrow, help me!"

"Did you hear that?" I whisper.

Hazel pauses and stands still as the sound of a mocking feminine voice floats over the walls.

"We're close." Hazel's voice is barely audible.

As quiet as we can be, we sneak through the labyrinth, listening for the sound of Black Annis's voice. We have to backtrack a couple of times when we realize we're moving farther away from the noise.

Left. Right. Right. Left. Right.

We come to yet another crossroad, and somehow, I just know this last turn will lead us to the center of the cave. Hazel leans up against a damp wall and braces herself, preparing to face the witch. I watch as a visible transformation settles over her. Her eyes harden, and her stiff spine straightens. The angle of her round lips becomes more severe. She tugs her elderwood bracelet off her wrist, and it forms into a dagger. I can tell it alters with ease due to the sheer amount of magic welling up inside her old body. She's at the peak of her power, the Elder Mother through and through. Hazel weighs the gray dagger in her hand before looking to me. Then she shoves it my way, holding the weapon handle-side out, almost like an offering.

I stare at her, bewildered. "What are you doing?"

"Take it," she commands.

"What? No! Are you crazy?" I half-whisper, half-yell.

"Black Annis will sense my power once we're in range of one another—she'll expect me to have some sort of defense. I don't want to lose the dagger to her. But she already believes you are unarmed and helpless."

I give her a dubious headshake. "What am I supposed to do with it?"

"Just hold it for me, keep it safe until the time is right."

I reach for the dagger, but I waver, hand hovering above the blade. "Are you sure?"

The Elder Mother lays the wooden knife in my hand and folds my fingers around the handle. "I'm absolutely positive. You're just protecting it for me, I don't need you to use it."

With a grim nod, I pull the dagger to me in a tight fist. The leaf pattern embedded in the wood imprints my hand.

Hazel smiles. "I'm going to need you to hide it, dear."

I flush. "Oh. Right."

I tuck the dagger into the back of my trousers, the waistband holding the flat of the blade against my spine underneath my tunic. It feels warm on my skin. I can feel the same hum in it I sometimes sense in the wheelchair beneath me. They're both buzzing with magic, just like Hazel.

The Elder Mother examines me. "Are you ready?"

I take in a deep breath, the bodice wrapped around my torso digging into my ribs. "As I'll ever be."

Hazel reaches out and pats my cheek before taking the path on the left. My chair, ever obedient, follows her and wheels me into the lair of a witch.

THE CAGE

The center of the labyrinth reminds me of a throne room in a ramshackle castle. Its ceilings are domed, cracked, and cavernous, with smaller versions of the globe that hovers above the maze levitating throughout the room, washing it in the same eerie blue glow. I'm beginning to grow sick of the color. The only other hue cutting through it is a fire blazing in a makeshift hearth in the corner of the room. The clash of the warm fire and cold blue magic is startling.

On the other side of the room is a large, mysterious mound covered in a sheet of black fabric. It's as tall as it is wide, almost the size of my bedroom back at the glade. I can almost see a shimmer of blue light trying to shine through the dense fabric, meaning there's a lot of Black Annis's witchcraft in use under the cloth. The skin on my arms prickles. My mother and the faeries aren't anywhere in sight.

My eyes drift to the far edge of the oppressive room, where there's a large dais. Atop the dais is a throne made of rough-hewn stone, its edges as jagged and dastardly as the creature lounging in it.

Black Annis lies across the rock, thin legs thrown over the

side of an arm and an elbow on the other. Her hand supports a brimming bowl of toxic fruit.

"You found me, pet. You're better at Hide and Seek than our other game." Black Annis smiles as she pops a dark belladonna berry into her mouth. "Looks like you found your friend as well."

Hazel and I stay put at the entry of the room, far away from the witch. I see the Elder Mother narrow her eyes at Black Annis, and I swear I can see the magic buzzing like a hive of wasps beneath her skin. It seems to swarm in reaction to her hate. My wheelchair and the dagger behind my back hum too, calling out to their kindred magic. A warmth blossoms through my heart, and I can only guess being surrounded by Hazel's magic is affecting me in strange ways.

"And a powerful friend, it seems," Black Annis notes, rolling a berry over her black tongue while she appraises the Elder Mother. "Your magic is coming off you in waves, crone."

"I am no crone. I have never and will never be an old witch like you," Hazel spits.

Black Annis spears a berry on her iron nail and waves it in Hazel's direction. "You have a lot of fire in you for someone so old."

I almost laugh. Little does the witch know, in just an hour, Hazel will start to de-age and become a lot more youthful.

"You and I have seen hundreds of years, probably thousands combined. At least I've kept my fire. You let yours fizzle out when you sold your soul to become *that*." Hazel gestures to the witch's gaunt frame.

"Oh? And what would *that* be?" Black Annis sucks the berry from the tip of her talon. Juice runs down her finger, discoloring her blue skin, matching the rotten color staining the inner portion of her lips.

Hazel's mouth curls. "A power-hungry hag. I know you reached a lot lower than the dirt just to get this scrap of magic.

Now look at you, gorging yourself on poison to keep from starving like a stray dog."

I can see rage stiffening the body of the witch, and I touch Hazel's arm, pleading, in silence, for her to hold her tongue.

Black Annis gives me an exaggerated frown, full lips pulling into a pout. "I don't like your friend, pet."

The Elder Mother bares her teeth. "Stop calling her that."

"Hazel," I whisper, trying to get her to stop. Angering Black Annis might end in a catastrophe. We're meant to be stalling her, in hopes Rush will arrive, not provoking her.

"If I don't? What will you do to me, crone?"

The witch is baiting Hazel now, and an uneasy wave roils in my gut.

"Why don't you step down from your mockery of a throne and find out," Hazel goads her.

Black Annis sets her bowl of toxic fruit on the ground and swings her bare feet to the floor. She claps her cerulean hands together. "Threats! I love threats."

Then she pushes her way up from her throne, shift swaying around her calves as she strides down the three steps off the dais. She stops at the base and spreads her arms wide. "Let's see what tricks you have up your sleeve," she calls to Hazel.

I meet the Elder Mother's crinkled eyes and give her the barest shake of my head. I don't sense Rush in the room, and I haven't yet seen my mother. This is not the time for her to make her move against Black Annis. We need more time. Everyone needs to be free first. Where in the world is Rush?

Hazel's gaze flickers to the dagger hidden against my back before she pivots back to face the witch. Her jaw clenches, her blue eye alighting with icy fury, and her brown one burning with the molten rage of a forge. I know she wants to strike down the witch where she stands. Blessedly, the Elder Mother stays still by my side, her lips clamped shut.

Black Annis lets her skinny arms fall to her sides, disappointment settling over her face. "Nothing? Well, alright." She sighs. "Since you're no fun, you might as well go stand in the corner and think about all the rude things you've said to me." With a dismissive wave, Black Annis turns, flicking her long charcoal hair over her shoulder.

Hazel shakes with unbridled fury as the witch's back faces her, her eyes glowing a raging shade of purple. This is it; this is the energy she said she would try to gather. I can see sweat collecting on her brow from the power and concentration of sculpting the trees' magic into a weapon.

Hazel all but explodes, launching a blast of energy next to Black Annis's head, just missing her by a hairsbreadth.

My heart sinks.

The hag snaps her head to the side with a snarl, and the next thing I know, Hazel is enveloped in a cocoon of Black Annis's magic, her face frozen in a mask of shock. The only thing she can still move is her eyes, which stare at me with terror. This was not a part of the plan.

The Elder Mother's feet start to lift off the floor.

"Hazel!" I try to grab ahold of her sleeve as she drifts toward the corner of the room. "Stop it! Let her go!" I shout at the witch, but she isn't where she once stood.

Black Annis materializes across the room, leaning up against the covered mound. She gives me a lazy grin.

I forgot about this little trick of hers, the ability to move through the air, traveling from one place to another in the blink of an eye. This must be how she stalked me through the labyrinth. I heard her coming from many different directions before she cornered and infected me. Does her magic have any limits?

"Don't be so sensitive, pet. We're just playing. But your friend Hazel has been naughty, and she needs some time to reflect."

I'm beginning to think I'm not the sensitive one here. "You're just scared." I feel my brows draw together.

Black Annis lets out a twinkling peal of laugher, head thudding against what sounds like iron behind her. The noise clangs through my ears, making my skin prickle again. I have to fight the urge to scratch at the bumps.

"Scared? Of a little old lady?" The witch continues to giggle.

I grit my teeth. "You said it yourself, you felt her power. She could drown you in it like the ocean tide. You're scared of the Elder Mother."

Her eyes widen. "Oh, is that who she is . . ." A smile slithers across her lips, and I regret my outburst. "Well, this makes things a lot more interesting."

Black Annis disappears again, only to reappear in front of Hazel. She leans in so close to her face, their noses almost touch. Hazel blinks in rapid succession. I can imagine the scent of cloying belladonna berries drifting from the witch's mouth, curling inside Hazel's lungs. I smelled it on her through the door of my home and again inside the labyrinth. The memory alone makes me crinkle my nose, as if the ghost of the scent lingers in my nostrils.

"The Elder Mother. How fun!" She taps Hazel's nose with a talon before winking out of sight.

Hazel's eyes narrow with loathing.

"You know of her, then?" I ask the empty air, turning my wheelchair in a slow circle. The last thing I want is the bogey standing at my back.

"Of course," she speaks behind me.

I whirl around, but she's across the room, once again leaning against the covered iron structure. She has an annoyed tilt to her lips. "I've tried to get close to her cottage for decades, but those nasty elder trees of hers won't let me get near."

A laugh slips past my lips. "Because they ward off evil." Both Rush and Hazel told me of the life and magic embedded in the trees. I give the bird pictured in the spokes of my wheels a light pat, giving a silent thanks to the elder tree it's made from for keeping Hazel safe. I have a feeling the two of us were destined to meet. The Pooka's prophecy and her role in it gives weight to the idea.

Black Annis issues a theatrical groan. "So I've heard. But now I have the crone in my grasp." She beams at me. "She'll make a wonderful addition to my collection."

My stomach heaves. I won't let the witch lay a hand on Hazel; her skin will stay right where it should be. I straighten my shoulders. "That's not going to happen, so you might as well let her go."

The witch scoffs, back arching off the metal behind her. "Now, why would I do such a thing? So she can use her little tree magic on me? Not a chance, pet. Naughty Hazel stays in the corner. I'll peel the skin from her frail bones later."

On the inside, I start to panic. How is Hazel going to kill Black Annis while she's frozen? She wasn't supposed to attack the witch when she did, and that put us at a disadvantage—not only because it was too soon, but also because she missed. The Elder Mother was never supposed to be off the playing board.

Once Rush gets here—if Rush gets here—he's meant to stay hidden and figure out a way to free the faeries and my mother. He needs to do this first and foremost before helping me, but I can't distract this monster on my own. I'm no match for the hag. She's already proven that she's not only lethal, but also much faster than me. If things go wrong, I know she'll kill me in an instant.

Black Annis trails her clawed hands over the black fabric she's been lazing against, watching me as she saunters around it. Despite my better judgment, I inch my chair forward in curiosity.

"Would you like to take a peek?" She teases me by lifting a small corner flap.

I swallow, hard. I have a hunch about what's under the drape, and I know it's going to be a heartbreaking sight to behold. "I think I already know what it is," I say.

Black Annis tears a slit in the fabric with the tip of a nail. A ray of light seeps through. It's the same light currently wrapped around Hazel. I spare the Elder Mother a look over my shoulder, and her eyes widen in warning.

"So, you got my message? The one I sent with your peeping gnome friend?" Black Annis picks through the cuts of leather hanging against her hip until she finds what she's searching for. She brandishes a slice of blood-flecked skin, the exact size and shape missing from Fern's arm.

I suppress an appalled moan. "Your message was received loud and clear."

Her face lights up. "Oh, good! Then you do know what this is." Without warning, the witch grabs a fist full of the black fabric and pulls. It seems to fall in slow motion. The first thing I see uncovered is the curved top of an iron cage. Next, the flare of magic that's been trying to penetrate the cloth. It shines so bright, it blinds me. Once the stars in my eyes clear, I see the glowing, thin-spaced bars and, lastly, the captives held behind them.

Packed together in the tight space are the faeries who were taken from the glade. I see the batlike faces of imps, emerald-skinned goblins, grumpy-faced brownies, and mossy-backed trolls.

Shielded in the arms of Bramwell is my mother, still clad in her bloodstained nightgown. Her hazel eyes are trained on me. Tears pool in her lashes, but they freeze before they can fall down her freckled cheeks.

They're all paralyzed with witchcraft, just like Hazel across the room.

I press a hand against my mouth to stifle a cry. There are fewer faeries than I thought there'd be, meaning the skins hanging in the banshee trees are all recent victims. And with how squished everyone is inside the giant birdcage, I can't imagine what the conditions were like when more faeries were crammed inside.

A small part of me is relieved the troll skin we found in the trees wasn't Bramwell, but I'll still mourn whichever troll it came from. I seek my mother again, and from what I can see, she appears unscathed. A knot in my heart loosens in gratitude as I scan the other side of the cage. Three identical green-skinned, curly-headed goblin girls sit huddled together with an older goblin man. It's easy to recognize them as Rush's half-sisters and father. They too look unharmed. This knocks a second knot in my chest loose.

"Ta-da!" Black Annis interrupts my probing, her bony hands thrown toward the shimmering bars. "Aren't they marvelous, pet?" She sweeps aside the fabric, letting it pool on the ground.

I shake my head, pulling my hand from my cold lips. "You're sick. Caging them like animals waiting to be sacrificed. You are a true monster."

The witch clicks her tongue. "Now, now. Does somebody else need to go in the corner?"

She swings around the bars, cooing at the frozen faeries inside like a crazy woman. As I watch her taunt my friends and family, all my pent-up anger begins to boil beneath my skin. I can't bear to see her mock them. I can't bear any of this, not anymore.

My body feels like a coiled spring ready to fly with rage, but just when I'm about to roll closer to the cage and the witch prancing around it, I feel a large hand on my shoulder. I seize up in surprise, but the scent of warm cinnamon wafts toward my nose and the hand gives me a comforting squeeze.

Rush is finally here.

DIGNITY

Some of the tension turning my muscles to stone leaves me with a sigh. I can feel the warmth of Rush's body at my back. I want to just sink into my chair and let his spicy scent envelop me, but the witch's crooning still grates on my nerves. It demands attention.

I can only hope Black Annis didn't see the abrupt change in my posture. The last thing we need is for her to find out about the half-goblin boy standing concealed behind me.

I scramble to think of a new plan. Hazel stands indisposed and paralyzed in the corner. My mother and the faeries sit in the cage across the room in a similar position. Even if Rush can unlock their prison, no one will be able to run free. I need a way to get Black Annis to release them. Persuasion is the least of my skills, but maybe I can try to appeal to her twisted love of games. I clear my throat to get the witch's attention. "If you won't let Hazel go"—I gesture toward the corner, so Rush will see where she's frozen—"then how about you let my mother go? I'm sure she didn't say any nasty things to you like the Elder Mother did."

Black Annis hums. "I don't think so, tricky girl. Your mother is going to be the next piece in my collection. I haven't taken a human trophy in years."

She drums her nails against the iron bars, gazing at her captives with longing.

My heart hammers in my chest. I can't let the witch harm my mother. "How about we play another game? I'll even give you something else in her place."

The witch's face lights up. "Are you offering your skin, pet?"

I gulp. Rush's fingers dig into my skin, clawing at me in alarm. I'm playing at something very dangerous.

"If it's what you want, then yes."

One moment, Black Annis is gripping the bars of her oversized birdcage, and the next, she stands in front me, clutching at my arm.

I jump in my seat, and Rush springs backward. My hands are slick with sweat, anxiety infiltrating my soul. I try to shove it away as the witch holds my wrist, tilting my arm to and fro, letting the clashing colors of witchcraft and firelight hit my skin. It looks ghostly pale, the blue veins in my wrist like snakes of frost under my flesh. She lightly skims her talons up my arm, leaving goosebumps in her wake.

To my horror, she bends down and sniffs at my skin, like she's trying to decide whether the offering is worthy. Her nose trails up my arm to my shoulder, dangerously close to where Rush's hand just was. That was too close of a call.

When the witch reaches my left collarbone, just above my thundering heart, she stops. She inhales deeply before dropping my arm in disgust and stepping away.

The witch gags. "This just won't do."

"What? Why not?"

"You're tainted, pet." She runs her hand over the skins swaying against her hip on her silver chain. "I could never add your facsimiled skin to my collection."

My face scrunches in confusion. What could the hag possibly mean?

"However, you could offer me something else." Her new smile is terrifying.

I don't even want to imagine what she has in mind. Yet my thoughts still drift. I visualize how hard it might be to work in the garden without thumbs. Or how difficult it would be to read with only one eye. At least if she wants a foot or two, I still have my wheelchair to get around and a decade of practice under my belt.

"What else do I have of worth to you? I have nothing else to give." I pray she'll allow me to keep my more essential limbs.

Black Annis sashays up the dais and walks toward her throne. She scrapes her nails over the jagged stone until she stands behind it, then drapes her arms over the back and rests her cheek in the crook of her elbow. Her hair spills into the seat like a blanket of ash. The witch's black eyes glisten as she accesses me. I can feel her piercing gaze search my soul for anything of value. I choke on the fire kindling in her gaze.

Her breath hitches, and I know she has an idea.

A mischievous grin curls over her dark lips. Dread wells in my chest, filling up the hollow spaces I sensed in the labyrinth.

"I know what you can give me, pet. It will be oh so fun." She picks her head off her arms and drums her skeletal fingers against her throne. The tip-tap of her iron talons against the rock makes me wince. I'm almost too afraid to ask what she has in mind.

A comforting hand brushes against my arm before disappearing again.

I take in a deep breath. "What would that be?"

"It's very simple, really." Black Annis saunters from behind her throne and back down the dais, stopping at the bottom of the stone steps. "I want you to give me your heart."

I let out a shocked laugh before I can stop myself. I can't

seem to stop. Maybe I'm finally cracking under the pressure building up inside me these last four days.

Just when I think I might lose myself to hysteria, I hear a dull thud come from the cage's direction.

My laughter cuts off.

I fight to keep my eyes trained on Black Annis. Her eyes narrow at me before she turns to the captives. Her clawed hands flex and she begins to slink over to the bars.

Intuition tells me Rush has gone over to the prison to find a way to spring it open. I risk a glance at the cage. From where I sit, I can see there's no apparent lock. The structure is made of only solid, shimmering iron bars, not a door or hinge in sight. It must be enchanted with witchcraft. This puts another wrinkle in our steadily collapsing plan.

"My heart? What does that even mean?" I ask as I focus back on Black Annis, trying to get her attention away from the cage.

It works. Partially.

Black Annis puts her hands on her protruding hip bones. "What would you do to get your mother back?" But her eyes slide back to where the noise came from. She's still suspicious.

I don't even hesitate before answering. I know the words flying from my mouth will capture her attention fully. "Anything. Absolutely anything. I offered you my skin, after all." I lay my hands over my wheels, preparing to do whatever the hag bids me to.

Her eyes widen, sound forgotten. This is just too good of an offer for her to refuse. Her spiked awareness and hunting stance relax as she smirks. "Then, I want you to walk to me."

My fingers tighten around the wooden rims, knuckles turning white. "I think you know I can't," I grit out.

Black Annis cackles. "Ah, but you can! I see the way your legs fidget. Use them, pet—come to me."

Another sound comes from what I would guess is Rush. I have a feeling he wants to kill the witch about as bad as I want to right now. Black Annis starts to turn her head toward the noise.

"Will you give me my mother back if I do?" I blurt, hoping to cover up the quiet sounds Rush is making in his anger and draw Black Annis's gaze back to me.

Her eyes meet mine, and my heart clenches. Pure devilry oozes from her as she grins.

"Play the game and get the prize. My rules are simple. Walk to me and we'll see how long your weak little heart lasts," she commands.

My stomach drops. There it is. I can get my mother back if I try to stumble my way to the witch. I once told Rush I would drag myself across the forest floor to reach my mother. But can I truly stand and risk my heart crumbling to pieces?

Hazel, Rush, and my mother would never lower themselves like this to her.

I try to build myself up in preparation for facing Black Annis.

Confident. Strong. Poised.

I'll have to tear down everything I've constructed if I want to save my mother. I'll have to cross the bridge over my moat of anxiety, burn it down behind me, and return the key to my jailer, succumbing to my shortcomings once more.

Can I break myself apart like this?

All I have to do is serve my heart up on a platter for the witch, losing my self-worth and pride in the process. How simple.

Cowardly. Weak. Inelegant.

I'll do anything for my mother if it means returning her and the faeries to the glade in one piece. Even if it means they go back without me. With a tremble in my chin, I push myself to the edge of my wheelchair. I glance at my mother, glad I can't see her frozen face morph in fear. More tears pool in her eyes.

I let my eyes wander around the bewitched bars, hoping that

at least once my gaze runs over the invisible Rush. He might forgive me for obeying the witch's demands eventually.

I glance back at Hazel; her multicolored eyes are misty. She reminds me so much of my mother sometimes. Her disappointment will be equally as painful.

Letting my body crumble in on itself, I slide to the edge of my chair and plant my feet firmly on the floor. As soon as I stand, my heart will start overworking. This is a huge risk to my life. Though, I have a feeling if I don't at least try to make it, living through this will be the least of my problems.

I peer up at Black Annis across the room, the sheer glee on her face making my throat sore with repressed tears.

I push myself up after blowing out a long breath, and my head begins to swim. Sweat is already prickling across my forehead and down my back. I feel like I'm going to throw up. My feeble legs wobble beneath me, making me stagger my way across the ground. One foot forward. My heart gives a painful throb. Two feet forward. My heart skips a beat. My teeth pierce my lower lip as I fight back tears of pain. I refuse to give Black Annis the satisfaction of seeing me cry again. I'll keep that last shred of dignity to myself. With any luck, I'll survive this, and one day it'll be ready to be replanted and lovingly tended to. I have to have faith I can grow it once more, nurse it back to life as I've done for straggling plants in the winter garden, if only my heart keeps fighting.

Black Annis cackles as my knees buckle beneath me. My underused legs are so tired. I sit with them sprawled beneath me, my elbows the only thing holding me up. I feel like everything I am is disintegrating on this cave floor. I can feel my heart pounding through my skin. It's all I hear in my ears as I grow hotter and my heart palpitates harder. I have so little of myself left to give to the witch, but I have to keep going. For my mother. For the faeries. For the Elder Mother and Rush.

I look to the cage on the other side of the room again, the

expressionless faces of the creatures inside staring back at me. I search the empty air and shake my head, begging Rush, wherever he is, not to do anything rash, including coming to my aid.

I imagine my actions only seem like defeat to Black Annis.

"Come on, pet," she jeers, knowing the next step could kill me. "Just one more step and you can have your mother back."

I glare into the hag's eyes.

"I promise."

Hazel's last words of warning ring in my ears.

"No matter what, you can't trust a thing she says. Black Annis will lie through her pointed teeth."

I know she will never let my mother and the faeries go. She's probably planned on killing me all along. Wrath and determination spread like wildfire from the tips of my toes to the top of my head. Black Annis lives to toy with people, but two can play this game. If it's a real game she wants, it's a real game she'll get. Except this time, we'll be playing by my rules. I force my legs back under me and push up from my elbows.

Confident. Strong. Poised.

The knife presses up against my spine, humming in tune with my resolve. My heart blooms with warmth in answer to its call. Maybe I misinterpreted the Pooka's prophecy. Perhaps the elder who's supposed to restore my mother isn't the Elder Mother herself, but the elder dagger flush with my skin. Maybe I'll be the one to save my mother by vanquishing the witch with the wooden blade.

Black Annis might strip me of my life, but she'll never take away the experiences that made me who I am. I used my instincts to slay Jenny Greenteeth, one of the most fearsome bogeymen in history. And I faced becoming wheelchair-bound as a child and kept my heart fighting with a strength grown men wished they possessed. I adapted to my new life with grace and blossomed into the poised young woman I am today. The anxiety I've carried with me most of my life hasn't been able to stop me from embarking on this journey to save my mother. Why should Black Annis stop me now? I *will* be sending my mother and the faeries home tonight, no matter what.

I try to get my feet back under me again, but my body refuses to cooperate. It knows I've reached my limit. The witch watches me struggle with a smile.

That's when Rush loses his composure. He appears across the room with a thunderous look on his face.

"Rush! No!" My cry causes him to hesitate; he looks torn between helping me and advancing on the witch. But he doesn't get the time to choose either. Black Annis throws her hand up without even looking at him, and he's frozen in his spot.

"Ah, there you are," she croons as she eyes her new captive. "I knew I smelled a peculiar mix in the air. Where have you been hiding?"

A sharp pain in my chest leaves me dizzy. "Leave him be. This game is between you and me."

"Fine," the witch sighs. Using her witchcraft, she pushes Rush toward the cage and out of the way. "This is getting boring. You're taking too long." Something new gleams in her eye. "Let me help you." Black Annis's magic wraps around me. My legs glow a sinister blue as they straighten beneath me. Against my will, I am forced to take the final steps toward her. My heart cries out in protest. I have never felt it beat this fast, not even the day I collapsed in the garden.

She's killing me.

Black Annis makes me stop in front of her, leaving me to sit back on my haunches, my bony knees aching. I fold my hands in a show of compliance and gaze at the witch through my damp lashes. I'm gasping as I try to catch my breath.

"Look at you, kneeling before me like an obedient little girl." Ardor drips from her voice. "What a dutiful daughter you are, pet."

Fake supplication slips over my face. "I did what you asked. Please let my mother go."

"Let's not be hasty. The fun has just started!" Black Annis licks her lips. She's lapping up my false surrender like the belladonna berries she sucked from her gluttonous talons. "Your weakness is a delicacy, pet. I want to savor every drop."

"Make no mistake, witch," I pant. Spittle leaks from my lips, my dejected mask splitting at the seams. "I might be on my knees, but this does not make me weak." I stare up into her onyx eyes. "It makes me cunning."

Black Annis throws her head back, dragging her nails along her throat as she howls with laugher. I take the opportunity to sneak my hand behind my back and reach under my tunic for the handle of Hazel's dagger. It warms against my palm.

"Cunning?" She giggles. "Come now, pet, don't make me laugh."

"You have no clue what I'm capable of."

A lethal sort of calm spreads through my body.

Black Annis leans down until her vindictive face hovers above mine, sweet poison curling from her tarnished lips. "What is a damaged doll like you going to do?"

"This," I answer with one last heaving breath.

I rise to my knees, grabbing onto the witch's shoulder as I thrust upward and pull her body onto the blade in my hand with my last bit of strength.

My aim strikes true.

The elderwood dagger protrudes from the center of Black Annis's emaciated chest. She looks from her wound to my eyes, shock written all over her monstrous, beautiful face.

Black tar bubbles past her lips and down her chin.

I hear a gasp behind me as Hazel tumbles free from the magic holding her captive. To my right, the bars of the giant enchanted birdcage start to melt away. The faeries and my mother take in heaving breaths, released from Black Annis's magic. Rush drops from his blue prison and runs for his family.

The orbs floating near the ceiling flicker. Black Annis is losing her hold on her witchcraft as she dies.

I push the hag away from me, releasing the dagger's handle, letting it settle in its new home in the witch's breastbone. In a stupor, she staggers toward me, lips frothing with black bubbles as she bares her needle-like teeth. I'm so mesmerized by her horrific appearance, I don't see her hand swinging toward me until it's too late.

Black Annis's talons cleave across my chest.

The sound of my skin tearing and my chest cracking open echoes throughout the domed room. I wash the witch and her throne in a shower of my blood as agony sears through every nerve in my body.

I think I hear screaming as I fall to the floor.

KINDRED

I'm dying—no question.

I can feel the frigid air whistling through the open cavity that used to be my chest. Blood bubbles past my lips, creating a watery wheeze every time I try to breathe in. I can't bear to look at the killing blow Black Annis has delivered to me; I don't want this to be the last thing I see. I can only stare at the flickering blue orbs above me, trying to ignore the fuzzy gold hovering at the edges of my vision.

I hear my heart crackling in my ears with every weakening beat. The sounds clattering around the room drift in and out as I'm submerged in an ocean of pain.

"Sparrow!" Hazel's scream sounds muffled.

I tilt my head against the floor to watch her feet running toward me. I feel and taste blood as it dribbles out of my mouth and down the side of my jaw, pooling on the cold cave floor. Wrath hardens Hazel's aged face as she scowls at the witch staggering about, the dagger still embedded in her chest. I watch from the corner of my eye as Black Annis tries to pull the blade free. The Elder Mother's arm shoots forward, hand curled into a claw.

"No!" she bellows.

Her entire arm glows a brilliant purple as she blasts her energy toward the witch. The power hurtling across the room is cosmic. The elder trees must have lent her everything they have, and she sculpted it into the perfect shot.

My head lulls as I watch the magic affix itself to Hazel's dagger. Tiny tree roots begin to grow from the handle, burrowing themselves into Black Annis's chest. They tread through her tissue like parasites. The hag, kneeling on Death's door, claws at the roots, trying to rip them out before they nestle too deep.

Then, all at once, the roots stop growing, having anchored themselves to Black Annis's body. There's a moment when everyone pauses. Even the witch stops her scrambling, and the air hangs heavy with anticipation.

Black Annis's eyes widen as she gapes at the Elder Mother. It's the look people get when they finally gaze upon Death's pearly face. A sight I'll see very soon.

Suddenly, the witch's body explodes, spraying the room in a rain of flesh and sinew. A slab of her cerulean skin lands right beside my face, splashing in the puddle of dark blood seeping from my mutilated body.

The room dims, losing its blue hue. Not a trace of Black Annis's witchcraft is left in the room. The only thing lighting the cave is the fire burning in the hearth, though everything appears brighter with the gold light in the corners of my vision. It gives the room an odd, hazy glow. And now, where the witch once stood, is a full-grown elder tree. It blooms with creamy elderflowers, showering the rocky throne on the dais behind it with blossoms, masking the scent of death in the air.

Hanging from one of its branches is the chain girdle that dangled from the witch's waist. The leather pieces shaved from her faerie victims sway among the flowers. They hang over the carnage that once was the hag who killed them. I can sense victory with their every swing.

Hazel made the elderwood dagger, and its roots burst through Black Annis, turning it into a full-grown tree like she said she could do. I can tell that she's killed the witch once and for all. Never again will Black Annis haunt the glade and surrounding forests.

A death rattle gurgles in my throat.

The room becomes a flurry of action. My mother now kneels by my side. My blood soaks into her nightgown, adding fresh stains to the ruined fabric. The underside of her face lights up gold as she leans over me. She's angelic.

"Oh, my little bird," she cries, palming at my cheeks. My eyes strain to focus on her. "Come on, sweetheart, look at me."

"Mother," I gasp through the blood.

"I'm here. You're going to be okay," she sobs. "You're going to be just fine, you hear me?"

Light throbs at the bottom of my vision. Is this what dying is like? Is this glow heaven coming to receive me?

Rush runs to my other side, slipping in the blood and gore coating the rocky floor. He freezes above my body, shock written over his features. He stares open-mouthed at my mother, but she presses her thin lips together and shakes her head at him.

"What?" I croak.

My mother won't meet my eyes.

"Rush?"

With bleary eyes, I gaze up at his sickly green face. His wet silver eyes dart from my blood-drenched face to my chest. I must be a horrific sight to behold.

My curiosity gets the better of me, and I glance down.

I'm stunned into silence—even the blood burbling out of my body seems to quiet. All that's left is the crackling sound coming from my chest.

My sternum is split open, my flesh peeled back in thick flaps. I can see my muscle and tissue parted to reveal my broken breastbone. Black Annis's iron talons cut through my bones like butter. But this isn't the worst part. Nestled in the center of the butchery is the source of the crackling—a heart made of splintered elder twigs, wrapped in the golden glow of a troll charm. And the snapped pieces of wood grind together in their glow as they fight to continue beating. It's a sound that will haunt me for the rest of my very short life.

"Mother?" My voice cracks.

She still won't meet my eyes. She leans over and picks up a piece of twig lying beside my arm, coated in blood. She twists it in her fingers.

Tears start to run down my face.

"What am I?" I weep.

"I'm so sorry, my little bird," she whispers, her gaze focused on the piece of my heart in her hands.

Bramwell lumbers up behind her and lays a craggy hand on her shoulder. Then he peers into my eyes with repentance.

Rush finally kneels on the ground, sliding the pieces of Black Annis's body away from me with his foot. His hands tremble as he latches onto my sticky fingers. He focuses on my eyes and not the changeling heart sitting in my chest.

He gives me a sad smile. "I always knew you were a special one."

I can't even muster a reply—my world is fragmenting around me as I die. My head swirls as I stare at the wood in my chest. I didn't invent the golden light giving the room a hazy glow, and it wasn't heaven receiving me. The changeling heart in my sternum is illuminating the bitter-cold room, and its light splashes across my mother and Rush's face.

Hazel draws herself into our group, a forlorn expression on her face. I'm like a beacon, drawing moths toward me with my glowing heart. As she comes closer, I see some of the wrinkles around her eyes and mouth smoothing out. She's de-aging, losing power by the minute.

I can't help but notice she doesn't seem surprised by my elder-twig heart.

"You knew what I was, didn't you?" I rasp, blood flying from my mouth.

Rush squeezes my hand.

She nods. "I did, my dear."

I choke as I inhale. "And you never said anything."

Her brows furrow. "That's not entirely true. I could tell you didn't know you were a changeling when I met you, so I left you little hints here and there. But it was never my story to tell."

My mind flits back to all the times I thought the Elder Mother was blatant in her mysterious ways. When I first met her, and she interrogated me about my family. She looked lost in thought when I told her there hadn't been a changeling in the glade in years. This must have told her how clueless I was. Then, when she told me the elder trees would give their bodies to me to use for my wheelchair, she said they felt a kinship to me. It was their twigs they were sensing inside me all along. They weren't just judging my good character.

The hollowness I felt in my chest when I was infected with belladonna finally made sense. Only in my delusional state was I able to feel what was missing inside of me. If my brain hadn't been so muddled, I would have known what I truly am. There were so many signs I missed. When Hazel and I entered the center of the labyrinth, she was buzzing with magic. My wheelchair and the dagger behind my back hummed back, calling out to their kindred magic. A warmth blossomed through my heart. The surrounding objects made of elder trees called out to the Elder Mother, including my heart.

I've been so blind.

How long has my mother been keeping this from me? How long have I not been myself?

My changeling heart makes an awful, grating noise, fresh

pain razes through my chest, and I let out a shuttering gasp as my eyelids flutter.

"Sparrow!" Rush crushes my hand in his. "Hey, stay with me. Okay? I just got you back today!"

I train my gaze on him. Even sitting in a pool of my blood, with a bruise on his cheekbone, and tears in his eyes, he looks like a faerie prince—my knight in shining armor. I attempt to lift his hand to my lips for a parting kiss. But then I see the red thread attached to our pinkie fingers. It's coiled around our hands and trailing up our arms like veins, wrapping us up in strings of kismet. Now that I'm dying, the invisible red thread of Fate is no longer so invisible. The Elder Mother told me the thread would never stretch, tangle, or break, regardless of the time, place, or circumstances. But I can see the bow around my little finger beginning to fray as if the Moirai from my storybooks have come to cut my thread, severing me from life and my destiny.

I give Rush a weak smile, sure my teeth and gums are shining red with blood. "It seems like Time is letting Death cut our thread short. Hazel was right."

He sniffles, sparing a glance at the Elder Mother standing above my head. Her hands tangle at the end of her messy braid.

"About what?" he asks.

"Everything. About me, destiny . . . falling in love." I let out a wet cough, the open cavity of my chest squelches. "If I had more time, I would've fallen so in love with you. I would've followed you on any adventure just to see you smile."

Rush laughs as he cries, letting go of my hand to brush the hair on my forehead away from the wound Jenny Greenteeth gave me.

"I've been searching for something on every one of my travels. I never knew what it was until the first day of our journey together." He runs his thumb over the corner of my eye, catching my tears before they fall. "Want to know what it was?"

My sternum whistles as blood blocks my throat.

"A home," Rush divulges. "I always had it in my head that a home had to be four walls and a roof. Maybe with a nice hearth and a comfortable bed." He wipes his damp cheek off on his shoulder. "But I was so wrong. Home is a stubborn, witty girl who loves her mother more than anything. Someone so brave it almost kills me with fright. Home is green eyes and pale skin."

If I had air left in my lungs, I'd be sobbing. I saw the way Rush gazed at my home at the glade and Hazel's cottage with longing. I realize now, with startling clarity, I've caught him looking at me the same way many times.

"You're the home I've been searching for, Sparrow. So please, I am begging you, don't leave me when I've just found you."

I struggle for air, my broken bones, splintered heart, and blood all slowly asphyxiating me. The troll charm around my heart, brightening the fire-lit room, starts to flicker.

"No. Sparrow? No, no, stay with me!" my mother pleads, finally meeting my eyes. Her words reflect around the room, reaching the ears of all the faeries huddled off to the side with tears streaming over their stricken faces.

They roll to the back of my head.

"No, no, no," she repeats. I feel her hands grabbing onto my cold arm, and Rush's hand cradles the side of my head.

A terrible silence follows, almost like everyone is holding their breath for me.

"Hazel!" Rush's cry is so sudden, they all jolt around me. "The prophecy! We were all wrong. It was never about Sparrow's mother."

"What?" my mother whispers.

I hear the Elder Mother's lips part. "A daughter of the trolls . . . the wretched Pooka was talking about Sparrow being a changeling the whole time!"

"What are you two talking about?" my mother demands.

"It's a long story, ma'am." Rush pats at my cheek. "Hold on just a little longer, love."

If I weren't dying, I'm sure my heart would've fluttered at his term of endearment.

"Hazel, the Pooka said *'only the elder can hope to restore her.'* You're Sparrow's only chance—you were meant to save her!"

I hear Hazel sink to her knees. Her dress rustles next to my ear, her voice thick with emotion and doubt. "My magic has passed its peak. I used quite a bit converting it to those blasts, but I still have some. Though it will begin to drain away very soon."

"Please," my mother begs. "You have to try and help her. I already lost my little girl once. I am not going to lose her again."

My heart shutters, the twigs popping. It pauses long between beats now, stealing my barest breaths away.

What did my mother mean, she lost me once?

"I'll give her everything I have left. It's not going to mend her bones nor her skin. She could still bleed out."

"We need to get her back to the glade," my mother presses.

Rush strokes my cheekbone. "We need to stabilize her before we move her. I won't let her die in this cave." He sniffs. "I can already smell Death coming for her."

My mother exhales heavily through her nose. "Okay, do it," she instructs Hazel.

I hear Hazel rubbing her hands together before suspending them above my chest. I can feel her radiating body heat, warming my torn flesh as it cools from blood loss and Death strides toward me.

"I am so sorry, dear, but this is going to feel like purgatory itself." Hazel grimaces.

The Elder Mother's dwindling magic shoots through my heart like an arrow. My eyes flash open as I shriek, my back arching off the stone. Rush and my mother hold my body down as I thrash. I hear the twigs of my heart snapping back together, starting to mend themselves with the help of Hazel's elder-tree magic.

The pain is too much for me to handle. The edge of my vision starts to go, as if Death is beckoning me into her darkness. I'm almost ready to collapse into her embrace when Rush calls out to me, "Sparrow!"

The last thing I see is the fated red thread drawn between us, beginning to fade. My screams echo off the domed ceilings as I pass out, torn between choosing Death or Fate.

DEATH AND FATE

Death and Fate.

Eternal sleep and astral destiny.

A chance for my exhausted body to rest or an experience designed to fill my life with love.

I'm tired.

Fate sits in her humble chair beside an abandoned spinning wheel, hand weaving tapestry after tapestry. Her red thread winds around her body, weaving through her hair, hanging from her fingers and trailing from her feet. With nimble fingers, she intertwines the façade of serendipity and fortuity into her grand designs.

Death sits next to her on the ground with a pair of sharpened shears. She plucks threads from the bottom of the tapestries, reverently untangling them, giving them a chance to work themselves back into the motif before cutting them loose. She sheds a tear with every snip of her blades. Her sorrow covers her in a black gauzy shroud.

They beckon me.

I sit at their feet as they work. They tell me tales of passion and loss, luck and demise. Sewing the future and clipping the present to create a beautiful effigy of the past.

Working in tandem, they create and destroy, but every so often, they stop. Time gifts them a few moments so they can let humanity decide for themselves. Let them make their choice between following their thread to destiny or lying down to sleep. Death and Fate look at me.

Choose.

My chest hurts. But I miss my home.

Fate holds on to the long end of my thread that connects to a beautiful boy. Death holds on to the tail of the bow looping around my pinkie. Do I let Fate weave it back into her tapestry, or do I let Death finally set me free?

I'm so tired.

They each extend their other hand to me. It's time.

I make my choice.

THE CHANGELING

Awareness comes rushing back to me with a sharp inhale, and the sounds of warbling birds fills my ears. The skin on my forehead and chest feels tight and sore, and the memories of my encounters with both Jenny Greenteeth and Black Annis slam into me.

My eyes snap open.

Early-morning light pours in from a square window. I recognize this window; I've known it for the last eighteen years.

I'm home.

Everything is in its place. My wool-filled mattress is plush under my aching body, and my quilted blanket is tucked snug under my chin. There's the worn trunk at the end of my bed, my oak desk, and the cabinet filled to the brim with books. The book I took with me on my journey is back, securely in its place.

My elder-tree wheelchair sits in the corner of my room. It's the only new addition.

If it weren't for the pain, and seeing my enchanted chair, I would think I'd dreamed a terribly long, vivid nightmare.

Unfortunately, I did not.

With stiff arms, I tug my quilt down. My old, blood-drenched clothes have been removed, and I've been dressed in one of my mother's billowy nightgowns. Through the loosened ties around the neck of the dress, I see the stitches running along my chest. The sutures are an awful sight. They're in complete disarray, most likely from being stitched with haste in the middle of a witch's dark labyrinth.

The path Black Annis's talons carved in my skin glares back at me through the wandering thread. My skin is red and puckered. I'll have horrific scars for the rest of my life . . . my faerie life.

I feel along my head and find neater stitches going through my brow. Though they may be ugly, these scars will show I survived. I've taken part in vanquishing two legendary hags and lived to tell the tale. I've been confident, strong, and poised, chaining my anxiety before it could drag me under.

To be honest, my anxiety will probably never go away, the panic welling in my marred chest being an obvious testament. However, this doesn't mean I can't be stronger and overcome it on my best days. When my mother needed me, I defied the odds to be there for her. I left the safety of my home, pushing myself into a world that wasn't built for a disabled girl like me. Though scarred, I did come out on the other side.

But I am not who I thought I was.

My whole life, I believed I was human, just like my mother, and to say I'm surprised to find I'm a changeling would be an understatement. Even now, my throat becomes thick.

I push down my tears.

I've cried enough to last a lifetime.

Anger builds inside me, making my cheeks feel flushed. I feel—deceived. My life has been just one big fabrication my mother and the trolls wove together. The fact that they all kept this secret from me stings. How could they hide my true identity from me?

My door creaks on its iron hinges as it opens. My mother sticks her head in through the door, our eyes locking. "Oh!

You're awake." She steps into the room. Her ochre-brown hair is up in her usual bun, and she wears one of her homespun dresses with an apron tied around her waist. Beneath her hazel eyes are dark blue smudges. She looks exhausted.

She shuffles across the room and takes a seat on the edge of my bed, bringing the smell of fresh-baked bread and honey with her.

"How are you feeling?" she asks, folding her freckled hands into her lap to hide their anxious shaking.

I huff a laugh, the question feels too absurd to answer.

"Of course . . ." My mother gives me an awkward smile, like she already knows exactly how I feel. She smooths a stray hair behind her ear with her berry-stained fingers, and a lapse of silence hangs between us.

I pull at a loose thread in my quilt. "When did we get back from Black Annis's cave?"

"About two weeks ago," she answers.

Startled, I glance back at my mother's tired face. "Two weeks?"

She nods. "Your friend Hazel has had to continue working on your heart every night. She said the recovery and blood loss took a lot out of you." Her eyes wander to the scars peeking out from beneath the nightgown I wear. "I imagine your body needed the rest. There was more than just your heart needing mending."

I feel her words, I feel beaten and bruised, and I'm not looking forward to the time it will take for my skin and bones to heal. I turn my head against my pillow, gazing at my wheelchair across the room. "Where are Rush and Hazel?"

"Hazel is somewhere around the glade. I'm sure she's playing with the younger faeries. The way she ages is such an odd thing." I hear a smile slip into her voice. "Rush is probably not far. The boy has barely left your side. When he isn't with his family, he's here reading to you. He's read the myth of The Minotaur about five times over."

My lips twitch. Reading to me as I slept like a fairytale princess . . . a boy after my own soul. I want to see him as soon as possible. I turn to my mother to ask her to bring him to me when I see the brokenness on her face. My breath hitches. "What's wrong?"

My mother buries her face in her hands, shaking her head.

I nudge her with my foot. "What is it?"

She pulls away her hands to reveal her bloodshot, teary eyes. "I'm so sorry, my little bird. You never should have found out."

I grind my teeth together. My mother never intended to tell me I was a changeling. She would've kept this secret from me forever. "How could you say that to me? Don't I deserve to know what I am?"

She grasps at my hand, lying on top of the quilt. "You're my daughter! Isn't it enough?"

I peer into her weary eyes. "I'm not your daughter. Not really, just a pale imitation of a human girl." I let out a rueful laugh. "I'm a daughter of the trolls."

My mother squeezes my fingers as she purses her lips, clearly hurt by my words.

"Was I ever real?" My voice shakes. "Am I just a copy of the daughter you once knew?"

My mother shoots up from my bed. She wraps one arm around her stomach, the other hand pressing against her wounded heart. "Oh, Sparrow." She paces across the room. Neither of us exchanges words for some time, and I just watch as she burns a trail over my hardwood floor.

Back and forth. Back and forth.

Guilt eats at me. I regret hurting her, I just wanted her to understand how painful it is to be lied to. But now that the fury is fading from my twig-woven heart, I know this was wrong of me.

"I'm sorry."

My mother pulls to a stop, stricken still by my apology.

"It's okay, sweetheart. I know you're upset with me. I shouldn't have kept this from you. I was so afraid of how you would react." She comes to sit beside me again.

If we're going to have a heart-to-heart, I want to face my mother, not lie here like a prone child, stewing in my own suffering. "Will you help me sit up?" I plead.

"Are you sure?" My mother gives me a worried look.

I reassure her with a nod.

She stands from the bed again and stoops to slide her arms under my armpits. Slow and careful, she shifts me up in the bed. My ribs and breastbone twinge with pain, almost taking my breath away. I feel my grimace the entire time.

Once I'm situated, and my pillow is fluffed to perfection, my mother sits back down, and I cradle my throbbing torso as she begins to speak.

"You are my daughter, Sparrow, and you always will be. I love you with my whole heart." Her shoulders droop as she stares at her hands. "But to answer your question, yes, you are a duplicate of my human daughter. But, in a way, she is still you. The trolls were able to embed her memories into the changeling body they crafted—your body." She reaches out to touch my knee. "You two have the same soul; I've seen it every day of your life. You're one and the same."

That would explain why I have memories of a childhood and a time before I became wheelchair-bound. It may not have been my body running through the glade, but the memories still feel like mine. I can still feel the dewy grass between my toes and the scrapes on my knees.

I lay my hand over my mother's. "What happened to her?" I whisper, afraid of popping the bubble of truth we're in.

My mother wraps her fingers around mine. "She was very sick. The village doctors told me when she was born—her heart never developed right in my womb. She was never supposed to survive past a couple of years. But true to your spirit"—she squeezes my hand—"she fought for her life and carried on like any normal child. But around her eighth birthday, I started to notice how tired she would get during the day. There were just dizzy spells and nausea at first, until she started to faint, and she could hardly stand up for ten minutes straight without her vision going black."

I remember those days like they were yesterday. The home-cooked meals I loved so much tasted like ash in my mouth. I was hardly able to eat anything before I started gagging. There were days around the glade where I could only be out of bed for a few hours at a time. I napped so often, I lost track of my days. My disorientation always made it feel like I woke up in a different world. Realizing those memories were made in a different body is something that will take time to sit well with me. Maybe even years.

My mother rubs at her forehead with her free hand. "Then, that autumn day in the garden came along. When I got news from the gnomes she had collapsed—well, I had never run so fast. When I got there, she was going in and out of consciousness. A gnome was there by her side, stroking her head, telling her everything would be alright. But my heart shattered then and there. I just knew her time had come."

I feel a heaviness settle in my chest. I remember Fern at my side, comforting me until my mother arrived. Anything past this is a blur. I spent time drifting in oblivion until almost a month later, when I woke to my mother and the trolls telling me I would be wheelchair-bound. I suppose during that month, the human Sparrow died and I was made.

I know it takes time for the trolls to craft a changeling's heart. Hazel told me they had to petition her as the Elder Mother for the elder twigs they used. And the funny thing was that Hazel, unknowingly, had a part in creating me.

My mother's gaze falls on me again. "She died that night. I was so overcome with grief; I couldn't stop screaming. The whole glade was on high alert, thinking a bogeyman had paid us a visit."

I feel the sadness saturating my face. I don't want to imagine my mother in so much pain. "What did you do?"

My mother reaches out to smooth my tangled hair.

"I dragged Bramwell into the house and begged him to do something. He tried to tell me there was nothing he could do to save her, but I wouldn't listen. Only when her body started to become blue and stiff did I realize he was right."

"Oh, Mother, I'm so sorry."

"It's okay, sweetheart, because Bramwell thought of a way to bring you back to me. I spent weeks in bed, barely moving, barely eating, before he presented me with an elder-twig heart. He offered to create a changeling in her place, one with the same memories, the same everything. She would even be eight years old, just like my poor girl had been. It would be like she never left me." My mother smiles to herself. "I jumped out of bed so fast the room spun. Bramwell and the trolls began crafting your body that day." She sighs. "It was so magical, little bird. You looked identical. My heart filled with love and hope again, just at the sight of you, and I made the decision right there that it would be best to keep your true nature a secret. The faeries and I didn't want to cause you any more distress."

Hazel was right; my mother had ensured who I was. Still, I'm in awe of my mother's strength as her story unfolds. Although, part of me still feels like something is out of place. "If Bramwell created this new changeling body for me, why am I in a wheelchair? Why wouldn't he make me whole and healthy?"

"He tried, my darling, but changelings are meant to be indistinguishable from their human counterparts. They take on the same face, personality, and memories if need be. Sometimes the troll's charms are so accurate they take on other physical traits too. The heart you have now has always been far from weak, but the magic making up your body treats it as if it were. The laws of magic mimicked my little girl's illness down to every last detail. Still, a heart made of twigs and magic can be fragile, and the troll's charms aren't always perfect. We knew a wheelchair would be the only way you'd be able to get around again."

The enchanted twigs beating in my chest feel heavy. This changeling body of mine will never know what it is to walk, but I'm just grateful for the memories passed down to me. Through them, I know just a taste of that freedom. It's going to take time for me to accept this truth. In some ways, I feel like an impostor. A piece of me doesn't feel like I can take full ownership of my memories, nor the way my face appears. I look at my mother again—but she will always be mine. She feels like the trolls are her parents despite her blood, and I can do the same. I was given a chance at life, and I'll honor my mother's first daughter by putting her memories and soul to good use. I'll live a long life full of joy and love.

"I understand why you kept it from me," I say. "It's a lot to process, but I'm so thankful you told me, and I'm trying my hardest to forgive you . . . I love you. But this rift I feel from a secret like this will take time to mend. I hope we can do it together?"

She brushes her fingers over my stitched forehead.

"Of course we'll get through this together. I love you too." She stands from my bed and tucks my quilt around me. "Get some rest, sweet girl."

Then, she walks to my bedroom door and slips out, shutting the door behind her.

I rest my head against the wall behind me and gaze up to the ceiling. I repress the urge to feel jilted. Almost everyone in the glade knew what I was before I did. Even the Elder Mother knew. I should've picked up on her hints, especially when she told me she could see specks of golden troll magic all over me.

Black Annis smelled the elder twigs inside me. She said my skin was facsimiled; she called me a copy. I'm beginning to question my intelligence now, and it prompts an awkward chuckle from my throat—I missed *every* sign right in front of me. But I won't be naive any longer. I know my mother's secret. I'm a changeling, a faerie through and through.

DESTINY

I spend the next hour staring at the warm-colored woodgrain in my bedroom ceiling, trying to find pictures in the whorls like I used to with the puffiest clouds in the summer skies of my childhood.

Can I really say it was my childhood?

I still can't wrap my head around the difference between my mother's human daughter's memories and the memories of my changeling mind. My mother will claim they're all the same, and maybe I'll agree with her one day, but for now, it's too strange. They feel the same, but knowing they've been taken from one body and reshaped to fit another makes them feel like they should feel different. Though the more I search, looking for rough edges or something bent out of shape, all I find are perfect, slotted pieces of the puzzle that composes me.

A light tap raps at my door, hesitant and meek.

"Come in."

Ever so slowly, my door squeaks open. Then there's a pause before slippered footsteps pass the doorway.

Hazel shuffles into my room and closes the door behind her before leaning up against the wood with her hands pinned behind her back. She wears another black dress, not unlike the one she wore on our journey, except this dress rustles around her knees instead of brushing against the floor. It fits her youthful appearance. At this time of day, she and I are almost the same age.

"Hi." She speaks low.

I give her a gentle smile. "Hello, Hazel."

She stares at me, chewing on the corner of her lip. The girl seems nervous to see me.

"I heard you might be having a fun morning," I comment. "How did you find the company of faerie children?"

The question earns me a gap-toothed grin. "Posy, Primrose, and Poppy are quite the group of rambunctious goblins. I don't know how Rush keeps up with them. I was only a year or two older than them, and I was having a hard time."

"Do they seem to be recovering well from the horrors of Black Annis?" I ask.

Hazel's face drops into a frown. "Rush told me they're having nightmares. I think in time, their minds will heal, but for now, returning to their normal routine is helping. They're strong little girls."

I nod in agreement, brushing my fingers over the tender slashes across my chest.

"You know, they won't stop talking about you—all the fairies, actually. They go on and on about what a hero you are, their knight in shining armor."

I snort. "Rush was supposed to be the knight. I thought I was supposed to be the queen."

Hazel playfully bows.

"You're correct, Your Highness—The Changeling Queen, slayer of witches."

I laugh as light as I can with my fractured bones, but as my laughter fades, my smile dissolves. I haven't yet faced the changes the truth of my identity will bring. How will knowing I'm a changeling impact my life? Hazel already knew what I was and accepted me and my cobbled-together body before our journey even started. What about Rush? Now that I've lived through Black Annis's attack, will his feelings for me cease to be? I'm not at all who he thought I was.

Hazel rises from her bow. Sensing my inner turmoil, she takes a tentative step toward me. Besides her childlike fear at the lake, this is the first time I've seen her waver. Where did her confidence go?

"Come here, mage," I beckon her, patting the space on the bed beside me.

Hazel's timid as she steps up to my bed before curling up at my side, careful not to touch my sore body. She shifts down until she can rest her head against my shoulder.

I tilt my cheek against the top of her head, the silky strands of her hair tickling my face. She reaches out and wraps my fingers into her hand. We sit quietly, soaking in each other's company, and I reflect on all we've been through together.

Hazel breaks the silence first.

"I'm sorry you had to be the one to use the dagger," she whispers. "It was supposed to be me."

I readjust my head against hers. "It's okay. Nothing really went according to plan, but, in the end, everything that needed to happen did."

"You didn't need to crawl to the hag. You didn't need to almost lose your life. If I had—"

I shush her. "There is nothing you could've done different, Hazel. Black Annis was threatened by you—she was going to take you out of the equation from the very beginning."

"I could've kept my mouth shut, but I was just so angry. Every word the witch spoke was like poison to my ears," Hazel simmers.

I pinch her palm.

"Ouch!" She pulls her head off my shoulder to give me an incredulous look. "What was that for?"

"For feeling guilty, which is very unnecessary. You said it yourself, everything happens for a reason. We never could've changed the outcome of what happened. The Pooka's prophecy is proof." I grab back on to her hand. "I was always meant to get hurt, and you were always meant to save me. It was our destiny."

Hazel glares at me before settling her head back onto my shoulder. "You're right . . . but I still don't like it," she grumbles.

"At least you admit it. Now, where's the confident Elder Mother hiding?"

Hazel stiffens beside me. "I left her behind on the cave floor in a pool of your blood."

I touch one of the raised lines on my chest with my free hand again. They're going to take some getting used to. I can't stop feeling them. It's almost like I'm reminding myself that everything that happened was real, not just a figment of my twisted imagination.

"Was this your handiwork?"

She grunted. "Rush and your mother's. It's why it looks like such a mess—two people should never work on the same sewing project."

I chuckle, but then groan at the pain in my sternum.

"How did they even manage to find the supplies to stitch me back up?"

Hazel's body relaxes beside me. "With my little remaining magic, I took some of the twigs that broke off from your heart and transformed them into needles. We pulled the loose threads from your ripped-up tunic and they got to work. Rush was like a mother hen the whole time. If you weren't bleeding out, I would've smacked him."

I hum. "Sounds like him. Considering the conditions they were in, they did well."

Hazel scoffs at me.

"Don't get me wrong, they're downright ugly, some of the worst stitching I've ever seen. But I lived. Now I'll have some tough-looking scars." I think about Rush with a smile. "Not even the Moon herself would mess with me."

"You're ridiculous." Hazel snorts.

"Just a little."

We watch the dust motes float through the air. The light shining through my window illuminates them, making them sparkle like flecks of gold. They dance in the air and drift throughout the room.

"Do you have to go back to your cottage? I'm sure the elder trees need you."

Hazel shrugs, her head bumping against my neck. "Eventually. I might stick around the glade for a little bit longer. Make sure your heart is healing right. The trees won't mind; I'm taking care of one of their own."

I turn to peer at the top of Hazel's tawny head.

"If my heart came from their twigs, and the trolls are considered my parents, does this mean the elder trees are my grandparents?"

Hazel almost falls off the bed from laughing so hard. I beam at her smooth face. At this point, she's almost older than Rush's nineteen years, and I realize as I study her that I'll miss the Elder Mother. I've become used to seeing her ever-changing appearance daily. It'll be heartbreaking when she returns to her home and I'll have to settle for occasional visits.

Speaking of home, how did I even get to mine?

When Hazel recovers from almost falling and sets herself safely back on the bed, I question her. "How did we all make it back to the glade? I don't remember a thing."

"Ah. You were unconscious the entire time. It was probably a combination of pain, my magic, and the troll's charms. Any time my magic built up enough, I worked on your heart, mending the splintered pieces and growing new twigs. You lost quite a few to Black Annis's claws." She glances at my ragged skin. "Rush and the trolls all took turns carrying you in a makeshift sling using the cloth covering the cage. We almost walked for a full day once. It took less time than our journey to the cave did." She meets my eyes, her blue and brown depths looking traumatized. "Everyone was desperate to get you home."

"Even the trolls?" I always felt the trolls were absent parents to their changeling children before they all left the glade. I felt like they always preferred the humans they acquired, like my mother, but hearing Hazel tell me that the trolls were concerned for me changes things. Maybe I had the wrong impression all along?

I think back to my relationship with them growing up. I always thought the trolls were distant with me, but really, they were always there. They found me my first wheelchair, paved the paths around the glade, and even left me gifts in my shoes during Christmastide. They acted as my parents in little ways but let my mother do the rest because she wanted it, and I didn't even notice.

"Even the trolls," Hazel answers. "They were incredibly worried. I'm sure seeing your mother so frantic didn't help. They did everything within their power to assist me." Her eyes drop to my chest again. "They strengthened the charm over your heart and mended the worst of the wounds to your body."

"They have healing magic?"

The trolls are just full of surprises. I thought I knew everything there was to know about the faeries living at the glade, but the journey to rescue my mother has proven me wrong. I've learned a lot along the way. I'm still learning more now, and I supposed I will for the rest of my life.

Hazel bobs her head side to side, weighing her thoughts. "Not exactly. They crafted your body, so they were able to 're-craft' some pieces. They wouldn't be able to heal a human or any other creature." She gestures to the sewn split in my brow and the carvings in my sternum. "Obviously, they can't fix superficial things, but they were able to repair the worst breaks in your bones and your destroyed muscle."

"Well, isn't everyone just brimming with secret talent," I muse.

"Not everyone."

"Oh yeah?" I raise my uninjured brow. "Who?"

Hazel nudges my knee. "Your goblin boy, of course. He's been an open book since day one. It's no secret how much he adores you."

The makeshift heart in my chest flutters. I want to see him, bad. But I don't want him to see me like this again. I want to shed this borrowed nightgown, don my own clothes, and see him underneath the sun. I've missed the green glimmer in his umber skin. "Do you know where he's at?" I ask.

Hazel gives me a knowing look. "Last I saw, he was at the barn. Your mother gave him some elderberry honey cakes and cream to bring to the imps and brownies."

It sounds like he's taking over the chores I had around the glade. Warmth spreads to my toes. I can't help but feel like he's reintegrating himself into the way of life around here, for me. And I pray it doesn't change—I pray he won't leave on one of his adventures again.

I start to peel the quilt away from my body. "Will you help me?"

Hazel scurries off the bed. "What are you doing?"

"Oh, calm down. I'm going to have to get out of bed at some point, and there's no time like the present."

"You're insane."

"Yeah, yeah, now help me up," I demand.

With care, Hazel grabs my hands and pulls me forward until I'm sitting up on my own and no longer relying on the wall behind me. My body aches; it feels like a giant got hold of me and crushed me between its fingers. I try to suck in even breaths to ease the pain.

Hazel has to help me swing my weak legs over the edge of the bed. I haven't been able to stretch them in weeks. I almost miss my old rickety wheelchair. Pushing myself with my toes always helped me keep some of the muscle in my calves. It'll be grueling, but I'll have to work on building muscle tone up again.

I glance down at the nightgown hanging on my thin frame. I need to get rid of it *immediately*.

"That just won't do," Hazel teases, pointing at the white cotton. She strolls over to the trunk at the end of my bed and lifts the warped lid. She rifles through my neat, folded clothes, throwing them in disarray. I sigh at her carelessness. Then she pulls out black trousers and my best blouse. The shirt's flowing jade fabric matches the color of my eyes. Its neck will fall under my collarbones in a straight line, hiding the worst of my new scars. The long, breezy sleeves bell out around the wrists, reminding me of characters in the books I love so much.

This will do.

To the best of her ability, Hazel helps me dress. There are many winces and apologies, and a few tears, but we manage. Despite the struggle, it feels good to be in clothes of my own. After I'm dressed, I hold my smarting ribs as Hazel walks over to my elder-tree wheelchair. With a light tap of her fingers, it springs into action and wheels itself to me. The sparrow and elderflowers spinning in the spokes catch the mid-morning sun filtering through my window. The chair bumps up against the front of my knees, waiting for me to climb into it. It's going to be agonizing to transfer.

Hazel's brows pull together. "Ready?"

"As I'll ever be," I say, breathless now.

I yell the whole time Hazel helps me into the chair. If Black Annis wasn't going to be the death of me, my ribs and taut sutures are.

-

AFTER STRUGGLING to catch my breath and calm the pain zinging throughout my body, I make my way outside. My enchanted wheelchair saves me from the suffering of pushing myself while I sit straight-backed in my chair, trying not to aggravate my bones.

Hazel and my mother watch me from the doorstep of my home as I roll over the smooth paths toward the timber barn to find Rush. On the way out, there isn't a blood stain from Copsewood's body to be found. I don't know how to feel when I realize that. I won't have a physical reminder of the troll anymore, only the memories of his protection and his show of love from afar. Though I wouldn't want his blood to remind me of that and would much prefer he were here, I'll always have a piece of his charm living in my heart's twigs.

As I roll along the paths, I bask in the sun and the fresh smell of the fauna around me. Summer's here, and the warm breeze on my face feels glorious. I will never take a sunny day like this for granted ever again.

On my way to the barn, I pass many faeries and exchange hellos with a group of goblins, Rush's father included, who are on their way to the garden with stacks of wood on their shoulders. My best guess is they're going to build new trellises since Black Annis's rampage had started there.

I see a jovial Fern along the way too, his bandaged arm waving while he huddles with some of his gnome brothers. They sit in the plush grass, snacking on a small bushel of strawberries, warming their balding heads in the sun.

I even see Bramwell and the rest of the trolls sitting in a circle on the ground. They're exactly in the same place where I found them weeks before, crafting a changeling heart before I confiscated it. After spotting me, they lift their arms in unison, palms flat in the air in greeting. A drone of "Daughter" falls from their lips and floats toward my ears.

I raise my own hand in response. Not paying attention to where I'm going as I address the trolls causes one of my wheels to roll over something solid, and I hear a gasp of pain.

Rush stands in front of me, hopping on one leg while he clutches at his foot. I've rolled over the tip of his boot, crushing his toes inside.

"Rush!" I can't resist laughing even though it hurts my chest. "I am so sorry! I wasn't paying attention."

"I see that now," he whimpers while he puts his foot down with caution, testing his toes. Seeming pleased they aren't broken, he gives me a grin. "It's so good to see you awake. I've missed hearing your voice." He rubs at the back of his neck and rippled ears. "You have no clue how many times I've come to visit you and just wished you'd open your eyes. I read some of your books to you . . . I could only imagine your commentary." He gestures to the path behind me. "I was just on my way to see you again."

"Well, here I am." I smile.

"Here you are." Rush reaches out and brushes his thumb around the edges of my stitched brow. "I can't believe I almost lost you. Don't scare me like that ever again, okay? I don't think my heart can take it."

"Your heart?" I laugh. "Mine was the one that got shredded, and it turns out it's not flesh and blood. It's not even real."

The corners of Rush's full mouth dip down. "Of course it's real. You're as real as Hazel or me." He tilts my chin up with a knuckle. "Your heart may not have been what you expected it to be, but those twigs in your chest don't change who you are. You're still my Sparrow."

His Sparrow. I like the sound of that.

I've been so afraid of what Rush will think now that he

knows I'm a changeling, but it turns out my fear was for nothing. He still has feelings for me, and the thought makes a blush bloom across my face. "Yours, huh?"

Rush pulls his hand from my face and lets his fingers creep toward the pockets of his tan trousers, but at the last second, his hands fall. The time for hiding his emotions is over. "Heaven help me, but I've fallen in love with you. I feel this pull to you that's like . . . like Fate. And I'm starting to wonder if I've always felt it." Rush's fingers twitch at his side. "We're connected, you and me. I can feel it."

I smile to myself, wiggling my pinkie against my leg. Rush has no clue how true his statement is. As I promised, someday I'll tell him about the red thread connecting us. I saw it as I balanced over the line of life and death, and I know it's real. But for now, I just want to enjoy this moment, this connection that is purely *us*.

"What about your adventures? I would follow you if I could . . ." I point to the scars peeking out from the top of my blouse. "But I don't think I'm ready yet."

Rush takes a step closer to me, catching my hand and pulling it away from my wounds.

"I'm done with adventures. I told you I'd been searching for a home." His perfect teeth practically sparkle in the sunlight. "You are my home. This glade is where I belong."

I take in his silver eyes. "So, you're not leaving?"

"Never," Rush answers, his dimples creasing his cheeks.

"Good," I state, pulling on his hand until he hunches over.

I grab the collar of his crisp, dove-gray shirt, balling it in my fist as I pull his face to mine. Our lips meet like they were always meant to be together. This half-goblin boy is my destiny, and I can feel it in the softness of his lips. It reflects in the way he returns my kiss with reverence and braces his hands on the arms of my chair. I try my best not to smile against his mouth. I feel like I have a flurry of moths caged inside my changeling heart, trying to burst free with my happiness.

I don't fully know who I am anymore, but in this tender-hearted moment, I know who I want to be.

I want to be Sparrow. Confident, strong, and poised. My mother's little bird, a friend to the Elder Mother, and the love of Rush's life. No matter what it might entail, I want to be a daughter of the trolls.

ACKNOWLEDGMENTS

Growing up, I always wanted to be an author. I tried time and time again to concoct an idea, but they never seemed to stick. I never felt that I had a story important enough to tell, that was until I became disabled. I spent my whole life being healthy and able bodied until I became completely blindsided in 2018 by an untreatable chronic illness that put me in a wheelchair.

After that, reading fantasy books was difficult. I couldn't connect with characters as easily and I couldn't put myself in these fantastical scenarios full of adventure and incredible feats. I can't even roll over carpet, how could I picture myself traveling through a forest alongside these characters?

This is how A Daughter of the Trolls was born. I wanted to give people like me with disabilities and chronic illnesses a character to relate to. I found a way for Sparrow, who has a similar illness to me, to go on an adventure that is…not very ADA compliant. Not to mention, I got to share my struggles and frustrations of being wheelchair bound without being paralyzed through Sparrow. There are so many stigmas when it comes to being disabled, this is not a one size fits all world and we are not meant for molds. Thank goodness I learned that disability is not inability.

None of this would've been possible if it weren't for the endless support I received. My parents will always be my number one fans, and they've done nothing but believe in me and tell me how proud of me they are. I love you Mom and Dad!

Thank you for always being surprised by the words that come out of me. My older sisters, you wonderful fools, you never finished reading the first version of my book but thank you for supporting me either way.

Huge thanks to Whimsical Publishing & Illustration for your faith in my story. I am so glad you felt like this was one worth telling. Thank you, Micheline, for your hard work and friendship, you've been such a blessing to me.

Thank you to all the YA book boxes I've worked with through Instagram and all the friends I've made there. You all put me on this path to becoming an author by letting me create makeup looks for you. Years ago, God opened those doors for me, and I am still baffled to this day that this is what came out of it.

And of course, thank you dear reader for delving into this world I created. I hope you've fallen in love with my characters the way I have and that you've come out the other side with memories of a story you'll never forget.

ABOUT THE AUTHOR

McKenzie Catron lives in sunny Arizona with her personal dog Finn and service dog Grimm. She is a wheelchair bound creative makeup artist fighting against disability stigmas one book and body paint at a time. When she's not writing young adult fantasy novels you can find her over on Instagram sharing her art. (@mckenziecatron)

Made in the USA
Columbia, SC
24 July 2023

20722765R00152